A Generation
of Vipers

A Generation of Vipers

Sarah Yarwood-Lovett

embla
books

First published in Great Britain in 2023 by

embla
books

Bonnier Books UK Limited
4th Floor, Victoria House, Bloomsbury Square, London, WC1B 4DA
Owned by Bonnier Books
Sveavägen 56, Stockholm, Sweden

A CIP catalogue record for this book is available from the British Library.

ISBN: 9781471415685

This book is typeset using Atomik ePublisher

Printed and bound in Great Britain by Clays Ltd, Elcograf S.p.A.

Embla Books is an imprint of Bonnier Books UK
www.bonnierbooks.co.uk

MIX
Paper | Supporting
responsible forestry
FSC® C018072
FSC
www.fsc.org

For Granny and Granddad: Sarah and Bill.
Natural storytellers and mischief-makers, with cores of
true grit to carve your own path.
This is for all the adventures 'up the wood', the wildlife
spotting and picnics in every lay-by of at least three
counties.
And for approaching everything armed with complete
conviction, and a full flask of tea.

Chapter 1

DI James Clark trudged towards the white police shelter shielding the forensic officers and the evidence they toiled amongst. The white tent billowed and surged in the wind, straining at its tethers as if about to fly away across the desolate heath. James would have given anything to do exactly that.

Instead, he turned his collar up against the driving rain and scanned the grey horizon for his DCI, Val Johnson. The heath's small car park, in the shadows of the nearby charcoal columns of Pendlebury's Heath Rise estate, was teeming with police vehicles, but no new car had arrived. James's shoulders slumped. He still had to prove his worth in this role, and it didn't bode well that Val wanted to join him.

The dark storm clouds, swollen with rain and unseasonably oppressive for a July afternoon, added to his foreboding. It made Furze Heath, stretching out beyond the car park, look especially forbidding. To him, it had always looked grim and barren – short, spiky red-brown grasses made the landscape look scorched, with bronzing bracken and bristly scrub leading to copses of conifers and scattered birch trees. But it was criss-crossed with paths – the main two leading around the periphery to the north and east – and the common stomping ground of the residents of Heath Rise.

All his colleagues knew the Heath Rise estate well. Too well. A sixties architect's dream of modern high-rise living had, over the decades, descended into blocks stricken with poverty, bored teens, casual violence and an imploding community. His Chief Constable saw it as a blemish on their county's record in England's South-East. Even though James wasn't a particularly religious man, whenever he was called out there, the thought *There but for the grace of God* always streaked through his mind.

These days, call-outs to Heath Rise happened less and less: as the tower blocks had fallen into disrepair and dereliction, people had moved out. Now the place was almost abandoned.

The general gloom made him keen to get on with the investigation, to have something to actively think about. At the cordon around the shelter's perimeter, James pulled the white protective suit over his clothes, glad for once of the extra layer, then the blue boot covers and gloves. Ducking under the cordon, he skirted around the Scenes of Crime Officers and approached the pathologist kneeling over the prone body.

Dr Saunders looked up, her body tensing when she saw James. 'Is Val here?'

When James shook his head, she stood up. 'Then we should wait. You could talk to the person who found our victim?' Her head jerked towards a pair of police constables speaking to someone sitting on the ground. His gaze followed her gesture, but James could only make out the silver blanket wrapped around the civilian's shoulders, flashing between the bodies of the officers. His team would take thorough notes, and Saunders' solicitous concern grated, especially as her focus always lasered on the body and – *usually* – taking him through her findings.

'I'm sure Val wouldn't mind if we made a start.'

'This isn't just a body, James. This is a cold case waking up.' She nodded at the estate, then the crammed car park. 'And we're not exactly being subtle about it, are we? The press will have a field day. *Again.* We've at least managed to get the cordons up and a tent, but I'd really like reinforcements.'

James's mind dredged unsolved cases. Something about a connection to the heath wormed in his brain until he gaped. 'Oh, God. Of *course.*'

Saunders nodded. 'I remember the helpful headlines last time. *Heath Hunter on the Prowl.* And this is exactly the same MO. Same type of victim. Young woman. Early thirties. And . . .'

She cut her words off, causing James to stare. 'What?' When she hesitated, his irritation prickled. Signalling his expectation that the Doc would take him through the key evidence – like normal – he dropped to one knee near the body.

But she didn't join him. 'James, wait . . .'

As he looked up at her, seeing her check again for Val, he had to stop himself from throwing up his hands in exasperation. Now he was DI, it would be unusual for his superior to turn up anyway. *Why did she need to be here before they could start?* It was ridiculous.

With a sigh, Saunders crouched, the body between them. 'OK, look, I wanted to warn—'

'Oh, for God's sake!' James bit back the words as soon as he'd said them. He didn't know why he felt so unsettled, or why Saunders was being so cautious. Maybe she felt as uneasy as him. He shot her a contrite glance, but her lips had set into a resigned line as she gestured at the corpse.

The woman's naked body was turned away from him; she was lying on her side, and her skin was stark white against the dark, peaty soil, and mottled with bright green and yellowish bruises, as if mouldering. Saunders pointed at the lacerations criss-crossing her torso and arms, filled with blackened, crusty clots.

'These stab wounds haven't bled much, so I'm assuming they were made peri- or post-mortem. And the cause of death is probably strangulation.' Saunders' voice was clipped. But James concentrated on what she said, following her gloved finger as she traced the lurid red mark around the woman's neck. 'Scratches around the mark of the ligature, which I imagine will match her own skin under her nails . . . And bleeding from mouth and nose.'

A prickle ran up his spine as he registered the victim's short brown pixie-cut hair, plastered to her head with mud and rain and blood. Crimson bruises leached up her neck, camouflaging a gently curving cheek . . .

'Now, look, I wanted to warn you . . .'

But James wasn't listening. He blinked. *It couldn't be. No . . . No . . . Not Nell?* He rocked back, the horizon spinning. Fear and nausea swept through him, flashing slick, sickly heat over his body. Flinging himself sideways, he just managed to clear the cordon before he retched on bare soil.

Wednesday 6th July – 2 p.m. (two hours earlier)

Eyeing the heavy clouds overhead, Dr Nell Ward changed into her steel toe-capped boots, yanking the laces tight, and pulled on her waterproofs.

As she regarded Furze Heath, her frustration grew, and she ran her hand through her brunette pixie-cut. From this car park, in the south-west corner, one path ran northwards and another extended east across the heath. Both looked endless, reminding her just how far she had to lug the reptile traps, or refugia.

She'd already laid out hundreds of similar traps – metre squares of bitumen-backed roofing felt – for the snakes to bask on or under, while they heated their cold-blooded bodies enough to go hunting. But, while those refugia had lasted for all the reptile surveys she'd being doing since March, now that they'd been vandalised and thrown around by locals, Nell had to replace every last one. Ideally, with something a bit harder to tear up.

It had taken her ages to lay out the original traps – and they weren't nearly as heavy as the metre squares of corrugated iron she'd now decided to use. It was going to take her all afternoon, if not well into the night, to replace them all across the heath. *And* she'd have to bring back the squares of roofing felt that the locals had ripped up, rendering them useless for the survey. Nell almost wished at least one of them had been bitten by one of the site's poisonous adders. Then they might not do it again.

But this was one of the perils of a site near a town. And Furze Heath didn't look especially ecologically valuable. The area around the car park was used as a general dumping ground. Bushes were strewn with litter. A fly-tipped mattress with rusty springs was half submerged in a shallow pond. Bike-tyre prints streaked up and down the sandy dunes. A hollow, which Nell saw would be sheltered from the wind, had stout logs arranged around the charred remains of a small fire, orbited with crushed beer cans.

She had to admit that the heath looked unprepossessing. Mounds of purple heather and bracken were dotted with thorny gorse bushes, shrouded with a red mist of fescue grass, and, generally, the landscape looked bleak.

But appearances could be deceptive. The species here would be unusual, specialised for the acidic conditions. Anywhere else, and managed with more attention than the local Wildlife Trust could afford, it could be *buzzing* with wildlife – although the Trust's occasional mowing did prevent the heathland from progressing to woodland. And with Furze Wood bordering the heath to the north, that encroachment was a constant threat.

Nell already knew from voluntary surveys with the local bat group that a disused railway tunnel curved to the west, beside a pillbox, both hosting hibernating bats.

When the tunnel had been used as a local hangout, covered in graffiti and strewn with beer cans, the bat group had been driven to put locks on the iron gates at both ends, along with a polite sign explaining how fragile the habitat was. With hundreds of bats of multiple species in one place, a disturbance could decimate local populations. The approach had worked – several bat species now hibernated there safely.

The reptile surveys she'd just done across the heath, plus the information from the desk-study data, confirmed that specially protected sand lizards and smooth snakes (as well as the four other native reptile species) were present – with a suitable habitat for breeding, overwintering, hunting and basking. *And* the county's only pair of nightjars might be nesting on the site.

And Nell knew that all these species might qualify this area as a Site of Special Scientific Interest.

Dragging her mind back to the task in hand, Nell called the office. She didn't expect the line to connect, because it rarely did – but this time the line crackled with Sylvia's familiar voice.

'EcoLogical Soluti . . . Sylvia . . . eaking.'

'Hi, Sylvia, I'm at site. Going to be here for a while.'

'You're . . . brea . . . ing . . . up,' Sylvia said. 'I ca . . . derstand what . . . u're sayi—'

Nell stabbed the red phone icon, shoving the useless, signal-less phone in her pocket. It suited her. She didn't have time for friendly chatter, and she didn't want to talk, either.

Ever since Rav's accident, Nell couldn't make herself care about social niceties. It took all her strength not to buckle under the weight of worry, fear about how he felt, gnawing guilt over what had happened . . . Nausea churned in her stomach. It never went away.

At least this site meant that she could work near Pendlebury Hospital's Spinal Unit. Near Rav. But her chance of seeing him today, ideally before his parents arrived for their usual evening visit, was slipping away. She'd have to get a move on. Even though she expected the visit would be full of their increasingly awkward exchanges, where she'd have to hold in the endless questions that she knew he didn't want to answer and instead try to make pointless, stupid small talk. Every visit made Nell feel more and more distant from him. She didn't know how to bridge the growing gulf. But she had to keep trying.

So she focused on her work. She wouldn't be able to charge Brandt Developments, the client, for today's unscheduled ecology survey. The species here might be interesting, but they'd already wreaked havoc on the site's tight timetable and even tighter budgets, and Nell knew the viability of the project was hanging in the balance. She'd pared the costs back as much as she could. Free visits like this, to salvage the sabotaged survey, had to be minimal.

Checking her map, she memorised the placement and numbers of the traps in the first section. Matching these new traps to the old ones would mean she could continue her work with minimal disruption.

Nell walked to the back of the van, slung low over the back wheels with the weight of the traps that she'd have to heft about for miles. Jamming a can of spray paint into one pocket, she pulled on thick work gloves and yanked the top four of the black-painted corrugated iron sheets towards her and out of the van.

She held two, sandwiched together, in each hand, and the metal bit into her palm, the weight dragging them out of the already cramping grip of her fingers.

A heavy raindrop plopped on her face, joined by another, then another, in rhythmic acceleration, until she had to rest the sheets in one hand against her leg while she pulled her hood up against the deluge. Great. Something else to slow her down. She shivered, and not only because of the dismal July day. The nearby blocks of flats cast a grey, cold shadow over the area. The stark, imposing buildings made her feel uneasy, somehow.

As she walked across the car park, she hesitated. A beaten-up Toyota saloon approached, crunching over potholed concrete, then turned towards her and cruised into the otherwise deserted car park like a hunting shark.

Nell's heart pounded as the car slowed, then stopped beside her. She dropped the metal squares and strode back to the van, sliding her hand into her pocket, gripping the car key in her fist like a weapon. With her other hand, she squeezed the cap off the spray paint.

The Toyota caught up with her. The window lowered. A man leaned out.

'You up for some business, sweetheart?' he asked, a leer on his face.

Wednesday 6th July – 4.30 p.m.

'James? I'm sorry ... I wanted you to wait for Val. She won't be long. And I wanted to warn you that while that poor woman looks like Nell, she *isn't* Nell.'

James shook his head, but the horizon swooped again and he steadied himself while the blotches in his vision swam away. As he started to get to his feet, a pair of scruffy, steel toe-capped boots walked into view.

His head jerked up but, as he tried to stand, he staggered sideways, clutching a tent post.

'Whoa!' Saunders steadied the post, before James could pull the entire tent over, and was then accosted by a member of her team.

But the owner of those boots grabbed him. James could barely believe it.

'Nell? Jesus. I ... I ...'

She dropped her silver blanket as he hung onto her, gripping her arms hard.

'Are you OK, James?'

'I ... I thought it was *you*.' His panic was subsiding but his voice still tremored.

For a moment, their eyes locked. James wanted to hold her fiercely against him again. But they weren't a couple anymore.

'How come you found her, Nell?' he asked.

'I'm replacing our survey equipment that's been vandalised by locals. I'd been going for about an hour when I got this far. A load of roofing felt had been chucked in the ditch, and I had to collect it all up. I stepped down into the ditch at the top,' she pointed at a shallow indent between the prickly gorse, 'and followed it down, gathering up all the pieces. Then I . . .' she swallowed. 'I saw her hand.'

James looked to where Nell pointed, studying the surrounding earth and vegetation.

'I backtracked when I saw the body. I called 999 straightaway. To be honest, it was lucky the call got through. There's barely any signal here. After I saw the body, I made sure I didn't trample any evidence. I spotted a partial footprint and took a photo. I was worried the rain would erode it.' She glanced at James. 'I've given an account to your officers. But I imagine I'll need to make a statement at the station?'

'Yes, as soon as possible would be best, if you can. Did you see anyone while you were working?'

'Only when I started, at about two o'clock. Some charmer pulled into the car park asking if I'd like to sell him sex before I got started. I told him to sod off, then I got in the van and drove away. I waited down a side street until I saw his car go past, then I came back here to get on with the work.'

'Got a description?' James didn't need to ask the question. Nell's observation skills always made her an unusually helpful witness. But he noticed her tone was more aggressive than usual, like she was on a short fuse. People reacted differently when they found bodies, but this wasn't Nell's first. Had the man in the car park freaked her out, or was it something else?

'Yes. Late forties, early fifties. Wearing a thin red V-neck jumper which didn't do much to hide his man-boobs and spare tyre. Complexion of a heavy drinker, red and thread-veined. Driving a silver Toyota Corolla, reg HY07 SOR. Dent on the offside wing. Your colleague took the details.'

'Why didn't you end the survey? Come back another time, or with a second person?'

Nell flushed. 'It's . . . complicated. If I make a fuss about the locals, it'll get passed off to someone else. And this is our closest site. It makes it easier to see Rav.'

'Ah. Yeah. Of course.' James winced, both at the name of Nell's partner and the reminder of his horrific car crash. 'How's he doing?'

Nell shrugged. 'Not great.' Her lip trembled and she bit it as she half turned from him.

'Hey.' He reached out, then stopped short. He couldn't hug her, even though he wanted to. But his movement towards her was enough for Nell to fling her arms around him and sob into his shoulder as if her heart was breaking. He could kick himself. *Of course.* This was why Nell was so distraught. Nell blamed herself for the accident at her family's racetrack during the annual Finchmere Classics event. It had only happened two or three months ago. As he looked over Nell's back, James saw Val walk towards them, her owlish face, framed by her swaying grey bob, set in a frown. He released his embrace and patted Nell's arm.

She loosened her hold and stepped back, wiping her eyes. 'Sorry.'

'James.' Val's staccato greeting was a verbal salute as starchy as her suit. 'Is this our witness?' As Nell turned, Val gaped. 'Nell?' With typical self-control, she immediately recovered her composure. 'It wouldn't be a crime scene without you being involved somehow, would it?'

Dr Saunders interrupted the reunion when she approached them with a SOCO. 'We've found her clothes – leggings, running top, underwear and trainers – under those bushes over there. But no phone or wallet. Nothing amongst her belongings to immediately ID her. And our SOCO needs to ask our helpful civilian a few questio—' She stopped abruptly as she looked at Nell. 'Nell? What are the odds?'

Nell smiled at the pathologist, then followed the SOCO, who led her away from the investigation team to talk to her.

As her gaze slid to James, Dr Saunders huffed a breath, eyes wide. 'I wanted to wait for you, Val, especially given that, from what little we do know about our perpetrator, they have a distinct *type*.'

Saunders' confirmation made dread uncoil in his gut. *If the killer's type is exactly like Nell, is she at risk?*

Wednesday 6th July – 6 p.m.

He typed the words that he used to end his blog carefully: *I left her on the heath. Keep an eye on the news. Police were all over it by evening.*

Chat bubbles appeared instantly, then the message: *How did you do it?*

His smile accompanied the surge of power. They can wait.

More chat bubbles appeared . . .

With another spike of satisfaction, he logged out.

They can wait all night.

As he fired the remote at the TV, the solemn tones of the local news reporter filled the room. 'An as yet unidentified woman's body was found on Furze Heath, Pendlebury, this afternoon by a member of the public. Police attended quickly and a section of the heath is closed while this tragic death is investigated. Chief Constable Trent had this to say.'

The uniformed, grave-faced man stared from the screen. 'We are appealing for witnesses and are keen to hear from anyone who may have been in the area. If you've seen anything relating to the incident, please contact the local team.' A phone number appeared as the article ended on a picture of the heath, police tape fluttering.

Watching the clueless police scrabbling about made his lips lift into a smile. Even if they were faking the gravity they only reserved for certain victims. But his sense of power was short-lived as the camera focused on a familiar sight, throwing him into turmoil.

'. . . And, finally, Pendlebury's Heath Rise estate, which had been scheduled for long-overdue development, is now at risk from spiralling costs. Following financial pressure from rising construction budgets, lead construction company, Brandt, have pushed back against what they describe as overzealous and onerous council requirements incurring prohibitive subconsultant fees. This may mean that, despite efforts of local residents and councillors to regenerate this neglected area, the development could now be scrapped.'

His blood boiled as he watched the spokesperson from Brandt, standing in front of *that* tower block, saying, 'This development will bring much-needed regeneration into a long-neglected area, creating affordable, quality housing in an otherwise exclusive and expensive town. We hope the council agrees to reduce their onerous demands, and that our contractors will revise their costs to get the proposals back on track. We appreciate local support – every letter to the council makes a difference.'

Bloody contractors! Can't organise their way out of a paper bag. That place wants knocking down! Every last sodding brick! How bloody hard can it be?

Pacing to the window, an idea took hold. *Maybe, just maybe, something could be done . . .*

Returning to his desk, a search soon brought up news of the development. Protests filed on the council's website said that proper ecological surveys hadn't been done. A further search found that the contractor had hired an ecology company – EcoLogical Solutions – with the work being led by Dr Nell Ward.

Clicking on her biography on the company's website, her picture was unexpected. He stared at her photo, his pulse thundering as heat flashed over his body.

Just my type . . . I bet she thinks she's a career woman, too . . . And I know just what strings to pull.

Chapter 2

Wednesday 6th July – 7 p.m.

'Let's be clear here,' Val said to the team, assembled around the incident board. 'This isn't only a newly opened cold case. This is a blot on our record. My views are well known: our initial investigation of the first case was poor.'

James saw the team around him shift at her direct criticism of their predecessors' work – conducted when Chief Constable Trent was a DI.

'Then, the next two cases were investigated under me, as DI,' Val admitted. 'We failed to amass enough evidence to even narrow down realistic suspects.'

James saw her regret at letting down the victims and their families. But she forced an encouraging smile.

'Now, with the capabilities we have, and with *this* team,' she looked around, making eye contact with all of them – DS Ashley Hollis, DC Ed Baker, DC Hesha Patel and him, their DI – 'I want this to be the last time we need to revisit this case.'

Ashley leaned forward, a corkscrew of her afro falling into her bright hazel eyes. 'This is the fourth victim. So now this is a serial killer we're looking for . . .'

Ah. That's why Val had wanted to be at the scene from the outset.

'Will you be calling in Dr Underwood?'

At the mention of the Behavioural Investigative Advisor, James understood why Ashley was so enthusiastic, and he wasn't surprised at her obvious familiarity with the case. With Ashley's background, *of course* she would have trawled any cases with the slightest hint of psychological analysis.

Their working relationship – and friendship – was still on a tender footing since his promotion. But they'd seen what horrors could happen when they didn't work together the way they needed. So James felt a surge of relief at not only understanding why Ashley would want to lead on this case, but also knowing that she'd be the best person to do it. He smiled at her, tilting his head, and she replied with a firm *I've got this* nod.

'These four murders all happened in the last twenty-eight years,' Val summarised. 'The victims had different backgrounds. The first victim, Amanda Richards, was strangled, then stabbed. She was a heroin addict and likely sex worker. Her partner was in prison. It was *assumed* that she was probably killed in her flat at Pendlebury's Heath Rise estate in 1994 by a punter, while her young son was playing outside. Poor kid ended up in care.'

She nodded at James, who was trying to assemble the incident board now that they'd dug out the files. He hadn't expected to be providing summaries. He fumbled with the folder. 'Um . . .'

'Second was Julia Beckett,' Ashley stood up. 'A young, single mum, attacked by the children's playground near Furze Heath in 2009. Her toddler was found later in the park.'

James mouthed, 'Thank you,' and pinned up the photos of the women, noting the years they'd been killed and marking the map with the locations where they'd been found.

'She wasn't linked to the first crime originally,' Ashley continued, 'because she was found fully clothed and strangled, but not stabbed. But the ligature marks – very distinct, but unclear as to what caused them – link all three victims. The third of whom was Kelly Granger, a beautician at a local salon, killed in 2017 on the industrial park between Furze Heath and Pendlebury. The fourth is our current victim, found on Furze Heath today. With the same ligature pattern.'

James blanched as he observed the faces staring out at him. All young women, with cropped brown hair. All slim, all probably reasonably healthy except the first, emaciated victim. And all killed on or around Furze Heath. Where Nell insisted on working.

Val joined him at the board. Her sharp grey eyes homed in on the assembled evidence like a hawk plucking a mouse from a meadow.

'The situation is clear, I hope.' She turned to the team. 'We're looking for a serial killer. Who, judging from this pattern, is getting more active.'

With no lead on who this latest victim was, Val had asked Trent to appeal for witnesses on the local news earlier. But they were scratching around for a starting point. James began to see why Val had been stumped.

Dr Saunders had warned them that this perpetrator had shown a high degree of forensic awareness, and James found himself praying he wouldn't be the third DI who failed to catch this killer.

Wednesday 6th July – 10.30 p.m.

Nell had watched the vermilion sunset blaze over the heath ninety minutes ago. But she was finding it hard to concentrate on the bats for tonight's activity survey as she walked the transect along the east path. Her eyes kept straying to the northern path. She couldn't see it now the place was in darkness, but she knew police tape flickered behind a uniformed officer, who stood where the tent had been earlier.

The fingertip search by a team of SOCOs had continued until dusk had fallen. Seeing Nell lugging the metal traps around the site, then number them with spray paint, had made James ask, 'What crucial ecology is this for this time?'

When she'd replied, 'Reptiles,' he'd just shuddered and said that one day he'd learn to stop asking her questions.

It had been a relief when James had confirmed that her team could continue surveys outside of the police cordon. But James had not been keen about her doing the work. She had to agree that the site was creepy, in the darkness, after what had happened only a few hours earlier. But there were other things to consider. And they mattered more to her.

She couldn't help hoping that she'd find something useful. It was why she'd spent most of this survey scouring the ground, and bushes, sweeping the terrain with her headtorch.

A chatter filled her ears, through the earphones attached to the bat detector. She checked the frequency – 55 kHz – and recorded the soprano pipistrelle bat. Her headtorch shone towards the side of the footpath, and something dazzled the beam back at her.

Nell's heart thudded in her chest as she crouched and directed the light into the dense gorse. Another glint made her adjust the angle. And then she saw what it was: an iPhone, screen upwards, on top of a damp-looking wallet.

Immediately, she texted James, then reached into her pocket for her high-powered torch, standing stock-still so she wouldn't trample any evidence.

As if fingertip surveying for signs of a protected species, she crouched, methodically searching the area. The worn grassy path had a few bare patches of mud, pitted with puddles after the unseasonable rain. Her pulse raced as she made out a print . . . then realised it was her own.

Turning back to the bushes, Nell could imagine the wallet and phone being dropped in, from directly overhead, so the branches would hide them. Examining the gorse, she spotted a small object snagged on the criss-crossed thorns and beamed the torch on it. Olive green, easy to miss. A button. With 'Craghoppers' inscribed around the circumference. As if it had been snagged from someone's clothing when they'd leaned over the bushes.

Thursday 7th July – 7 a.m.

James could have kissed Nell last night, when she'd called in the phone and wallet, complete with driving licence and business cards. They'd also found an Apple Watch. And a button.

So, now they knew who their victim was: Amy Fallon – a thirty-two-year-old architect, a partner at Sapani Associates (very high-end, James noted), living alone in Pendlebury.

On the heath, SOCOs had taken Nell's boot prints and extended the police cordon to include the path where the items had been hidden.

James and Ashley had visited Amy's parents, who lived in the next town, immediately. This was the part that never got easier. The couple had been having a perfectly ordinary evening, until he gave them the news that blew their lives apart. Her mother's words still echoed in his ears. She'd described Amy as sociable, independent, no partner as far as they were aware – although lately, she'd seemed to have something on her mind.

Now, as James searched Amy Fallon's penthouse, which occupied the entire top floor of a converted warehouse, he wondered what could have been worrying Amy. Her home gave frustratingly few clues. One entire wall of glazed bi-folding doors opened on to a roof garden of leafy shrubs. A telescope looked over a glorious view of the Nye River, castle ruins and Pendlebury beyond.

He walked over to the tilted drafting desk, positioned so that someone sitting at it could soak up the panorama. With a gloved hand, he pointed at the plan. 'If I wasn't a detective, I think I'd have been an architect.'

'You astonish me,' Ashley deadpanned as she bagged Amy's laptop. 'This place would seduce anyone into the job, though, wouldn't it? Very aspirational.' She arched an eyebrow. '*Provided* you're a partner in the firm, with a string of awards.' She gestured at a bookcase, empty except for variously shaped crystal trophies etched with accolades like *The RIBA Reinvention Award*. 'And you get yourself featured in *Architectural Digest*.' She picked up the magazine placed prominently on the coffee table, with Sapani Associates named on the cover.

The wide, open-plan space tested James's architectural and interiors knowledge. A cluster of sculptural Herman Miller chairs looked more like an art installation than a living space. Photography books were stacked on the modular coffee table. Behind him, a Calacatta gold marble waterfall island housed a sink and induction hob in front of a wall of handle-less matt-black cupboards. They contained unreasonably healthy food that made James question his life choices. The clutter-free lifestyle made it challenging for him to find anything to go on.

With feet shuffling in protective booties over the herringbone porcelain tiles, they worked methodically around the rooms.

The bedroom was as minimalist as the rest of the flat. No personal pictures; just one navy wall hosted an oil painting of streaks of blue and apricot, evoking an ocean sunrise. As he checked under the low, wide bed and the mattress, Ashley went straight for the en suite. As he'd passed the door, he'd seen it was lined with petrol-blue and bronze slate, with high-end toiletries in the shower alcove. He moved to the bedside drawers.

'Hey, look at this,' Ashley called. Peering round the doorway, he saw she'd opened the cupboard, hidden behind the vast mirror. It contained an assortment of teeth-whitening treatments and medication.

With her gloved hand, Ashley held up a prescription box bearing Amy's name. 'Follicle stimulating hormone. That's interesting. What do you reckon? Defective gland, cancer or IVF?' She began to bag up the cupboard's contents.

'That's a question for Dr Saunders,' James said. He returned to the bedside table, under the suspended glass globe light. The top drawer contained a Kindle, rosehip facial oil and lavender pillow spray. The lower drawer contained a vape kit, with three small bags of cannabis.

As he bagged it, he called out, 'Got some weed here. Doesn't look like it's medically prescribed. So that's another question for the Doc – how extensive was Amy's recreational habit? And is that a lead for us?'

Thursday 7th July – 2 p.m.

As Nell drove through Pendlebury Hospital's main car park to the smart, modern Spinal Unit, she found that there were no spaces. Jolting over the field that served as the overflow car park, she pulled up and took a breath.

The now-familiar sensations of a heavy heart, coupled with an inextinguishable glimmer of hope, carried her through the doors to the Spinal Unit. *Today could be the day Rav actually talks to me.*

The peaceful space was a perfect square around a lush, accessible courtyard, reached via bi-fold doors, which were often open in the summer. Light poured through, filtering off the blossoming shrubs and hawthorn, rubied with berries, where a chattering of dunnocks fluttered.

Inside, on the other side of the wide corridor, were patients' private rooms, looking out on to more gardens. A kitchenette, open to everyone, and staff offices were at the top end of the square, beside reception. At the opposite end was the Physical Therapy suite. A lift led to the first-floor café, where food and drink could be enjoyed all day, along with the view – from the rooftop terrace – of the town, castle and river, surrounding downland and the heath.

The space was designed to be calming. Nell wished it would have that effect on her.

It had been ten weeks and six days since Rav's crash on her family's racetrack. Nell's mind replayed the images, which were still horrifically, starkly clear. The optimism of that day rolled in like a tide: the fizzy anticipation of Rav's parade lap on the racetrack, following the relief from solving both a ruinous fraud and a murder. Rav had been so excited that Nell's father would let him drive his beloved classic Alfa on the track, and Nell's heart had sung with the hard-won approval from Rav's family, who had finally accepted her as Rav's girlfriend, and as a friend to Rav's teenage sister, Aanya.

As Nell recalled the lap, her heart thudded. Rav had fallen back from the more experienced drivers, then had to floor the gas, speeding around a tricky blind bend – only to be confronted with a pile-up of crashed cars after one had had a blowout. He'd swerved and hit some debris on the track, which had sent the Alfa rolling, landing on its roof.

Burning, sick dizziness flashed heat all over Nell's body at the memory.

The days that had followed, when Rav had been in A & E and Nell could only watch glimpses of activity from the sidelines, had been terrifying. She'd heard murmurs about ruptured organs, then learned from Aanya that the steering wheel had damaged Rav's spleen, and emergency surgery was needed to remove it.

She'd watched him being whizzed along the corridor for an MRI, returning ages later with the news that his L2 fracture would need bolts straightaway – meaning more surgery.

Rav's orthopaedic surgeon, Mr Rennie, had said that they'd know more when the lumbar contusion subsided, which could take up to twelve weeks. Rav's bruised, battered body was almost non-responsive as he lay on the hospital bed, hooked up to a drip of morphine.

Those first few days had been brittle with tension and heartbreak. Nell had walked a tightrope: she could sense that his family didn't want to see her, and was desperate not to add to their grief by upsetting them, knowing she was a constant reminder of the cause of Rav's accident. But she also couldn't bear to leave Rav's side. She ached to pour all her love into his recovery. And she hated the thought that, if she wasn't there, he might think she'd abandoned him.

Her training had helped her here: like any good ecologist, she'd instantly tuned in to how his family used the hospital habitat – usually evenings, almost every day. So Nell had restricted herself to daytime visits, considering the lengthy suite of surveys at nearby Furze Heath a gift. She could dovetail Rav's visits with the site work *and* avoid Rav's parents.

But occasional run-ins had been inevitable. They'd all been there when Rav came out of surgery, even though Nell had segregated herself and tried to blend into the background.

The potential long-term complications had been laid out clearly but kindly by Rav's surgeon, Mr Rennie. Rav's parents had fallen into each other's arms, and hugged their daughter Aanya, while Nell stood alone, rejecting the words. She knew the daunting list would cast fear into Rav's heart once he heard them, too: spinal injury, loss of bladder control, erectile dysfunction.

Rav's mother, Neeta, had gone into full doctor mode. Nell heard her insist on the facts, the unvarnished prognosis, to manage expectations for herself, the family and her son.

With gentle empathy, Mr Rennie had taken Rav's mother to one side, ironically nearer to Nell, to give Neeta the professional respect she needed. 'Dr Kashyap, at the moment, there's a lot of uncertainty. And you and I both know what that means. Rav has a lot of hard work ahead of him, a vast amount of pain to deal with, and he'll need a good dose of luck on his side. But he is young, fit, healthy, muscular. And don't underestimate how important a supportive family can be.'

Nell had hoped that might mean she'd be welcomed in Rav's support network. But though Neeta and Rakesh had been polite, they were also distinctly frosty. At least Aanya would give Nell an occasional unguarded update, and tell her the things that Rav held back from her.

As she stood in the corridor, the open door to Rav's room gave Nell a glimpse inside, and she drank in the sight of him. Day by day, he was looking thinner. She knew he'd hate that too, especially losing the muscle definition in his arms – he'd always had a bit of swagger about his sculpted, climber's physique. His kind face was gaunt; his ready smile had vanished, his irreverent humour replaced with frowns and continual frustration. And today his face convulsed with pain, his forehead sheened with sweat.

As Nell crept closer, she saw the trainer moving Rav's limbs, lifting his legs, encouraging him to move, lift, wiggle his toes. Rav grunted with the effort, exasperation etched in the tension across his face, the clench of his jaw.

'Arrrghh!' His body, which had barely moved, flumped into the mattress as he stared at the ceiling. His frustration rolled towards Nell. She could practically feel the pain ripping through his body; the agony was so clear in his squeezed-shut eyes, the twist of his mouth, his ragged breathing.

His physical therapy had had several knock-backs. Nell was at a loss as to why, and what she could do to help. But she rarely saw the struggle first-hand.

'I know this PT is hard work. I know it hurts,' his trainer said. 'Take a break, we can try again in a few minutes.'

Rav shook his head. 'Enough,' he gasped.

His trainer sighed. 'OK, but if we rest today, let's *really* try tomorrow.'

Rav nodded. He looked exhausted and flooded with pain, as if it swelled through his body and all he could do was be carried along on it, rather than trying to resist it.

The trainer left the room and Nell's next step brought the rest of Rav's bed – and, beside it, his sister Aanya – into view. She slouched on a chair, texting, her glossy raven hair shining under the harsh halogen lights. Nell tiptoed into Rav's sight-line. As he gazed at her, Nell wondered if she'd imagined the flicker of pure love – right before his face hardened.

She pulled up a seat. 'That looked painful.'

Rav nodded.

'Any progress?'

Rav shrugged.

'I'm going to make myself a coffee. Do you want one?'

He shook his head, almost angrily.

Nell's face burned as Aanya's head snapped up to look at her. She liked Rav's younger sister, but it was humiliating to come here every day and face Rav's rejection in front of one or more of his relatives. It made her feel like a stalker. Or an obsessive ex who just wouldn't get the message. *Is that what I am? Should I just stay away?* But she couldn't. It would feel like the worst betrayal.

'I'll grab one with you.' Aanya got up, pocketed her phone and followed Nell to the kitchenette.

'You've got staying power, I'll give you that,' Aanya said.

Not trusting herself to speak, Nell nodded.

'Not like you've got anything better to do, though. You'd only be out bat-bothering.'

Nell couldn't help her small smile at Aanya's irreverent humour. Sometimes she sounded just like Rav. An icy ache gripped her heart. She swallowed what was left of her pride and asked, 'How is he?'

'Not great. His trainer is doing everything possible to motivate him. But he's not even trying. Don't ask me *why* he's being such an idiot. You'd think he screwed his head up, not his legs.'

Nell gasped, but Aanya was unperturbed and checked her buzzing phone, as Nell put a coffee pod into the machine and pressed the 'brew' button.

'How's his prognosis looking?' Nell hated having to ask, but not knowing was killing her.

'The contusion has gone down a little. But still not enough. The doc said it would take time. He's had some tests. Since they've taken him off the morphine, they've found out he's got really bad neuro-nerve-something pain. So now they have to try out a load of drugs on him. But that's why his PT is so *agonising*. I think that's why he can't get on with it. He's never been gym-shy before, has he? But the doc said that if the drugs don't make a difference, and if he doesn't start using his muscles, then he won't regain his mobility.'

Nell didn't disguise her shock. She hadn't realised it was that bad. *Rav hasn't let me.*

'I know, right?' Aanya shrugged. 'He needs to get his arse in gear – *literally* – and build some muscles up before he can even begin his proper PT. But he's got no *drive*—' She bit her words off at the unfortunate expression, looking shamefaced.

But the word *drive* convinced Nell that Rav's reluctance to speak properly to her stemmed from him blaming her. She clamped her lips against the river of apologies that threatened to gush out. They'd make no difference. 'Can I do anything?'

'What do you think?' Aanya huffed out a long breath, suggesting to Nell that perhaps she wasn't the only one who was being kept at arm's length. Which only worried Nell all the more.

'I don't know what it's going to take. If there's any news, I'll keep you posted. But he really needs to respond to his treatment soon – or he might lose his chance to ever be able to walk again.'

Friday 8th July – 8 a.m.

James recoiled from the sharp, searching stench of formaldehyde that permeated the pathologist's lab. He should have waited to have his breakfast after this. He swallowed hard and bent over the dead young woman lying on the autopsy table.

'I was right. Asphyxia by strangulation. With that same sort of ligature,' Dr Saunders said. Her index finger traced the lurid, purple-brown band between thin scarlet lines, indenting the white throat. 'That's consistent with the cyanosis of the lips and nailbed, caused by lack of oxygen, and the enlarged tongue and larynx.'

James glanced at the neatly filed, unvarnished nails, blotched with bluish marks, and the blue lips. 'Any idea what this distinctive ligature may have been?'

Saunders beckoned James to a screen suspended on the wall and scrolled through some magnified pictures of the victim's neck. 'SOCOs took these photos at the scene, and I've taken these other ones in the lab.' Her eyes followed the line of the ligature. 'If it was something like a rope or a shoelace, you'd see an imprint from the material – or the edges, if it was a rigid belt. But we just have this sort of ringed pattern, here.' She pointed at a patch, a few millimetres square, which appeared blurred.

She moved aside so James could see. He frowned at the image on the screen.

'The ligature hasn't left any fibres,' Dr Saunders continued. 'And there's no fingerprints or any other residue from the perpetrator that I can find.'

'Not much to go on,' James said as they walked back to the table. 'But it suggests someone who may have given the attack some forethought to make sure they didn't leave any evidence.' He glanced up hopefully. 'Too early for any DNA analysis, I suppose?'

'I've taken some samples to process. I'll let you know.'

James nodded. 'Do you know why she might have been taking follicle stimulating hormone? Anything come up that might indicate a reason?'

'I didn't see anything abnormal.' Dr Saunders scrutinised the notes. 'Pituitary gland was normal size, and there were no tumours.' She looked at James. 'Must be IVF.'

James made a note to double down on the search for a partner. Unless Amy was planning motherhood alone.

'Any signs of a sexual attack?' He hated having to ask.

Saunders shook her head. 'No. None. But there are signs of drug use. Cannabinoids in her bloods. And her lungs show signs of severe chemical injury: corroded, like they've been subjected to poisonous gas.' She gave an unhappy shrug. 'That doesn't indicate a heavy habit, that's just vaping for you. Apart from that, she seems healthy. Fit, toned, a final breakfast of quinoa and chia seed porridge.'

Dr Saunders looked at James as she walked around the table. 'But there is something that might be useful to consider . . .'

James gazed at her across the woman's body. 'Yes?'

'You don't need anything *like* this level of force to strangle someone. And the other injuries,' she nodded along the torso, 'like I said at the scene, were all made at the time of the murder or just after – not before. The perpetrator would have needed both hands to apply the ligature, and there are no injuries to the victim's hands or inner arms to indicate she held them up in defence and, equally, no marks to suggest her arms were restrained. So, it's my professional judgement that all these stab wounds were made immediately after the victim died.'

James studied the wounds scattered along the torso, legs and arms, now cleaned into dark slices, shadowed with bruises on the pale skin. He frowned. 'These are all different sizes, different directions . . .'

'Yes, I knew you'd notice. Different depths and angles, too.' She raised her hand over a few of the marks, miming holding a knife and bringing it down in line with one of the wounds, then another.

James watched. 'That suggests to me that this was quite chaotic. Frenzied, even.'

'I've examined a lot of victims,' Saunders said. 'This is a very violent attack. It's like the perpetrator was just filled with . . . *rage*.'

Chapter 3

Friday 8th July – 4 p.m.

'Congratulations!' Nell sang the word with the rest of the crowd. Her parents, Hugo and Imelda, raised their glasses, along with Nell and Sylvia's colleagues from work. Sylvia beamed at Conor, now her fiancé, who'd been joined by two of his – very obviously ex-military – friends.

Nell was overcompensating for somehow being behind this social curve. She hadn't realised that Conor and Sylvia were even together, let alone engaged. *Had Sylvia said something and she'd missed it?*

Conor wasn't only her mother's security detail, he was like family to Nell, and Sylvia was her best friend at work: she must have been horribly neglectful not to notice. But it had been unusually discreet for Sylvia to omit tales of her dating life from office chatter. Especially as Nell had inadvertently brought the couple together.

Intuitively, Sylvia leaned in to whisper, 'Given your connections, darling, I didn't want to go public with this one, unless it had legs.'

The blush under Sylvia's unrepentant smile gave Nell a reprieve of relief: while she'd been open about casual dates, once Sylvia had realised that this relationship was more serious, more precious, she'd guarded it carefully. Ever glamorous, it wasn't the scarlet silk wrap dress, perfectly coiffed blonde curls, ruffling in the summer breeze, or the immaculate makeup that made Sylvia glow. It was sheer happiness.

'We're *so* delighted for you,' Imelda said.

Nell could see how happy her mother was for them; no wonder Imelda had mobilised the estate hotel to lay on a lavish picnic. The restaurant's terrace, framed by the elegant orangery, was the perfect setting in the afternoon sun. Sandwiches, pies, quiches and cakes were flanked with silver ice buckets of Finchmere sparkling wine.

Conor hadn't meant his request for time off to turn into fuss. But Sylvia had embraced the small celebration. And the summer evening, overlooking the verdant rolling downs, with the gentle hum of bees from the apricot roses rambling up the wall, was gloriously romantic.

'We got you a little gift.' Elliot, the Founder Director of EcoLogical Solutions, was a diffident, self-effacing fellow, dressed like a geography teacher in cords and a shirt. In winter, all his tweed jackets had elbow patches. 'But before I get carried away with the celebrations, may I check that you'll still coordinate the company's anniversary fair next week?'

'Of course! Although everything's already organised.'

'Naturally!' Elliot laughed.

He was happy to let Erin, Nell's over-confident mentee, take over the moment. 'We're *so* excited for you,' Erin gushed. 'You didn't give us very much time to come up with something – but we did! Here.' She gestured at Tom, their new intern. He was constantly yawning and downing energy drinks, lacking the eagerness that their interns usually had, and needed a bit of prompting to do anything. Like now. Erin prodded him again, and he got the point and handed an envelope to Sylvia.

'A proper certificate will follow. This was Colette's idea, if you hate it; mine if you love it.' Erin flicked her dark glossy hair and stuck her tongue out at their mapping expert. Colette responded with a Gallic shrug, never goaded, despite Erin's best attempts.

As Sylvia opened the envelope, Conor leaned in to read the email from the Woodland Trust. 'Oh, how *wonderful*!' She nudged Conor. 'This is one of our favourite spots. And now it'll have an extra acre of trees.'

'*And* a bench, with *your* names on it, overlooking the view,' Erin added.

'How romantic.' Sylvia smiled at Conor. 'I'll have to persuade you to conjure up one of your epic picnics.'

'Ah.' Conor's Irish accent was warm with emotion. 'That'll be no hardship. Properly under your spell, aren't I?' He tweaked her cheek. 'Smitten from the moment I laid eyes on you.' Nell remembered that eventful night – and what Rav had done – and knew Sylvia would regret he wasn't sharing the occasion. 'Didn't know *then*, of course, what I'd be gettin' into.'

Sylvia shot him a knowing smile over her glass. 'Oh, darling, you *still* don't know. A lady has to have *some* element of mystery!' Her eyes danced. 'We're having the ceremony in Ireland, to make it easier for Conor's family. And we've just confirmed the date. It'll be in September.' She side-eyed her fiancé. 'Can't hang about, can we? At *your* age.'

'Sure, dear.' Conor grinned. 'Besides. When you know, you know.'

'Ahh!' The comment invited top-ups of drinks and cheers of, 'I'll drink to that!'

Nell smiled her congratulations and clinked glasses, but her heart ached.

Friday 8th July – 4 p.m.

After delivering Amy's computer to the tech team, James had followed up on where she might have scored her supply of cannabis. He'd asked the team for any cash withdrawal patterns, finding that she made one every fortnight.

Her card transactions, and texts about meeting friends, showed that the Coach Inn, near her place and the river, was a favourite for Sunday lunch with friends. But she went to the Copperhead pub in the town centre every other Friday, right after withdrawing the cash.

The Serious and Organised Crime Unit had said they were aware of a variety of low-level drug-dealing in Pendlebury, as well as a few county-lines investigations. But they had no links or intel that put the Copperhead pub on their radar. With no names or ID to work with, James had free rein to make his own enquiries there.

Today would have been Amy's next visit to the pub, and James found himself sitting at a table with a stunt beer and something very engrossing on his phone to read. His eyes flicked around continually, guessing who the regulars were, and who belonged to the Friday after-work crowd.

A couple of older men propped up the corner of the bar, and knots of workmates of various ages, complaining about their tough week, took up the rest of the polished counter. A few tables of colleagues enjoying after-work drinks were getting gradually louder. A surly teen hogged a Trivial Pursuit machine, which was at least mercifully quiet.

One man walked in, on his own, in jeans and a very fitted shirt, the top three buttons undone. James guessed he was in his early forties but invested heavily in his preservation. His thick, dark hair had a wave, like he'd just run his fingers through it. His dark facial topiary, around very bright white teeth and a prominent nose, was so precise that it looked tattooed. He hefted a black sports bag on his shoulder and sat in the corner. James imagined him doing card tricks, pulling rabbits out of hats; he did *not* expect what the man did next.

When one of the regulars left the bar and joined him, chatting, the newcomer reached into his sports bag and coaxed out a python. It was about as thick as his wrist and maybe one metre long. And then, as if it were a puppy, he handed it over. The second man draped it around his shoulders, holding the questing head in one hand and stroking it soothingly, while the woman he was with took a photo. Whatever the men said next made her shake her head, her blonde waves bouncing.

James approached the less busy end of the bar and spoke to the barman. 'Unusual clientele.' He tilted his head in the python's direction. 'Doesn't it bother any of your regulars that a dangerous snake's about?'

'Nah.' The barman laughed. 'Bit of a novelty, if anything. People often come up and ask me if this is where the Snake Charmer hangs out. They always stay and have a drink, usually come back, some of them become regulars. So, as far as I can see, it's good for business.' He tapped his nose. 'Got to have a USP in this game. He's all right. And that royal python couldn't do any damage. Queenie's harmless. It's fine by me.'

Back at his seat, James saw the barman's words come true as more folk drifted towards the man with the snake. Apparently, a reptile companion was the ultimate icebreaker. And the man did indeed charm everyone with his charismatic smile and laid-back manner – women especially, if the blonde woman who'd refused earlier, but now had Queenie draped over her arm, was anything to go by.

Trying to catch bits of conversation, James heard some ask about keeping snakes, where to buy them, which breeders to trust. The man gave out his number – willingly to women, more grudgingly to men. He recommended species to keep, advising, 'The key thing is to really care for them, not do anything to cause any stress. That's how they remain healthy and docile, which is what you want.' The more attractive women, James noticed, were invited round to see his species for themselves.

As people returned to their seats, a few chatted to the teen at the quiz machine on the way. James judged that their bodies were occasionally close enough for money and substances to change hands unseen. While the young man jabbed at the buttons, James wandered over.

'Got any gear?'

'Sorry, Granddad.' The teen kept his eyes on the machine, continued stabbing the buttons, getting all the questions right in rapid time. 'Not me.'

'Know where I can get some?' James asked.

'Not here.' He stabbed the final button in his game, making the machine light up. 'And I don't know why you're asking me.'

'Because it looks like you've got all the answers.' James gestured at the youth's perfect score. 'Or that you at least hang around here a lot.'

'Righto.'

'Do you?'

'Unavoidable when your dad's the owner, innit? Me and my mates meet up here before we go out.'

'Ah.' James shot a glance at the barman, who was leaning on his folded arms, watching James closely. *Oh well, in for a penny . . .* Fishing out his phone, James brought up a photo of Amy, and showed the lad. 'Have you seen this woman in here?'

'Police, are ya?' He pressed another couple of buttons, getting all the questions right again.

'Yep.' Blocking the view from the rest of the pub, James discreetly showed his badge. 'I know she came in here. I need to know who she spoke to on a regular basis.'

'She comes in every other week. Has a couple of drinks and leaves. Quite sociable. Always chats to the regulars.'

'Did she make a beeline for anyone in particular?'

'Oh, yeah. Our resident David Attenborough over there.'

Saturday 9th July – 6 a.m.

Nell's alarm blared in the dark silence of her bedroom. For a nanosecond, she felt fine. Then she remembered The Accident. Pain hit her chest like a tonne weight, like it could pin her to the bed. A black rush of renewed grief flooded her heart.

It was an effort to move, as though her bed were made of quicksand. She ached to curl up, cocoon herself in the duvet. It was Saturday. She could sleep . . . *But today could be the day she and Rav might actually have a real conversation.*

The thought roused her. As if knowing that just a smidgen of encouragement was needed, a velvet paw stroked her face. Nell's bleary eyes met Jezebel's bright golden ones. Another pat was followed by a purring head-nudge. 'OK, OK, I'll feed you.' Dragging herself up, Nell went to the utility room, served the required food, refreshed the water and unlocked the cat flap.

With Jezebel occupied, Nell checked Pipsqueak, unzipping the large mesh enclosure on the counter. Her latest rescue bat might be tiny – weighing less than a pound coin – but pipistrelles were mighty. That was lucky, because her injuries had been extensive; a little boy had found her on a garden path, after what Nell suspected had been a cat attack. It was why Nell kept Jezebel in at night, so her deadly cat couldn't hunt the protected species.

Indignant chatter filtered through Nell's gloved hand as she unfurled Pipsqueak's wing. The tears and inflammation around the joint were healing well. Squirming, Pipsqueak bared tiny teeth, determined to reclaim her independence.

As Nell refilled the food bowl with wiggling mealworms, Pipsqueak seized one and scurried up the enclosure's wall to eat it under cover of a draped tea towel. Her chatter told Nell that she'd eaten the first mealworm quickly and wanted to be left in peace, thanks, to finish the rest of them. So, after hurriedly cleaning out the base of the cage and refreshing the water, Nell shut the enclosure. A tentative nose snuffled out from behind the tea towel, and Pipsqueak returned to her food.

Upstairs, Nell cleaned her teeth, and noticed how red and raw her eyes were from insomnia and tears. She showered, functioning on autopilot.

Determination set in. Rav's parents' visits were less predictable at weekends. If she could face breakfast, she could go to the hospital, and maybe today would be the day that she could get Rav to talk properly, and start the therapy he needed.

Sunday 10th July – 9 a.m.

James looked up as the door opened, and waved at Dr Saunders. 'Don't usually see you over this side of the building!' he said, smiling.

Saunders held up a folder. 'Just want to put something on your radar. Have you got a minute?'

James nodded and gestured towards the table, where the Doc lined up four photos and four files from the folder in a precise order.

'I'm still puzzling over the ligature, trying to work out what it could be. So I've blown up all the photos from all the cases. It's a strange pattern, see?' She pointed at the close-up of the imprint on reddened skin.

'It's always the same *kind* of overall pattern. But when you zoom in, it's more complex. Here it seems almost zigzagged. Here, possibly coiled. Here, it looks looped.'

She pointed at the four photos, and James saw exactly what she meant.

'When I measured and overlaid the pattern, despite the few minor anomalies at the micrometre level, statistically they're all a match with each other.'

'So it's not just the same *type* of ligature, it's the *exact same one*, each time?' James clarified.

At her nod, he suggested, 'So, what, different sections? Sides? Placement? Pressure?'

'Yes. Possibly all of the above. But I really want you to think about that pattern, in case you're searching someone's house and it's staring you in the face. It's very distinctive, unusual. You'd think it would be easy to work out. Yet it has us stumped. Again.'

Monday 11th July – 11.30 a.m.

Sylvia placed a mug of steaming coffee on Nell's desk and leaned in to whisper, 'Offer Erin some help. She's struggling over there, and she won't ask.'

Glancing over, Nell saw Erin huff at her screen, then cross out notes on a map on her desk. Nell grimaced. 'There's a reason she won't ask me, Sylv.' Erin's massive crush on Rav had spawned into jealousy of Nell and was festering into blame for his accident.

'I know. But she's your mentee, isn't she?' Sylvia jerked her head. 'So mentor the poor girl.' She shot Nell an innocent expression and sipped her ginseng tea.

Nell took the saucer of Bourbons that Sylvia had brought and scooted over on her chair to offer them to Erin. 'Whatever you're stuck on, chocolate biscuits are usually the answer.'

Erin eyed Nell and huffed again. But she took a biscuit and pointed at her screen. Through a mouthful of crumbs, she fretted, 'I'll never get my surveys in before the season ends in September. Or on budget.'

'You've got Little Popplington *and* Coney Thicket *and* Vexing Bottom, right?'

'Yep. All with multiple breeding-bird surveys, bat surveys and badger surveys. All with tonnes of surveyors. Last-minute cancellations due to un-forecast rain have blown my budgets and my schedules. So now they're all impossible.'

'Same has happened to me,' Nell said. 'I combined the dusk bat surveys – this week they're about nine thirty to midnight – with the dawn bat surveys, from about 3 a.m. until 5 a.m. Then I asked two surveyors to stay on to do the breeding-bird transects. Then one person can either stay on for any daytime surveys, or swap with another surveyor. See if that works.'

'OK.' Erin's tone was grudging. But she was squinting at the schedule.

'Our Great British Summer will hone your dark art of juggling plans.' Nell attempted a grin, nodding at the window, where rain sluiced down the glass.

But Erin ignored her attempt at rapport. Nell thought at first that it was because she was concentrating. But, no, it was because Erin was still avoiding talking to her: after she'd revised the schedule, plugged the new numbers into the budget and smiled in relief, Erin elbowed past Nell to Sylvia's desk.

'Sylv, the desk-study report I reviewed for Nell's Furze Heath site has *heaps* of species. We all expected the summer roosting bats in trees, hibernacula with winter roosting bats, and reptiles. *But* the data from the British Trust for Ornithology has a record of *nightjars* there. They're *super* rare. Imagine if we confirm they're nesting? It would be great for a magazine article! I reckon I could persuade Tom to write it.'

Nell frowned. Usually, Erin would run that by her first. But Sylvia, always hungry for marketing pieces, was encouraging. 'Oh, yes. Give me the hook.'

'Nightjar populations have decreased by ninety per cent in the last fifty years. So having them on a local site is *incredible*! I thought a piece on their population, habitat and how we'll mitigate the nearby development could be interesting? I'll get Tom to organise an evening walk so we can all hear their calls.'

'Terrific! I'm sold. Put a draft together and let's see where we can land it.'

Nell agreed it was a great suggestion but, before she could say so, Erin had bounded out to see if Tom had arrived back from site yet. Just then, Elliot beckoned Nell into the meeting room.

He waited for her to sit, then said, 'I've thought about your kind suggestion to help the business continue to pay Rav's wages, since he has no income protection. Are you sure you're happy to work here voluntarily while I pay him?'

Nell nodded. She oversaw their operational budget; this was the only way Elliot could afford to pay Rav. And she was more worried than ever since Aanya's update – and the fact that Rav still hadn't confided in her *and* still hadn't started his exercises over the weekend.

She knew that the obvious thing would be to resign from the job she didn't need and spend time with Rav. But, if she did that, Elliot would be *two* team members down due to her, in the middle of survey season, when work was overrunning. This way she could cover Rav's pay *and* his work. For the millionth time, she wished

Rav would accept help from her. But he wouldn't. Nor would his family. If Elliot could be her proxy, so be it.

'In that case, thank you, Nell. I'll email Rav today to confirm it. He shouldn't have money worries when he needs to concentrate on his recovery.' Elliot sighed. 'Although, with this and our new recruits, we'll need to be even more careful with budgets.'

'I know. I'm doing all I can—'

'Oh, I'm well aware of the lengths you're going to, Nell. Especially with Furze Heath. That's our major financial risk, so I'm very pleased it's in your capable hands.'

Monday 11th July – midday

Waiting in the reception of the spacious office building – converted from a Georgian warehouse, all high ceilings, exposed beams and glass walls – was his chance to scope out the company. He spotted their logo amongst others on the wall by the lift: EcoLogical Solutions, on the second floor. Two other men also sat on the low sofas, taking in the surroundings.

A steady stream of people in suits, checking phones, or in jeans, carrying coffee and clutching bags of sandwiches, flowed through reception. *Worker ants.*

Those two must be ecologists – a young, curly-haired, gangly man and a woman in her twenties, slim, short, with long dark hair – both lugged waders and nets. She looked familiar, from his search of the company website. *Erin . . . something.*

'Yeah, I'll make a start on that article after lunch. And I'm *so* ready for lunch,' the youth said.

'Do you ever stop eating?' *Oh, Erin's a tease, with that flirty smile.* 'Help me take these up, then I'll get on with the report while you grab us a sarnie, OK?'

Idiot, being ordered about by a woman. And she's ambitious. On a successful path? Or frustrated? The bloke's an intern or junior assistant, happy to follow direction. Sheep.

As the lift doors opened, Erin avoided colliding with the man stepping out. 'Hi, Elliot.'

Ah, the Founder and MD, who was asking: 'How did you get on at Little Popplington?'

'Finally good enough weather to survey in,' Tom said. 'I'll disinfect the kit now.'

'Thanks, Tom. Settling in OK?' Elliot asked as his employees stepped into the lift.

'Yeah, great, thanks!' Tom gushed as the lift doors closed. *Over-keen idiot.*

Turning, Elliot walked into reception, and approached with a smile and a handshake. 'Ah! All three of you are already here! Welcome. Let me take you all for our company induction, then you can meet the team.'

I can't wait . . .

Chapter 4

Monday 11th July – midday

James took the tray of coffee back to the incident room, as if hoping the caffeine would fuel a faster result. He jerked his head at Val and Ashley, who were itching to join him.

Dr Underwood, the Behavioural Advisor, was still sitting at the desk by the incident board, files open all around her, making rapid notes.

'Coffee?' He passed the cup with a smile. The middle-aged woman glanced up. Her brown hair was scraped back from her pale, round face into a tight bun, styled for practicality over vanity. Her black trousers, black long-sleeved T-shirt and black trainers (in mid-July) suggested an easy uniform for someone whose thoughts were occupied elsewhere.

Val offered her mug-free hand in greeting. 'Good to see you again, Dr Underwood. I'm DCI now. James is our DI. But I want to introduce DS Ashley Hollis, who has a background in psychology. Any insights into the psyche, the motive—'

'Ah.' Dr Underwood's eyes gleamed. 'Latest thinking is that it's a waste of time, a distraction, profiling for motive. What we *can* focus on now is the victims themselves, who are similar enough to indicate that the killer has a physical type.'

She moved to the board, which James noticed she'd rearranged a little.

'So, quick recap.' Dr Underwood pointed at the evidence as she spoke. 'Amanda Richards. Killed and left in her flat. The investigation – *if* we can call the brief foray the police managed into the murder of a drug-addicted prostitute in the early nineties that,' she exchanged a pointed glance with Val, '*decided* she was probably killed by a client, dealer or someone who was both, while her young son was out. The child was passed to social services. Amanda was found

35

on the bed, in her underwear, strangled and stabbed. You can see from the picture that there wasn't much blood, so the stabbing was some time after Amanda died from strangulation by some kind of ligature. Stabs were made by a small blade, a few inches long, like a small kitchen knife.'

Pointing to the next picture on the board, she said, 'Julia Beckett was second. Eighteen, single mum, found in bushes at the children's playground near Furze Heath. Her toddler was left in the park, suggesting that Julia was somehow lured or overcome with force. Police were alerted after her crying child had approached another young woman, who was there with her daughter. Julia was also strangled. She was found fully clothed and not stabbed.'

Underwood looked up again at the three detectives. 'So this attack might have been opportunistic, rather than planned. That might indicate erratic, risk-taking behaviour.'

'Third, Kelly Granger.' Underwood pointed at the next picture. 'A twenty-eight-year-old beautician at a local salon. Killed when she took her habitual shortcut between work and where she parked her car, across the industrial park between the heath and Pendlebury. Found half undressed behind the huge industrial bins. She was pregnant, which of course made her murder doubly tragic and very traumatic for her family. She was strangled with a ligature with that odd pattern. Stabbed once – it would have been immediately at the point of death – in the stomach, so a lot of blood loss, as you can see from this graphic photo.'

She pointed at the gruesome crime-scene picture. 'Maybe the perpetrator hadn't expected that, after the first victim hadn't bled much? It might explain why they stopped after one.' She made the gesture of a single forceful stab, then turned her hand up and shrugged.

'The fourth, Amy Fallon, was an architect and partner in her firm, found on the edge of Furze Heath last week. We now know that she was going for a run on Friday afternoon and took a route along the footpath that skirts the edge of the heath.'

'All these victims were killed at different times,' Val noted. 'So there's no pattern there, no times we could get Uniform out on the heath to deter the perpetrator.'

'No.' Dr Underwood shook her head. 'And no opportunity to broadcast messages or put up signs warning the public to be extra vigilant or avoid places at certain times.'

'But the MO is always the same,' James confirmed. 'Same ligature to asphyxiate, in particular.' He pointed at the photo of the enlarged pattern, next to the picture of Amy that showed all her wounds.

'It's interesting that he left most victims uncovered,' Underwood said. 'It suggests a lack of repentance. Killers who cover victims do so as an expression of guilt, fear of discovery or regret. Those that don't have no remorse – for the victim *or* the crime. As if they believe the act is vindicated or excused. Or even necessary. More than that,' Underwood emphasised, 'they believe they're doing the world a favour by removing the victims. Like it's a cull.'

James recoiled at the idea, shaking his head. The wall of photos, so like Nell, couldn't make it clearer that the killer had a type. *But what triggers the murders?*

Ashley leaned forward. 'Some kind of God complex?' she asked.

'If you want to put it that way.' Underwood shrugged. 'But I suspect it would be a more useful lens for the *victims* than the perpetrator. It makes me wonder if there's some reason why these women were attacked. Something in their characters that might have conflicted with the perpetrator's core beliefs? Or maybe they provoked something, *triggered* something in the killer?'

Monday 11th July – 1 p.m.

Nell was engrossed until Sylvia tapped her shoulder. 'Meeting,' she said, gesturing at the glass-walled conference room across from her.

Glancing over her computer screen, Nell saw three strangers, all men, standing around the large meeting table, with Elliot. They were shaking hands with Nell's colleagues who were in the office today.

Sylvia glided off, whispering, 'New recruits.'

Already? Nell hadn't realised that Elliot had sent out offers and had them accepted.

Inside the meeting room, with a flourish that made her engagement ring sparkle, Sylvia invited the three men to help themselves to fresh coffee and biscuits – a selection box rather than the more usual budget custard creams, showing this was a genuine occasion.

Nell tried to guess each man's specialism. The chap in the suit was definitely the Finance Director. Camo-man had to be the birder. That meant the man with the Instagram-ready trimmed beard must be the herpetologist.

Camo-man turned to Nell. He was thin, nerdy-looking, with short messy black hair sticking out above very hollow cheekbones. Creases around his brow and eyes suggested he was mid-forties. 'Hi, I'm Simon Slaker.' His accent was American or maybe Canadian.

Pointing at his head-to-toe camo – cargo pants, T-shirt and even an over-stuffed rucksack shoved against the wall, all in sludgy green and browns – Nell joked, 'I nearly didn't see you there!'

He stared at her as if she'd spoken in a foreign language. But he accepted her handshake, barely moving while his eyes continually darted around, observing in all directions.

'I'm Nell, nice to meet you.' She moved to the man with the immaculately groomed beard, prominent Roman nose and dark wavy hair. He could do with fastening a couple of shirt buttons, unless he was heading to a romance novel photo shoot. And his teal-coloured shirt was the right size for straining a little over his biceps. He seemed younger than Simon, but not by much – Nell guessed he was in his early forties.

'I'm Amir. Amir Massoud.' His eyes roved over Nell's face, his smile slow, his handshake lingering. Creeped out, Nell pulled her hand away and turned to the third man.

He leaned forward, one hand against his buttoned navy suit jacket, the other reaching out to give a decisive, single handshake. 'I'm Drew Deacon. Nice to meet you.' His cultured accent sounded self-conscious, and his brief smile didn't quite meet his blue eyes. Despite his receding hair, and ambition in chasing director roles like this one, Nell guessed he was the same age as her: mid-thirties, maybe slightly older. As they took their seats, she wondered if he had enough experience to add any real value.

Around them, colleagues hastily poured coffee, enthused over the fancy biscuits and greeted the new team members, between snatched comments about work.

'I'm glad a few of us are in today.' Elliot smiled at everyone sat around the table. 'This being field season, most of the team are out.'

Simon and Amir both nodded, but Drew looked puzzled.

'But,' Elliot continued, 'you *will* have a chance to see everyone at Pendlebury's Nature Fest on Wednesday. Under Sylvia's machinations, the gathering has snowballed, from our modest idea to celebrate EcoLogical's thirty years, into a town-wide event – a fun community day. We'll have stalls to showcase the different expertise we can offer as a consultancy and we'd love to include your specialisms, too. If you have any ideas, please tell Sylvia.'

Turning to her, Elliot said, 'Would you send them their invitations?'

'Of course.' Sylvia's ring caught the light again as her fingers flashed over her phone's keypad to unlock it. She searched her emails, typed quickly and smiled. 'Done.'

'Your partners are welcome, too, from the afternoon onwards. But, for today, at least the reduced numbers mean more biscuits to go round!' After the polite laughter, he said, 'I'm very pleased to introduce our new team members: Simon, Amir and Drew, welcome. You've all been highly recommended, so we're glad to have you aboard. Our biggest project right now is trying to keep the multiple surveys on track at Furze Heath, for the Heath Rise development, so you'll all be helping with that, one way or another. Nell is the project lead.'

The three men fixed her with intent focus. She shifted in her seat.

'Nell will take you through the project tomorrow and get you on site asap. But, for now, let's get to know you.' Elliot gestured. 'Drew Deacon has a strong track record as a Financial Consultant, and joins us as our first Financial Director, with a glowing endorsement from a trusted colleague of mine at the Board of Directors. Drew's gained a reputation in resolving complex financial challenges, so we'll make good use of his expertise at Furze Heath, where the overall costs are threatening the project's viability.'

Nell fought not to gasp out loud. She *knew* she was doing a great job of dovetailing work to squeeze the best out of their tight budgets.

And she knew the price she'd given the client was beyond competitive. *There's absolutely no feasible way to improve on my costs. Doesn't Elliot have any faith in me? I haven't missed anything, even with Rav . . .* She managed to stop her gaze dropping to the table and, instead, met Drew's laser-like stare.

'Drew, would you like to say a few words? Maybe throw in an unexpected fact about yourself, too, for fun?' Elliot invited.

Drew spread his hands. 'All I'll say for now is thank you for the kind welcome. I know this part of the world well, so I'm looking forward to working on a significant development here – and, of course, to seeing how the team can benefit from my expertise.' He sat back with an air of satisfaction, then hesitated. 'Oh, random fact? I'm a bit of a history buff. Especially WWII.'

'Nice to know, thanks, Drew. Amir Massoud is our new expert herpetologist. He's on the board of our local Amphibian and Reptile Group, and highly recommended by their chairperson. He'll oversee our reptile and amphibian surveys, and resume Erin's herptile training.'

Elliot shot an apologetic glance at Nell. But she couldn't blame him for needing to fill the gap that Rav had left. Erin's training couldn't be interrupted indefinitely.

Beside her, Erin sat up a little straighter, shook her hair so it shimmered down her back, and smiled. 'Good to know that we'll be working together, Amir.'

The smile he returned was slow, measured. Like he knew Erin would wait for it.

'And I'm told Amir is quite the snake wrangler, by all accounts?' Elliot said.

Amir chuckled. 'Yes, I have a few at home. Fascinating creatures. Will that do as my fact?' He shot the company another charismatic smile, then glanced at Nell. 'I look forward to working with you on Furze Heath. I know it well, since it's one of the few UK sites with all six reptile species.'

Before Nell could answer, Elliot cut in. 'Indeed, we'll need to make good use of your licence and experience for our mitigation plans.'

'Since the reptile work is so critical to the project's success, feel free to leverage my expertise and have me lead the project.' Amir smiled as he land-grabbed Nell's work.

Nell raised her chin. He could manage the reptile work, certainly, but he wasn't going to bloody well steal her project – the only one that meant she could survey *and* see Rav.

'We'll bear it in mind, thanks, Amir. And, last but definitely not least, Simon Slaker is our new ornithological expert. And we are very lucky to have him, judging by the impressive review from a friend, who's a Director at the British Trust for Ornithology.'

Simon gave a matter-of-fact nod. A pause drew out, with Elliot looking like he was willing him to speak. Eventually, he urged, 'Care to add anything or share a random fact?'

'The recent *Wildlife on Earth* series had some of my footage from the Orkney Isles. Some of my shots make it into *Nat Geo* from time to time. All of which means I'm a survival expert. You have to be, to get those shots.'

'How impressive!' Elliot enthused. 'Well, Furze Heath won't present quite the same challenges as North Sea-swept cliffs, but we do have a number of bird surveys for you to manage, so your specialism is welcome.'

'Yes, especially now we've found out that nightjars might be there,' Erin enthused.

'Ah.' Simon nodded. 'That'll be my data. I've monitored the breeding population there for a number of years. My knowledge of the site will be essential for the development. The mitigation plans will be exceptionally complex.' He looked at Nell. 'It would be advisable to involve me in any client meetings and key milestones.'

That went without saying, surely? But Nell nodded. 'Of course.'

As Elliot invited the rest of the team to introduce themselves, Erin jumped in.

'I'm Erin. I've got a Masters in Ecological Management. I'm a Field Ecologist, been here a year. Um . . . I've got a great crested newt licence and, um . . .' Running out of steam, she turned to Tom. 'And now Tom's just joined us! Tom?'

'I'm Tom. Intern. Learning loads.' He grinned, then stifled a yawn. 'Sleeping nil.'

'Sylvia Shawcross, Marketing Manager. Before I took this company in hand, I oversaw PR at Saatchi and Saatchi and, before that, cut my teeth as a journalist.'

Nell knew some of the reasons for Sylvia's major career change, but she was certain she didn't have the full picture . . . *yet*.

'I'm Collette, I do the mapping.' Collette's epic understatement belied her workload.

With the competitive edge her new colleagues had displayed, Nell laid out her credentials. 'I'm Dr Nell Ward. I'm the team's Principal Ecologist and project lead for Furze Heath, due to my wide expertise across multiple protected species and habitats. I'm a Chartered Ecologist with CIEEM—' She stopped as she noticed Drew's frown, then added, 'Our professional body. And I manage our team of ten field ecologists, as well as our operational budget, winning work and looking after our key clients.'

'Thanks, everyone,' Elliot said. 'Nell, what's the latest with Furze Heath?'

'We started this project in spring with the habitat survey and reptile presence/absence and population surveys. We've confirmed there are all six species on site: low populations of grass snake, slow-worm, common lizard, smooth snake and sand lizard; and high populations of adders. All of which we'll have to translocate if the development goes ahead. When locals vandalised the roofing felt traps, I replaced them with corrugated iron ones so we're ready to go if translocation is needed. Given how much pressure we're under to reduce costs, that was a pretty unwelcome additional job last Wednesday . . .' Her voice trailed off as the three newcomers stared: Drew stopped making notes, fountain pen hovering, Amir looked horrified and Simon's watchful demeanour froze until he asked, 'When that woman was . . . ?'

Nell nodded. 'The police cordoned that area off. But we're permitted to work around it.' She might have said 'we', but no one else had wanted to go there since the murder. 'We still need to complete surveys for bats and breeding birds at least, so our estimated upper costs are likely to apply.'

'Ah!' Drew's exclamation was ominous as he looked at Elliot and steepled his fingers. 'Before you see the client, Nell, I'd like to review your figures.'

Nell managed not to groan. *Of course he would.* 'Sure. I'll show you my budget tomorrow lunchtime, if that suits?'

'Great!' His eyes flicked over Nell's tense body language and he widened his smile. 'Let's brainstorm over a chocolate muffin from the bakery next door. My treat.'

Cakes or biscuits were currency amongst the young surveyors, whose days were active and long. But no one had ever been quite so self-congratulatory about it. 'Sure. Thanks.' She forced a smile and, noticing the time – 1.55 p.m. – she turned to Elliot and exchanged a nod. 'Lovely to meet you all. I'll have to head off.'

'Of course.' Elliot nodded vigorously and Nell stood, glad to escape.

Dashing to her desk, she checked which reports were ready for her review, prioritised them according to deadline, and downloaded the accompanying maps. She always took a pile of work to Rav's visits because the reality was, it helped to make conversation. She'd hoped that talking about work might help to show him he had things to offer, and might spur him into action. It hadn't worked yet, but she wasn't exactly overrun with other options or ideas.

As she disconnected her laptop and packed her bag, the meeting room door opened and Elliot strode out.

'You still here?' he called, hurrying to his desk.

'Taking some work with me.'

Erin's voice drifted through the open meeting room door. 'Hey, Sylvia, Tom's agreed to write the article. What word count should we aim for?'

'Oh, you're both *too* fabulous.' Nell heard Sylvia practically purr with approval. 'I've got some bites. I'll check what they want. There's one spot where, if we catch them on a slim week, we may get a full page. And now we have Simon's talents, we'll surely have some incredible photos, too.'

'Sure. I've probably got some already. I'll dig them out,' Simon offered.

But Drew interrupted. 'What's this? What article are you doing about the heath?'

'Just a nice ecology piece,' Sylvia said. Nell bit back a smile at Sylvia's vague explanation, and how she averted attention. 'Amir and Simon, why don't you come with me and see if there's anything you want to add to our anniversary event?'

As Sylvia swept them out of the meeting room to cluster around her computer screen, the rest of the team wandered back to their own desks – except Drew, who seemed to be waiting in the meeting room for some reason.

Nell soon realised why, when Elliot rushed back, laptop under arm. He walked in, and Nell heard him say, 'Here are our quotes for Furze Hea—' as he shut the door.

Nell froze and listened intently, realising Erin was doing the same.

'Thanks, I'll fine-tooth comb this, Elliot.' Drew's muffled voice resonated through the wall. 'And I've got some good news for you. I've already initiated the PR drive for Heath Rise. A nice fluff piece on its ecology to win some hearts and minds. Soften things up with the council and locals alike. Removing those barriers makes all the difference.'

Chapter 5

Monday 11th July – 5 p.m.

Rav heard his surgeon talking to him, but just couldn't absorb the words. His refusal to listen to Mr Rennie was a refusal to accept his situation. The surgeon looked at him like he expected a reply. Beside Mr Rennie, Rav's parents looked stricken. Rav gave a half-hearted nod, which made everyone staring at him frown. The surgeon added a note to Rav's file, then strode to the nurses' office to give some rapid instructions.

Through the door, Rav caught sight of Nell arriving; spotting his parents standing by his bed, their backs to the doorway, she slowed and loitered awkwardly outside his room.

'*Beta*, you heard the surgeon,' his mother cajoled. 'You *have* to start taking your therapy seriously. Your medication should be making a difference soon, but you need to find . . . some *motivation*.'

'Nell's here,' Rav said. He wasn't sure if he was saying she was his motivation, or if he was warning his parents, in case they didn't want to see her. Forced tolerance around his hospital bed wasn't exactly conducive to feeling better.

'We know you care about her, *Beta*.' His mother lowered her voice. 'But perhaps . . . perhaps it would be kinder all round to break it off?'

Rav stared at his mother, pushing himself up in the bed. 'What?'

'You aren't treating Nell like a partner. You're not confiding in her, so Aanya says. So how can she know what kind of future you two will have? That isn't fair to her, *Beta*. And even if you tell her how things really are, what if she says it is all fine and stays, but then reality sets in, and she decides she cannot cope? And if you two are not discussing things properly, you're not giving her a chance, are you?'

'Aanya isn't privy to all our conversations.' Rav couldn't believe he was trying to justify himself.

'Fine. So *have* you had a proper conversation with Nell?'

'I'm not your patient, Mum. You don't need to counsel me.'

'Oh, no! You're my most important patient. And your own worst enemy at the moment. I'm not blind. And, you forget, some things I have seen before, in my other patients. Don't you think I can see the pain you're in, and want to save you from having any more?'

'I don't think Nell will hurt me.'

'No? So why are you hurting her, then? Why aren't you trusting her? It is her future, too, that you're affecting. She might want to have children. Her family will be expecting it, no doubt. An heir for all their land and titles. You should think enough of her to give her the choice.'

Rav didn't know how to answer. Rakesh tugged his wife's arm, as if to say that she had said enough, and his parents kissed him on the forehead.

But, as they left, Rav saw Nell again in the doorway. Her face was even paler than usual. She exchanged an awkward, 'Good evening,' with his parents, and his mother was at least sheepish enough to turn and shoot an apologetic glance at him, acknowledging that Nell might have overheard her words.

Nell's hesitation on the threshold was a stab in his heart. He tried to smile. But a flash of pain made him wince and Nell took a step back. 'I'll get a coffee. Want one?'

He shook his head. His heart ached. But he knew he couldn't speak to her about his prognosis or their future. It would open floodgates that it just wouldn't be possible to close again.

Catching a flash of colour in the corridor, he realised that Sylvia, bright as a beacon in scarlet and leopard-print, was heading his way with Conor beside her in his trademark black suit. He tried to sit up a little straighter for the unexpected visitors. Sylvia intercepted Nell and they walked towards the kitchenette together, while Conor walked to the open door of his room.

'Knock, knock,' he said in the doorway. 'Feel like some company?'

Unable to refuse, Rav gestured at the chair beside his bed. 'Come in.'

'Here you go, bud.' Conor placed some magazines and Haribo on his table, within easy reach. 'How you doing there?' His matter-of-fact tone and expression, in contrast to the grief-stricken faces of his family and sympathy from his friends, made Rav feel a bit more normal. But then, Conor had probably seen a lot worse.

'I'm OK.'

'That so, is it? You look like you're getting a bit behind, like. With your training. If you don't mind me saying.'

Rav sank a little deeper into his pillows. 'Uh-huh.' So much for friendly conversation. Everyone was on his case today.

'Painful?'

Conor's question was straightforward enough that Rav could nod. 'Aye. Neuropathic? Like you're being stabbed all over.'

'It's like burning for me. Burns so bad I expect my skin to melt off.'

Conor sucked air through his teeth. 'Aye, that's a bastard. No wonder the training's tough. What are you doing, to deal with it?'

Rav shrugged.

'Ah. Are you *not* dealing with it, then?'

At another shrug, Conor jerked his head at the door. 'You *do* realise that she's not gonna leave you, right? However hard you try to convince her you're giving up, *she* won't. She's not made that way.'

Barely trusting himself to speak, Rav managed to grunt, 'It's . . . it's tough . . .'

'Oh, mate. I know what you're thinking. You've got all this going on, but all that's really going round your mind is the fear, isn't it? Fear that people are just being kind, saying what you want to hear, not what they really mean.'

Rav inhaled and bit his lip, stopping anything from spilling out.

'I've been there. So have a few of my mates. If you want to talk to someone who might understand, I'm here. Any time. But the answer is staring you in the face, mate. You've got to really *talk* to the girl. Look at her. She's not going anywhere. She's *here*. For *you*.'

He paused, as if giving Rav a chance to answer. But he couldn't speak.

'I've seen those who leave it too late. Or who accept it, but about a year on, when their muscles are wasted. And I've seen those who don't have this chance to squander. It takes courage to face it.' He punched Rav's arm lightly. 'But you've got plenty of that. You could be one of the lucky ones, who trusts it – right now, *today* – and gets on with living.'

Rav looked away, not able to meet Conor's knowing gaze. But the wave of despair welled up through his chest like a tsunami, thundering against his self-preservation. 'I . . . I can't bear to talk about it with her.' It blurted out, without him even knowing what he was going to say. 'I don't want her to look at me the way . . . the way . . . people *do* now. I know she's only here because she feels guilty.' He clamped his lips shut. He couldn't say what he really felt. He didn't want to put Conor in the position of having to offer unwelcome – pointless – protestations.

'Oh, she feels guilty, buddy.'

Surprise at his words made Rav look up and meet Conor's eyes.

'Her father's car, her family's event at their racetrack, knowing you'd be competitive and knowing her general love of speed – oh yeah, I've no doubt, sure she believes she encouraged you, and that this . . . outcome is very much her fault.'

Rav's throat was suddenly dry. With effort, he swallowed. 'See? She'll never be honest with me now, will she? If she blames herself, if she feels responsible, then she's obligated, isn't she? She'll never admit that she doesn't want me. And how could she, when I'm . . . like *this*?'

But Conor shook his head. 'Nell is pretty straightforward, Rav. She'll tell you how she feels. *If* you give her the chance. Just talk to her.'

Rav shook his head, chewing a trembling lip. 'How can I? I can't walk, I can't do my job, I don't know if I can have a family. I don't even know if she wants one, because we haven't even talked about that yet. We just took a future together for granted. But that was when I . . .' The lump in his throat made him unable to speak.

'Aye. You're afraid that, if you speak to her, she'll either be – in *your* view – honest and admit she doesn't love you anymore, or tell you that she *does* love you, but really she'll be burdening herself with you out of obligation. And *lying*.'

Rav couldn't answer. But he felt a treacherous tear slide down his cheek.

'So, is that what your surgeon said, about your prognosis?' Conor's tone was practical, still with no hint of pity.

Rav gave another shrug.

'You don't *know*?' Conor leaned forward. 'Trust me on this, mate. Don't lie here doom-mongering about what might happen. You're a smart lad. Arm yourself with facts and determination. You've got it in you, I know that. I've *seen* it.'

'What if . . .' Rav couldn't continue.

'Yeah, exactly, *what if*!' Conor said. 'What *if* the doctors think you can recover? What *if* you could do well if you got on with your PT? What *if* Nell doesn't feel the way you fear she does?'

Nell had an agonising coffee with Sylvia. She'd got the impression that her friend had recruited Conor for Rav's reality check. *And perhaps . . . just perhaps . . . he'll convince Rav to talk to me properly?*

The idea both raised her hopes and dashed them. As desperate as she was to have a real heart-to-heart with Rav, she didn't want him going through the motions because someone had told him to.

'OK, Nell, this is an intervention. I want to take you home and see how you're doing. Then take you for a bit of TLC. My treat, no arguments. Will you give me one evening?'

'No, Sylv, I'll wait—'

'Take a night off. Some space might help you both,' Sylvia suggested gently. '*And* I'll be done with you in time for your bat survey *if* we go now.'

At Nell's sigh, Sylvia marched off, calling, 'Come on! Let's both drive to your place, so you can get changed, and then we can go for dinner. TLC part one.'

Thirty minutes later, inside Nell's home, Sylvia didn't hide her open appraisal of how Nell was coping. But the converted flint barn was as pristine as usual, with stylish decor, furniture and artful touches reflecting Nell's travels.

The only thing Sylvia could consider remotely untidy was a crate of survey equipment by the door, where Nell had dumped various handheld metres for measuring water chemistry, bat detectors, cables and batteries in a disorganised tangle.

The copper-and-navy kitchen was typically gleaming. But, opening the custom copper fridge, Sylvia tutted at the stack of ready meals. 'Well, at least you're eating *something*.'

In the utility room, the washing machine churned and Sylvia raised an eyebrow, as though in approval of Nell functioning enough to put a wash on.

'The cleaners,' Nell confessed. 'Not me.'

'Very sensible.' Sylvia nodded, then peered into the large mesh enclosure on the counter. It was spotless. The pristine dishes on clean newspaper contained mealworms and fresh water. 'The bats are all right, I see.' She turned to Nell with a smile. 'I know you wouldn't entrust their care to anyone else. So that's a good sign. I'm glad to see that, darling. It's too easy to let things get on top of you when things are difficult. But you seem to be managing.'

Nell didn't know how to answer. Everything took so much effort. Even getting up. It didn't *feel* like she was managing. It felt like she was dragging herself through a swamp.

'Good. Now I've checked up on you, go and change and let's have dinner.'

'There's no need, Sylvia. You've seen for yourself that I have food in—'

'I'm not leaving you to a ready meal unless I must. Besides, there's TLC part two.'

'Oh?'

'Get changed, I'll tell you when we're there.'

With a sigh, Nell trudged upstairs and changed into a pair of jeans and a jumper. Clothes that would let her fade into the background. Forty minutes later, she was sitting opposite Sylvia, being presented with an amuse-bouche and dreading a drawn-out meal stretching ahead of her.

'Mmm. Delicious.' Sylvia beamed at her.

'So, what's part two?'

'I've booked a spa evening . . .'

'What, *tonight*?' Nell nearly choked on her compressed watermelon with feta crumb and microherbs. She took a long swig of water. *Oh, no.* She hadn't bargained for this.

As the waiter whisked away their plates and replaced them with starters of fresh scallops, which won a stream of superlatives from Sylvia as they ate, Nell tried to appreciate her kind gesture.

Eventually, Nell asked, 'So, what have you booked?'

'Massage, manicure, haircut, facial.'

'*All* of those?'

'Yes. I've timed it to perfection. I heard you telling Erin that bat surveys start at about nine thirty this week. We'll have eaten by seven thirty, so that's ninety minutes of pampering before I send you off to the bats.'

'That's devious planning, Sylv.'

'Yes, well, I have to be devious. I make no apology for it. And, while I'm laying down the law, I really don't like you surveying that place on your own, Nell.'

Nell's protest was cut off as their main courses were presented with a flourish. Lemon sole with tarragon velouté and baby vegetables. Once the waiter had left, Sylvia leaned forward. 'Conor's texted me about Rav.'

Nell's head jerked up. 'What did he say?'

Something in her gaze made Sylvia's face soften. She shook her head. 'He's not doing well, sweetie. I know the first round of surgery was a success, but he's lost all his *oomph*. His get-up-and-go has got up and gone. The nerve pain is a real setback. Conor thinks it's sent him spiralling a bit. And – friendly warning – his parents will be seeing him tomorrow for lunch and to speak to his trainer.'

Nell noted Sylvia's tactful note about visiting times. But Sylvia's account overwhelmed her with guilt. 'It's not surprising, is it? This is devastating for him. I can't imagine—' She stopped abruptly at the lump rising in her throat.

Sylvia began eating, her expression thoughtful as she eyed Nell. 'I don't think that Rav's lack of response is entirely down to injuries. I think . . .'

Nell's head filled with static. *Don't say it. Don't say it.* She couldn't bear to have her worst fears confirmed by someone else's calm, rational opinion.

'He needs something – some*one* – to fight for. To motivate him. In his recovery.'

Nell dropped her gaze to the table. 'I've tried to talk to him, Sylv, but he just won't open up. It's like we're acquaintances. He just won't confide in me.'

'And you've no idea why?' Sylvia pressed. 'You can't imagine what his reservations might be?'

Nell shook her head miserably, pushing back voices that gloomed despondent answers.

'Nell, for someone so intelligent and so observant, you can spectacularly miss all the signs when it comes to relationships, and what people do for love.'

'What . . . do you mean?'

'Have you looked up his condition? Got the medical facts?'

'Of course.' Nell stared at the velouté dissolving on her plate. Her phone was full of open web pages showing every possible permutation.

'So you know all the . . . *nitty-gritty* details?' She waited until Nell met her eyes.

Nell swallowed. 'Yes. And he has every right to blame me for what happened. If I hadn't encouraged him to—'

'Nell.' Sylvia leaned forward. 'Rav loves you. He doesn't blame you.' She shook her head. 'But you've never considered that he might not want you to see him like that?'

Nell's mouth dropped open. 'What?'

Sylvia shook her head. '*Think* about it, sweetie. From *his* point of view. You were in the early stages of a relationship. The best-behaviour, suck-it-all-in, socks-off phase. Now it's too real, too quickly. He can't control certain things at the moment. Maybe ever. Add that to the fact he's a physical guy: always had a great physique; scaled trees to save baby bats on a daily basis; saved you from drowning in a river, for God's sake – he's a classic modern hero. And now, *all that* has changed. Apart from what that means for how the rest of his life might be, don't you think he wonders if it will change how *you* see him?'

'But I go every day! He must know—'

'And every day he keeps these facts off-limits. To make sure you *won't* know.' Sylvia reached for Nell's hand. 'Sweetie, nothing in this world is constant. There's always a bend in the road that wasn't on the map. But he's afraid this is your crossroads.'

As Nell looked at Sylvia, tears spilled from her eyes. 'So what do I do? How do I convince him that he's wrong?'

Monday 11th July – 6 p.m.

He cracked his knuckles over the keyboard, then typed. 'Initial contact made.'

Typing bubbles appeared but, as usual, he ignored the questions. 'She's a real cold fish.'

Then he laughed as he added, 'But she'll be even colder when I've finished with her.'

Chapter 6

Stamping feet numb with cold, Nell blew a huff of air onto her gloved hands and rubbed them together as she scanned Furze Heath in the faint post-dawn light.

She drained the last of her flask of coffee, depending on the caffeine to see her through. She'd only snatched about an hour's sleep, between the dusk bat survey ending at midnight and returning for this morning's pre-dawn bat survey at 3 a.m.

Sylvia's revelations had whirled round her mind all night, making her plan a million different approaches to try to reach Rav. In the end, she found a way to be able to express her feelings, while giving him the power to do something about it, to make the choice. Now, she just had to wait for the right time.

But while she waited, she was freezing. At least while she'd been walking the transects, the activity had kept her warm. Now, the damp dawn air was chilling her, but she couldn't start the bird survey yet.

Setting the flask down and picking up her clipboard, she swapped the bat survey forms for the dawn breeding-bird survey sheet.

Shapes gradually formed through the veil of rising morning mist. Usually, watching the nocturnal world slip back into hiding as the day stirred around her felt like the reward for disrupting her own diurnal patterns. But today, she couldn't shake off a shiver of unease.

Where the hell is Simon? He'd been proactive in looking up the survey schedule and offering to join her. But waiting for someone was worse than just cracking on with the work. She loitered in the shelter of a cluster of gorse bushes, alert as a rabbit, jumping at every flutter of the birds they were supposed to be surveying.

Hearing a twig snap nearby, as if underfoot, and then a grunt, Nell shrank back into the thorns, clamping her lips against the automatic, '*Ouch.*'

The man strode past – not Simon, too heavyset and purposeful – a terrier scampering at his feet. The way he headed to the boardwalk across the mosaic of ponds showed he knew the heath well. The dog snuffled around the gorse, and Nell hoped the man wouldn't pause.

Thankfully, he marched on, and Nell let out a relieved exhale when the dog scurried after him.

As the sky lightened, birds flitted around her with clamouring calls. Seeing no one approaching, no one pulling up in the car park, Nell pulled out her phone to send an irate text: *Where the hell are you?* With a huff, she deleted it, deciding to be more tactful. After all, she didn't know why he wasn't there yet. Instead, she typed, *Hi, I'm at the heath. Can't see you – hope you're OK?* He probably wouldn't get the text; she only had one bar of signal.

Her phone was set to silent, so a beep behind her made her jump. Twisting round, a rasping whistle and the snap of flapping wings made her stagger back, then swear under her breath as a black redstart flew at her and then across the heath.

That was a phone – so is Simon here? Nell scanned the bushes.

With a groan, the ground under the gorse undulated. The strange serpentine movement was unexpected, and she jumped back.

'Nice job, disturbing that black redstart.' Simon huffed as he squirmed from his camouflaged survival bag. 'I've been trying to work out where that nest is for *weeks*. The male was displaying territorial behaviour. I bet I just needed a few more seconds. But now he's flown.' He ripped off his brown beanie and scratched his dark hair, then scrabbled to his knees. He'd obviously spent the night there. He *must* have seen her waiting for him.

'Why didn't you say something? To let me know you were here?' At least her voice sounded steady, even if she felt weak with relief, her arms limp with adrenaline.

He'd been stuffing his sleeping bag into its compression sack but now he paused, his back to her. 'Because I was busy. Watching.'

Nell took an involuntary step back, the back of her neck prickling. *Does he mean the bird . . . or me?*

Hauling on the sack's straps, he squashed his sleeping bag into a ball. 'Same as you would. We're observers. All good surveyors are.'

'Uh-huh.' Nell made herself sound agreeable as she tried to see if anyone else was near. *No one. Not even the dog walker.* They were totally isolated. She groped for an excuse to leave. 'I think we're too late to get a full survey in now. Let's reschedule—'

'No, it's fine.' Simon rolled his survival bag up and attached it, and his sleeping bag, to his rucksack. Heaving the laden rucksack onto his shoulders, he said, 'I'm ready. Are you?'

Tuesday 12th July – 7 a.m.

James listened as Ashley made the most of Dr Underwood's expertise.

'Can you narrow down anything like the killer's sex? Background?' Ashley asked.

'Male, almost certainly,' Underwood said.

'How are you sure?' James asked. At Underwood's surprised face, he clarified, 'I'm not challenging it, I just want to know *how* you're sure. Is it because Amy was left naked? Do you think there's a sexual element?'

'How many *female* serial killers can you think of?' Underwood asked.

'Er . . .' James floundered, recall failing him.

'Exactly.' Underwood nodded. 'There are fewer than twenty. Researchers have looked at why that is. And it boils down to a specific combination of brain damage, genes, environment and timing.' Underwood paused and plugged a USB stick into her laptop. She clicked on a folder and the screen filled with rows of psychedelic brains.

Ashley leaned forward, studying them as Dr Underwood explained, 'PET scans show that every single serial killer assessed has epigenetic brain damage near their orbital cortex above the eyes, which handles emotion and memory, and/or their anterior temporal lobe, which is critical for emotional associations, memory, language comprehension.'

Nodding, Ashley glanced at Dr Underwood. 'That's why how a psychopath processes emotion is often impaired in some way?'

'Yes. They also share a major violent gene, the MAOA gene. It's carried on the X chromosome, so passed from mother to son. If the son gets the MAOA gene on his single X chromosome, the gene is expressed in violent, aggressive behaviour. If the mother passes it to her daughter, it isn't usually expressed, because females have two X chromosomes, unlike an XY male, so the MAOA gene gets cancelled out by the second X chromosome.'

'So *that's* why more men are serial killers compared with women,' Ashley said.

'Precisely.' She looked at them with the rapt expression of an academic sharing a jewel of research. 'What's *really* interesting is the third factor: that the gene is associated with excess serotonin during development *in utero*. When that happens, the brain of that child and adult becomes desensitised to serotonin. That's *fascinating* because that's the chemical the brain produces to make people feel relaxed, happy. But, for people with this gene, with overexposure to serotonin *in utero*, it doesn't work the way it should.'

With a frown, Ashley asked, 'But not everyone with that genetic code and that epigenetic brain damage turns into a killer. So what causes that?'

'That's down to the final factor. Environment. In times past, we've questioned whether nature or nurture is the cause. From this research, I'd say it's both. If the gene *is* expressed in a violent way, it means the child has had a severely traumatic or violent encounter before puberty. We're talking *serious* abuse, extreme violence in the home, something happening *around* and *to* the child.'

She looked at the detectives. 'This is the tragedy of the things I research. Abuse can often beget abuse. For many, it's an endless, ongoing cycle. Some break it, but they're rare. Given all this, I also think they're remarkable.'

In the reflective silence, James made notes. He should be more hard-boiled by now, but the lottery of birth – that sheer *chance* – always affected him. He had to clear his throat before he could speak. 'So, we're looking for a male, then. Any idea on age?'

'Hard to say.' Underwood sighed. 'The first crime, assuming Amanda *was* the first, could be anything between, maybe, late teens to thirties. That was twenty-eight years ago. So your perpetrator would be between early forties and mid-fifties now.'

'OK, that's helpful,' Val said, though James detected a wince at the vast demographic.

'I know that doesn't narrow it down much. Bear in mind you're looking for someone with an abusive home environment as a child; a mother with a medical history of something like painkillers, antidepressants, opioids; plus, examples of psychopathic behaviour in the child, like animal abuse, arson, bed-wetting to a late age.' She tilted her head. 'The latter probably wouldn't have made it into any police reports, but you never know.'

Underwood squinted in thought. 'The social strata of the victims is interesting – the range of economic and education sectors. That could be random, or it may indicate some social plasticity.'

'And what about the victims?' James asked. 'He has a visual type. Is that usual?'

'Oh yes.' Underwood nodded vigorously. 'Yes, these killings are about reclaiming control. The victims will resemble someone he didn't, or couldn't, control. He's reliving some of the abuse encountered as a child, taking control by turning it on someone else.'

'Should we issue a warning?' James asked Underwood, but his eyes slid towards Val, betraying who he was really asking.

Dr Underwood shrugged. 'That's your call. Like I said earlier, there's no pattern to times of day, so any warnings will be too general to be useful. And it may not deter him; it may excite him, make him feel like he has to answer a challenge. So it could increase the danger, but I don't think this is about titillation. In answer to your earlier question, there doesn't seem to be a sexual element: no semen on the victims, although that could be due to forensic awareness – and no sign of penetration, either.'

'Can you predict if there'll be another attack?' Val asked.

Underwood pursed her lips. 'I can only see what you've already noticed. The attacks are becoming more frequent. And more violent.'

As Dr Underwood closed her laptop, and Ashley showed her out, James turned to Val. Before he could even ask, Val held up her hands. 'I know. You won't be able to concentrate until you know Nell's safe. I agree that you should warn her. I don't want to ask Trent for permission and, honestly, he's *irate* at yet more scrutiny being heaped on his original investigation of this case. He's not being terribly . . . cooperative. But James . . .'

The warning note in her voice made him look at her sharply.

'Even if we warn Nell, it doesn't mean she'll take any notice.'

Nell sharpened the focus of her binoculars, watching the nightjar hunker down across the heath beside a gate post that led into a sparse stand of conifers.

'See? I was right.' Simon's tone was victorious. 'They *are* often active around dawn, not just dusk.' His words suggested that Nell had doubted they'd see the rare bird. But she hadn't.

Trying to ignore her rising irritation over his incorrect assumptions, she watched the nightjar fan its tail, displaying accents of bright white feathers between its camouflaged markings. The pattern resembled snake scales and, together with the elongated eyes, made the bird look very serpentine to Nell. *Not that that was surprising . . .*

'I always think their cryptic field marks look a bit reptilian,' Simon was saying. 'So you might spot that common ancestry, between reptiles and birds.' His unnecessary lecture added to Nell's annoyance. Behind her binoculars, she bit her tongue. So he continued, 'Of course, *Archaeopteryx*, a genus of feathered dinosaurs, was thought to be the first bird, which would have dated bird evolution at Late Jurassic. But more discoveries suggest it may have been earlier.' He spoke in a full-on nerd monotone now.

'Yes, I know.' As soon as she'd said it, Nell felt her bluntness was rude, despite her annoyance at him assuming her ignorance.

But Simon smiled. 'Fascinating, isn't it? That the evidence is right there to even tell us how it flew.'

'Burst flight. Like a grouse. Good for a vertical getaway, but not for sustained flight.'

'Exactly. And we have the fragments of information that can tell an entire story. We know what a creature that existed eons ago looked like, and how it behaved. Makes you think, doesn't it? Of the data we leave behind, without even realising, long after we're dead.'

Nell's neck prickled at his words, and they fell into silence. At least that wasn't weird; ecologists spent a lot of time just listening.

The quiet was punctuated by staccato bursts of birdsong. Then, a peculiar churring call made them both hold their breath. As high-pitched as a nineties computer dial-up tone, and as rapid-fire as a pneumatic drill, it sounded more like technical equipment, or perhaps very frantic crickets. But it was the odd call of the nightjar.

It was incredible to see the rare bird's nesting site. But, despite her delight, Nell still felt uneasy. She itched to leave. The survey had overrun, with Simon reluctant to stop.

'Well, that's a great note to end our survey on,' she chivvied. 'Erin and Tom will be pleased.'

'Good. Well, you carry on, I'll take some photos.' Simon didn't even look up as he rummaged in his rucksack, then attached a massive telephoto lens to his camera. Lying flat on the ground, he focused, then snapped several pictures.

Astonished that extricating herself hadn't been the battle she'd feared, Nell headed back to the car park. But, as she walked away, she shivered. Glancing over her shoulder, she saw that Simon had stopped taking photos. His camera was still held up in front of his face, but his head was turned towards her. Watching her. Again.

Her pace picked up until she reached the car park. Another vehicle had arrived; it hadn't been there before her survey with Simon. Shielding her eyes from the morning light, she scanned the heather: Amir was bobbing up and down around the fringes of the shrubs.

What the— Holding her breath, Nell crept closer, seeing him refer to a clipboard as he walked and occasionally crouched. He was following a row of reptile traps. The ones she'd painstakingly replaced on the day of the murder. Realising he was checking her work, a barb of outrage made Nell stride over.

Once she reached him, she paused, folding her arms as he looked around and waiting for the scan of his gaze to bring her into view. Catching sight of her, he jumped – then waved.

'Nell! Hi! I'm just checking your reptile trap placement so I can move them to better spots. I want to make sure that when we start the translocation, these will yield ideal results.'

'I see.' Nell nodded at his map. 'I hope you're marking any changes.'

'Oh, yeah, sure. No worries.'

Nell drew in a sharp breath.

'Although, actually, I haven't had to move any,' he added.

'Shocking.'

'Eh?'

'It's almost like I might actually *know* what I'm doing.'

Amir recoiled, and Nell knew that, again, she'd been rude. Which just made it worse. She took a deep breath. 'Look, I think there's been some misunderstanding . . .'

Amir didn't answer. His dark eyes narrowed as he regarded her.

'Maybe it would be helpful for you, Simon and me, and Drew, to discuss our roles and responsibilities on this project?'

Amir just tilted his head. 'Whatever you think, Nell.' But he turned and continued checking her work.

Nell fumed all the way back to the office. At a red light, she sighed, glaring out of the window. Catching her fury reflected in the glass, she sighed again. She knew she was just as bad – always over-eager to share some brilliant nugget of information. Her new teammates were just trying to prove their value. And Elliot had asked them to collaborate on this project. She didn't have to be so bloody combative.

Her hands on the wheel shook. Everything felt combative these days. She was furious at the universe. It felt like the colour had been sucked out of her life. But she couldn't complain – she wasn't the one lying in bed, wondering if she'd ever walk again, was she? Having parked, she dashed the tears away with the back of her hand, steadied her breathing, gathered up her survey notes and walked into the office. At her computer, she used the hour before most people arrived to study the budget. She blinked as the numbers on her computer screen swam in front of her eyes. Her eyeballs felt gritty and hot in their sockets. As Sylvia arrived, Nell stood up. 'I'm going to brew a pot of coffee. Want one?' She tried to sound upbeat.

'Ooh, lovely. Yes, please. I've brought almond biscotti, if you'd like some?'

'Better not. Drew's threatened to bring me muffins.' Nell managed a comic grin.

'I'm sure my biscotti pip Drew's muffins any day.' Sylvia's silly riposte showed how pleased she was to see Nell in a lighter mood.

'Me too. But I'm trying to show willing. Going to be frustrating enough having him check my project management skills. I may as well get cake out of it.' She hesitated. 'And thank you for yesterday, Sylv. I spent all night thinking about what I could do. And you've given me an idea.'

Sylvia's smile trembled a little. She clasped Nell's hand. 'Oh, I *am* glad.'

A few minutes later, Nell returned with aromatic coffee and a plate of biscotti for Sylvia, who covered the phone's mouthpiece with her hand as she mouthed her thanks.

Grateful for the jolt of caffeine, and a new sense of optimistic purpose, Nell checked her costs spreadsheet a final time.

'Ah, I see you're ready for our meeting!' The booming male voice made Nell jump. She turned to see Drew peering over her shoulder at her screen. His face was close to hers, and she caught the unwelcome, sharp smell of his sweat. He stood, resting his arm on the back of her chair. Nell swivelled in her seat, as if to look at him, making his arm fall away. He staggered – but when he righted himself, he no longer invaded her personal space.

'Whoops,' Nell said. 'Yes, I'm ready for the meeting. We could start now?'

'Great.' Drew held up a paper bag. 'And I brought these.' He eyed Nell's coffee. 'Go great with a cup of joe.'

'I've just brewed some. You can grab a cup while I set up in the meeting room.'

Drew's eyebrows slowly crept into his high hairline. He gave a slow nod. 'Sure.'

Moments later, Drew joined Nell, sitting next to her to look at the laptop. He moved his chair closer, but Nell pushed the laptop towards him, staving off his overbearing presence.

'Thanks.' Nell took a muffin and began eating it as Drew read the figures.

'Seems a lot,' he said, frowning. 'These bird surveys. And bat transects.'

Wiping her fingers, Nell pointed at the spreadsheet. 'See how I've made one of the bird surveys free? That'll be Tom's nightjar walk, doing triple duty as survey, team-building outing and article. As *you* told Elliot, the positive news offers added value to the client.'

Drew's eyes narrowed, but he nodded. 'OK. But the bats? Is all that necessary?'

'Depends what habitat they remove, and the planting and lighting schemes. That's why our early input in the project makes such a difference to the budget. It's possible to design out all the impact to bats, and that would save a fortune. I'll explain that to the client.'

'And reptiles? A translocation? That's the major expense.'

Nell nodded. 'We can't avoid that one. Whatever happens, reptile habitat will be lost. We already know there's a diverse, ecologically valuable population there.'

'Yeah, but you ecologists all say that if you don't want a development to go ahead. Who checks up on you?' Drew asked.

Nell held in her surprise. It wasn't an unusual accusation, but she hadn't expected it from a colleague. 'Well, Amir told you that the site is known for its reptiles, and the desk-study data has a few old records, so they aren't current. *But . . .*' Nell opened her weather-writer – a clipboard with a folded clear plastic cover fastened with two poppers. Its design enabled ecologists to write in the rain and store samples. Reaching inside the plastic A-line 'tent' that had sprung up over the clipboard, Nell drew out a perfect, whole snakeskin.

Choking on his muffin, Drew spluttered chocolatey crumbs. 'Holy mother—' He covered his mouth, shuddering, then fussed over brushing the crumbs off his shirt. His lips stretched into a taut smile. 'Didn't expect a side of reptile with my morning coffee.'

'It's the sloughed skin of an adder. They're protected. So we'll have to move the population on site away from the development.'

Drew stared at the screen again. 'But you could reduce the cost of that.'

Nell noticed it wasn't a question, despite him knowing nothing about it, and fought back irritation. 'No. We absolutely can't. This fee assumes we'll easily find a site to move the adders to. Which hardly ever happens. If you compare it to actual figures of similar jobs, you'll see this is *so* close to the bone, it's basically unrealistic.'

'You drive a hard bargain.' Drew folded his arms.

Nell shook her head. 'If that was the case, we'd have healthy twenty per cent profit margins on all our projects, wouldn't we, rather than seeing how lean we can go.'

He glanced at Nell's budget. 'Fine. At least I can tell Elliot in our meeting this afternoon that you're doing a great job of handling tight budgets.'

Managing to keep her face neutral, Nell said, 'I think Elliot may have noticed that already, given all the years I've worked here.'

'I've no doubt.' Drew shrugged. 'I've seen how much he values the team. But he *has* drafted me in for my expert financial assessment. And I don't always see people being this creative, finding ways to add value, make good use of funds, demonstrate to the client how they can save whole rafts of work. It's impressive.'

Nell regarded Drew – and his meaningless flannel – in silence. He clearly had no clue about their work, and no idea which surveys were needed or not, nor how to combine them for optimal efficiency. How the hell could he assess if she was good at this or not?

When she didn't smile or say thank you, he simply held the door open for her. But as she walked past him, she felt his breath on her neck as he murmured, 'I *do* hope you're a team player, Nell. Elliot's asked me to evaluate that, too.'

Chapter 7

Nell steeled herself as she approached Rav's room. Her heart hammered like a woodpecker as she walked through reception and past the nurses' office. Rav was propped up on pillows, reading a book. She tiptoed to his bed. 'Hi.'

Rav's eyes lifted to see her. He looked exhausted.

She leaned forward. 'Morning, love. How are you feeling today?'

He swallowed. 'I'm . . . I'm in a lot of pain.'

Nell inched closer at the honest answer, studying him. 'Do the doctors know? I can—'

'Yes, they're on the case.'

'Can I do anything?' She looked at his bed. 'Can I make you more comfortable?'

'No. Leave it.'

'Let me help, if I can.'

'There's nothing you can do.' He closed his eyes, and she ached to reach out and touch him, but she held back.

'I love you,' she whispered. 'I know a lot has changed. But that hasn't.'

Seeing his cheeks tremble, she held her breath, hoping he'd open his eyes and look at her, talk to her. A tear trickled under his dark lashes and ran down the side of his face to the pillow.

'Nell . . .' He shook his head slightly. 'I can't . . . not today.'

Nell held in the sobs that rose in her chest, making her breaths shudder. She wanted to brush his tear away and kiss him. She wanted to shake him and yell, 'Why don't you believe me? Why don't you have any faith in how I feel about you?'

Instead, she reached into her bag and drew out the letter she'd written to him earlier. She placed it in front of the book he had propped open in front of him. But, if he registered it, he didn't respond.

Standing up, Nell squeezed his hand. 'OK, I'll see you soon.'

At the reception desk, she turned to see him open his eyes and stare at the letter. Nell jumped as Rav's parents walked past her. Neeta shot her a concerned smile, which made Nell want the ground to swallow her up. Her stomach dropped, heavy as a stone, expecting one of them to see her letter and somehow disapprove of it. Or read it. Or stop Rav from reading it. Even though she knew that was ridiculous, she glanced back.

Rav shoved the letter under his sheet, out of sight.

And a spark of hope flamed in Nell's heart.

James summarised the busy morning's work on the incident board.

He and Ashley had revisited the families of the second and third victims: Julia Beckett and Kelly Granger. It had been a difficult few hours as they'd tried to extract any new information that might help, but without causing further distress – and, worse, raising hopes – with the refreshed investigation.

In the Grangers' living room, Kelly was front and centre in every family photo, usually wearing something sparkly, shimmering makeup and glittery nail art, and her short brown hair spiked. The backdrops to the gatherings were elaborate and coordinated.

'She loved a theme for a party,' her mother had said in a soft Yorkshire accent. 'She'd always go t'town on decorations. Said it were important to have an *ambience*. She found some place to hire all that stuff from. Made playlists of music, invented cocktails, the works. Of course, that would have changed. She and her fiancé were wanting to settle down.'

'The files indicate that Kelly and her fiancé had argued a fair bit,' Ashley had said, gently.

'Aye, worried about money. Nowt out o' the ordinary. You know how it is when you're starting up a home together with a little one on t'way.'

James had known the file was full of statements and interviews with Kelly's fiancé. But he'd called DC Ed Baker, just in case, to see if Kelly's fiancé had an alibi for Amy's murder. A beep from his phone within a couple of hours had confirmed that he had: Kelly's fiancé had moved away and, at the time Amy was killed, he'd been at home with his new family in Sheffield.

With no leads from Kelly's family, James and Ashley had driven over to Julia's parents, hoping to find something there to go on.

When they'd arrived at the terraced house, James had seen there was no avoiding Julia's presence. Her school photos lined the walls; pictures of her with family were framed on gleaming side-tables. Photos of Julia with a baby, then toddler. Then pictures of a little boy on his own, in his school uniform, then as a teenager – about the same age as his deceased mum.

'Julia had her moments, like any of us,' her mother had said. 'She was eighteen. You never want to listen to your mum at that age, do you?' Her face trembled. 'I hate that time has frozen *there*, when our relationship was probably as challenging as it was likely to be. She didn't get to follow her dreams, I didn't get to see the woman she'd become.' She swallowed, took a deep breath. 'And don't ask me who little Tyler's father is. That was all the police were interested in last time. I still don't know. I don't even know if *he* ever knew. And little Tyler's had so much to deal with.'

James's eyes had strayed to the most recent picture of little Tyler, now a tousled-haired teen, towering over his gran. He'd wondered if he was imagining the slightly haunted look – and it made him wonder if Tyler remembered anything about the day his mother was murdered.

Tuesday 12th July – 11.30 a.m.

Nell sat back as the argument erupted around the meeting room table.

'Drew's right. Lone working is perfectly fine,' Simon asserted.

'I'm literally *never* going on my own, that's for sure.' Erin's face was resolute. 'It's a creepy bloody place. And that was *before* the murder.'

Sylvia nodded. 'Quite. And an extra surveyor is cheaper than legal fees and funerals.'

'I know I've . . . monopolised the heath surveys,' Nell said. 'But it's against policy and best practice to send lone surveyors at night. Just because I've gone alone, doesn't mean everyone's willing, nor that they should be, especially if they find the place creepy.'

'So melodramatic,' Simon muttered. 'I know the heath well and it's absolutely *fine*.'

'Except for the murder,' Erin retorted.

'But that area's cordoned off,' Amir protested.

'I don't think there's a line for that on the risk assessment – is there a flimsy bit of tape keeping out a murderer? Yes? Oh great, risk solved,' Erin countered, and she and Amir glared at each other.

'For goodness' sake. "Creepy"? "Never going on my own", "funeral costs" and risk-assessment hysteria.' Drew shot a conspiratorial glance at Elliot. 'Women, eh?'

Elliot cleared his throat and eyed the three new recruits. 'That comment is blatant sexism. And this is inappropriate. If *any* member of my team's professional assessment gives them concerns of *any* kind, then our policy is to send a minimum of two surveyors—'

'Of course. Apologies.' Drew glossed over the misdemeanour. 'But surely, with so many surveys needed, won't we be doubling up on site anyway?'

'Some, of course, and those are already combined.' Nell held in her sigh, having already explained this to him in their finance meeting. 'But that adds fatigue risk because it overloads the team. The surveys that are separate *have* to be done at different times.'

'So much for economies of scale.' Drew raised his eyebrows. 'So this will bust the budget, of course. But, if there's no other way . . .' He tilted his head at Elliot expectantly.

'Well, we could share locations via our smartphones,' Elliot said. 'Would that sufficiently allay any concerns?' He looked at Erin, who shook her head, then Nell.

'Partly,' Nell negotiated. 'I don't mind sharing my location and doing lone daytime surveys. But I will agree with Sylvia that two surveyors should go at night.'

Across the table, Sylvia mouthed, 'Thank you.' Her relief made her shoulders drop.

As they left the meeting room, Nell nudged Erin. 'Can we talk?'

They stepped aside to let the men pass, and Nell said, 'Something's up, isn't it?'

'Yeah, *too* right!' Erin hissed. 'You let that slimeball walk all over your budget and survey plans, when he *clearly* hasn't got a clue how we work, and you *are* at least good at *that*. So now he'll try it on with *all* of *us*! *Then* you let him dictate our *safety* policy! And *yesterday*, you let *him* take credit for *my* idea when he spoke to Elliot!'

'Oh, does it matt—'

'*Yes*, it *matters* to *me*. You may not need this job, *Lady Beaumont*. But *I do*. And *I* want recognition for my work! How will I ever be promoted if my ideas are presented as some *interloper's*? I can't disagree with Directors, but *you* can! You can quit any time you like. But us *little people* can't!'

As Erin flounced off, Nell groaned at the sight of the three new recruits loitering. Well within earshot. She tolerated Erin's belligerence because she knew that it was rooted in jealousy: Nell had all the things that Erin wanted but didn't have – namely, financial security, her own home . . . and Rav. But it wasn't professional, and it didn't set a good precedent about how she should be spoken to in the workplace.

And now, as if making that point, Amir was raising a critical eyebrow, his pause before speaking making sure that Nell knew he'd registered the exchange. 'I just wanted to say, nice work on those reptile refugia. I didn't actually need to move any traps. I did a quick survey and got some great results, *despite* it being a suboptimal survey month. Look!' He showed her some photos on his phone. 'Adders, a sand lizard, a smooth snake! Amazing!' He bestowed his charismatic smile. 'And you're right, let's draw up our roles and responsibilities so we all know what we're doing. Over lunch?' Amir suggested. 'At one?'

At Nell's nod, he gave her a thumbs up and walked away. Drew looked like he was about to say something, but Simon beat him to it. 'Nell, where do I save today's bird survey data and photos? If you have enough space on your server, I'll download everything I've taken on the site.'

'The folder's saved under the client name – Brandt – then site name. We should have plenty of space, and extra data is always welcome.'

With a curt nod, Simon moved out of the way. 'Good, finally,' Drew said. 'Nell, it's about time for the meeting with the Furze Heath client, isn't it?'

Nell glanced at the clock – 11.55. *Oh God.* 'Yes, in five minutes. Why—?'

'I'll join you.' Drew walked into the meeting room and set down his laptop.

Nell shook her head. 'There's no need, Drew. I'm sure you're busy—'

'I wouldn't dream of missing it,' Drew said. 'Shows the client that we're serious if the Financial Director joins the meeting, doesn't it?'

'Well, no,' Nell said. 'Rufus won't want to pay for a Director's time without good reason. We can't give the impression we're careless with his budget when it's so tight.'

'Oh, very laudable. But I'll add needed *gravitas* to convey our diligence.' Drew opened his laptop, displaying Nell's spreadsheet.

As she stared at him, stunned, he glanced up and looked beyond her, then stood to offer a handshake with a wide smile. 'Ah, Rufus! You're early! Good to see you!'

Nell turned to see her client, ready to introduce herself.

As Rufus shook Drew's hand, Drew glanced at Nell. 'A coffee would be great, thanks, love. Rufus? Can she get you anything?'

'Oh, a coffee for me, too. Thanks.' Rufus smiled at Nell.

How predictable. Nell managed not to roll her eyes. Instead, she extended her hand. 'I'm Dr Nell Ward, the Principal Ecologist on your project. We've only met so far over email or on the phone, so it's lovely to see you in person.'

'Oh! Nell! Great to meet you!' Rufus moved towards the table so they could take their seats.

'I *will* just see if someone can bring us all a coffee,' Nell offered. 'Give me one moment, then we can get the meeting started.'

Outside, Nell scanned the office for anyone willing to help. Erin was free to – but wouldn't. Tom was absent. Colette was busy. Sylvia met her eyes. To Nell's relief, she mouthed, 'Coffee?' and Nell mouthed back, 'Thank you!' as she dashed to grab her laptop, while Sylvia glided off to the kitchen.

But Nell returned to the meeting room to find Rufus and Drew consulting her spreadsheet on Drew's computer.

'My PR team will *love* the idea of a local interest article on a rare bird,' Rufus was saying. 'Great way to highlight how eco-friendly Brandt are. A bit of goodwill goes a long way for public support. And it softens up the council. That's a great idea of yours, Drew.'

Nell set her laptop down loudly, making both men look up.

'Ah, Nell.' Rufus pointed at the screen. 'Drew here was just showing me what he's done with the budget. The cutting down of the bat survey is great news . . .'

'There are a few ways we could reduce surveys – and costs – but it depends on the plans. Now they're under review, we may be able to design out some ecological impacts.'

'Oh?' Rufus was shocked. 'I didn't realise a reduction was contingent on the plans?'

'No . . .' Drew began.

'It *is*,' Nell said firmly. She gave Rufus a reassuring smile. 'But I've found a number of options.' She gestured at the plan of the site on her laptop. 'May I outline my ideas?'

As Nell discussed possibilities, she felt Drew's cold eyes boring into her.

But Rufus looked increasingly relieved. 'Thanks for all this, Nell,' he said. 'It's great that the project is *finally* financially viable.'

Once she'd seen Rufus out, she returned to the meeting room. Drew was closing his laptop. He looked up as Nell sat down. 'Drew, I need to discuss how that meeting went.'

'Oh?' He frowned.

'I know you wanted to show support, but some of your comments misled the client.'

Folding his arms, Drew appraised her. 'How so?'

'When you said the bat survey costs could be avoided, you didn't say it depended on designing out the scheme's impacts. Then, when we talked about the reptile surveys, your suggestion that a translocation meant just dumping them over the fence was—'

'A *joke*?' Drew made a face, implying Nell was taking this far too seriously.

'*Irresponsible*,' Nell said. 'It gives the client the impression that carefully selecting a site and moving the reptiles isn't strictly necessary and the cost is unwarranted.'

He stared at her in silence.

'If I hadn't corrected your comments, *you'd* have put Rufus at risk of breaking the law. When he's *specifically* paying us to make sure he won't. You can clarify *costs*, but you *can't* advise on surveys. Misunderstandings with clients are impossible to repair.'

Drew still said nothing, his eyes fixed on her.

'And don't turn me into the coffee-maker, or call me "love". Whether clients are present or not. I'll document the meeting, and this chat, in an email to Elliot. It can't happen again.'

His face remained impassive. Nell met his gaze, not minding the awkward silence: if Drew was going to insert himself in client meetings, he had to be clear on boundaries.

'Mea culpa.' He held his hands up. 'You make some good points. I've worked with various specialists, but not ecologists. Let me learn. Would you educate me over lunch?'

Nell hesitated. She hadn't expected that. Relieved at having an excuse, she said, 'I've already made plans to have lunch with Amir.'

'The more the merrier!' Drew smiled. 'Ask Simon and Elliot along, too.'

'Fine.' Nell shrugged. 'Let's grab a quick coffee and a sandwich from the deli.'

'Perfect,' Drew said.

Nell put her laptop on her desk and told Amir. He pursed his lips, then nodded and joined them. As Drew held the office door open, Nell saw Erin's scowl turn into an open-mouthed expression of disbelief as she watched them go for lunch.

Chapter 8

Tuesday 12th July – 1 p.m.

After the morning's concerted activity, James saw the signs of morale dropping across the team.

It didn't sound like Ashley was getting far, following up the only lead that had emerged from visiting the families.

DC Hesha Patel had followed up with the driver of the silver Toyota Corolla, who'd propositioned Nell around the time of Amy's murder. DNA samples had been taken, and his car had been impounded and forensically examined, all to no avail; also, his alibi – a sales phone call to one of his clients – checked out. Now, she was frowning at the incident board, searching for inspiration as to where to go next.

DC Ed Baker's search of the HOLMES database for local men in their forties to mid-fifties seemed to only be finding how extensive that demographic was, if his groans were anything to go by. All of them felt the pressure of time slipping away.

'Let's get lunch and take stock,' James suggested. 'Pub? On me?'

He'd never complain about having a caring family, but today was torture for Rav, with their unexpected morning visit and devoted ministrations. His mum fussed with his pillows, wanted to know what he'd eaten, asked about his flaming PT.

His dad read out articles from the *New Scientist* – in a ponderous baritone that carried down the corridor – that Rav was sure no one else wanted to hear. And every time he moved, he heard Nell's letter rustle maddeningly under his sheet.

He'd had to agree to a PT session to get them to leave. And as soon as they'd gone, he instantly felt mean for taking them for granted. He watched them walk away with a heaviness of heart caused by his perceived lack of appreciation for the people he loved.

He was in agony, wanting to read Nell's words. But now he didn't even know if he dared open her letter. *What if she didn't say what he hoped? What if she did?*

With trembling hands, he read the words, trying to make sense of them as they danced on the page. He scanned the lines hungrily, then re-read them, slowly.

She said everything he'd ached to hear, but he still couldn't believe this wasn't fuelled by guilt, or that her assertions were made either in ignorance of his situation or blind optimism of what was possible. The weight of her expectations, her hopes, was exhausting.

He kept coming back to the last line:

'I love you, Rav. If you don't feel the same, then you're going to have to tell me.'

'I don't fancy the deli for lunch. Let's try the pub.' Amir hefted his black holdall and pointed at the stylish Coach Inn, overlooking the Nye River.

Nell tried not to check the time. She didn't want to have anything that would take longer to eat than a quick sandwich, so she could get back to her desk and then . . . *Oh.* Her stomach dropped. *I've already seen Rav today.* The continual drive to see him slackened. She almost felt like she'd collapse, and realised just how much the thought of seeing him kept her going.

'Great idea. We won't often have the chance to have lunch together,' Elliot enthused.

Before Nell knew it, they'd been seated at one of the impressive sash windows overlooking the willows and ducks beside the river, with the castle ruins in the background. She was willing her lunchtime to fly by, sensing that it was going to be unbearable.

'Excuse me a sec.' Amir slid out of his seat, picked up his holdall and, with a nod at the landlord, joined a man at the bar. They spoke briefly, then Amir returned empty-handed.

'You forgot your bag,' Nell pointed out.

'Oh, I was just returning something.' He bestowed his charismatic smile. 'But thanks for checking.'

* * *

As soon as he walked into the Coach Inn, James spotted Nell reading her menu. She looked worn out, tense, sitting with three middle-aged men he didn't recognise . . . until a fourth joined them.

James jumped. It was the guy from the pub. The Snake Charmer – the man Amy Fallon had spoken to. James watched as Nell nudged the man and pointed towards the bar – and James winced at her friendly gesture with someone who was on his radar as a potential person of interest. When the man gave Nell an easy smile back and leaned in towards her, James practically bristled.

He walked over. 'Hey, Nell! Fancy seeing you here! How are you doing?'

'Oh, hi! James!' Nell's smile was brief. 'Nice to see you.'

But James, hoping for introductions, didn't walk on. 'Working lunch?'

At Nell's nod, he glanced around the table. 'Nice to meet you. I'm James.' He stared at each man, invoking a polite response. He heard mutterings: 'Elliot,' 'Drew,' 'Simon,' 'Nice to meet you,' but he was only listening out for one name. It was Amir.

He had to move aside to let the waiter take their order. But he'd got what he needed. 'Enjoy your lunch.'

Nell ordered a salad and gazed at the view, trying to let it relax her.

'Yes, you're right, the biggest expense will be the reptile translocation,' Elliot said.

'I did suggest we could just put them over the fence.' Drew chuckled into his wine glass, but no one laughed with him. Amir looked horrified; Simon tutted and locked eyes with Nell, and she found herself sharing a brief grin of understanding with him.

Elliot glanced at Amir. 'We've also got smooth snakes and sand lizards, so we'll need to get a licence for the development. And finding a suitable site to move them to will be a real challenge. Would any of your contacts know of somewhere?'

'I'm working on it, but it's really tough, for those species,' Amir said. 'If we can come up with a plan of action, I'd be able to speak to the biodiversity officer at the council.'

Their food arrived and Nell stabbed at the lettuce in her Caesar salad. 'I've been wondering if we could persuade Brandt to use the least valuable habitat. Then we could enhance the rest and retain the reptiles on site.'

'Would there be enough carrying capacity for the species?' Simon wrestled with tofu.

'Yes, if we're strategic,' Nell said. 'If we keep the north-west section of heath, and strengthen connectivity between the heath and woodland beyond with suitable planting, the habitat could even support a *greater* population, because we'd enhance the possible food reserves and year-round habitat. We could do that by digging a pond, or boggy area, and using the earth to create south-facing banks on the habitat edge. Build log pile hibernacula.'

Amir nodded. 'That would be ideal. If we can minimise how far we move them, we'd reduce their stress, and that would mean their fecundity rates won't plummet.'

'Excellent.' Elliot beamed. 'That'll make it easier for Rufus to get planning consent.'

'That's music to my ears,' Drew said. 'But wouldn't there be any safety concerns? I can't imagine young families being delighted that we're encouraging poisonous snakes to inhabit the green space around their new flats.' He shot a doubtful, sidelong glance at Elliot.

'The rougher habitat – that reptiles will prefer – is at the north-west edge, and furthest away from the new builds,' Nell explained. 'That works aesthetically, too, so the landscapers will be pleased. The green space can become increasingly manicured southwards, towards the housing, and that itself would create a buffer of unsuitable, exposed habitat that adders would be unlikely to cross. Around the housing, the paths and play areas will be artificial substrate. Chippings, or that spongy tarmac, would deter reptiles from getting close to the living areas.'

'Genius.' Elliot smiled at Nell. 'Colette can draw up a planting scheme with Rufus and get that underway today. And these enhancements will benefit all species present.'

'Yes, like your nightjars, Simon,' Nell said. 'If you advise us how to enhance the site for them, we can add that to *Erin's* idea for an article. It may get the scheme more support.' She didn't know why she was supporting Erin, after her outburst. But it was gratifying to see Drew struggle to hide a scowl as he sliced his rare rib-eye.

'Great, I have some ideas for that. I've already selected some terrific pictures for *Erin's* article.' Simon caught Nell's eye as he emphasised Erin's name, and she was sure she saw a hint of a smile on his serious face.

'Thanks.' Nell grinned at him. 'We could even involve the local Wildlife Trust? Put some investment into their management funds? Share the local opportunity for regeneration and ecological restoration. It'll give the development a high profile for all the right reasons.'

'Not bad,' Drew conceded. 'Rufus mentioned he needed something to improve Brandt's local standing. This would be ideal.' He held up his glass of red wine to toast the idea, stretching out to reach Nell's coffee cup. As did Amir, and then Simon.

She obliged.

Elliot smiled warmly. 'So what are the next steps on site?'

'We'll do the planting, so it can become established while we start the translocation,' Nell said. 'Then the fingertip search so we can install the reptile fencing around the construction zone and areas where we'll create habitat, like the pond and the bank. Then, we'll trap the reptiles from that zone and move them into the enhanced habitat.'

'Yeah, that'll work.' Amir nodded heartily. 'It's brilliant. My contact at the local authority will go for that, which will speed up the licensing process. I'll get onto it.'

Drew regarded Nell with a smile over his glass. 'So are we, in fact, going to simply put the adders over the fence after all?' His lips twitched. 'Was I – with no ecological credentials to my name – somehow right all along?'

Nell looked at him, wondering how to explain the difference the habitat creation made, then realised he didn't care about the technicalities. She caught the eye of both Simon and Amir, and shared a conspiratorial smile. Pleased with *their* endorsements – people who *did* care *and* understood – Nell's smile grew into a grin. 'Fine.' She threw her hands up. 'Mea culpa.'

* * *

Joining Ashley, Hesha and Ed, already deep in discussion, James could barely take his eyes off Nell's colleagues as he studied their dynamic.

He didn't even glance at the menu; he just repeated what Ashley had asked for. When the ravioli arrived, he ate on autopilot, too busy listening to his teammates, and watching Amir.

Nell still seemed starchy – somehow twitchy and unsettled. It could be worry about Rav, but James couldn't help wondering if her warning instincts were firing, too.

'I could do with some ideas to narrow down my search,' Ed was saying. 'I've got thousands of men in this age range.'

'Given what Dr Underwood said about environment,' Ashley said, 'what about filtering the search by seeing if any had involvement with social services in their early years? Especially where there's any reports of psychopathic behaviour as a child. You never know, it might suggest – or even include evidence of – abuse at home, or a mother taking medication or drugs.'

'Good point.' Ed made a note.

Hesha glanced at Ashley. 'Thinking about social services, what about trying to find the son of the first victim? He might remember something. He might have heard or seen even a small detail which might help? There's only a brief statement in the file. No guarantee he'll remember anything all these years later. But—'

'He'd have been nine, though,' James cut in. 'It'll reopen some trauma, so we should take advice on the approach. But we can't avoid it.'

'Yes, tread carefully there,' Ashley said. 'I've just spoken to Julia Beckett's son, Tyler, the toddler left at the park when Julia was killed. He's seventeen now, at college, and after all this time I think he still thinks he's somehow responsible for not noticing something or helping. Poor kid. It was a tough conversation and it yielded precisely nothing.'

'The first investigation should have been much more thorough,' Hesha lamented, as she emailed social services. 'It's a poor effort, honestly.'

Ashley raised her eyebrows at James. 'Trent's team, wasn't it?

Investigating the murder of a prostitute . . .' The unspoken criticism hung in the air.

James gave her an unhappy nod. 'I know that Val is having a tough time steering the investigation with him as our Chief Constable.' He shrugged. 'I know she's getting some high-level support. And it makes me wonder if there will be some damage limitation coming into play.'

'Like a strategic retirement?' Ashley asked.

James's raised eyebrows conveyed that he wouldn't be surprised.

'Would Val . . . you know?' Ashley finished her question with a head tilt.

'I hope so,' James and Hesha said in unison, then smiled.

As James sat back, his eyes strayed over to Nell. She was looking more relaxed, exchanging smiles – not polite, tight expressions, but genuine smiles – with her colleagues. His unease stirred as she laughed at something Amir said.

'Let's hope we get somewhere with your social services angles, Hesha,' Ashley said. 'Otherwise, I don't know how the hell we'll track down a middle-aged man with a God complex, who has no remorse and is possibly on some kind of culling mission.'

Oh, this is a fun game. She's softening up nicely . . .

Chapter 9

Tuesday 12th July – 5 p.m.

Nell pulled up outside Amir's house. Horribly close to Rav's place, but she tried to ignore that as she locked the car and ran up the steps to the Georgian town house.

It looked like Amir had a whole house to himself. Pressing the buzzer, she waited for him to let her in, for an hour of snake-handling training.

Amir opened his door with a smile.

'You found me all right, then.' He welcomed her into a smart kitchen. 'Can I get you a drink?'

'No, I'm fine, thanks. I spoke to Rufus. He's on board with our idea. He's happy to fund the habitat enhancements immediately, because it won't cost much if he doesn't get permission – but it will save us thousands in reduced delays if he *does* get planning consent.'

'Oh, great! I'll talk to the planning officer tomorrow morning. I know him, as it happens. I'm sure we can get a swift approval on that basis.'

'Good.'

'So . . . Do you want to see any while we're waiting for Erin?'

'Any . . . *snakes*?'

'Yes. Come and get acquainted with my girls. And if you want a closer look at any of them, just let me know.'

Nell tried not to shudder. Rav had helped her overcome her aversion. He'd been so calm when they'd done their herpetology training together. Nell didn't want someone else in his shoes. Especially not Amir, flashing his Mr Charisma smile. He seemed to think she was susceptible to his charms – and she definitely wasn't.

Amir led her up the stairs to the lounge. The room was low-lit, the walls lined with tanks under glowing ultraviolet lights. Each vivarium had a front-opening glass door and contained a unique landscape: sculptural driftwood, branches, large-leafed or bamboo plants, all strewn with bark chippings and leaves around plentiful fresh water.

Nell flashed with heat, and not just because it was warmer in here. From all sides around her, she heard faint slithers. Claustrophobia started to close in. She tugged at her top.

'You get used to the temperature.'

Uncomfortable with Amir's scrutiny of her reaction, Nell forced a smile. 'What have you got?'

'Couple of corn snakes, over here, royal python in here; over there, behind the bamboo, a king cobra.'

'A *cobra*?' Nell blurted out the question. 'I didn't realise you could keep venomous snakes.'

'Oh, yes. You just need a licence. But they're pretty cheap.'

Oh, comforting! 'What happens if they escape?'

'Well, you know the answer to that – if you think about it as an ecologist, instead of someone worried about snakes.' He tilted his head, encouraging her to answer.

'Sure. A cobra would die. Not warm enough.'

'True. At the moment, at least. Frankly, I'm amazed our government isn't using that as the main motivation for combatting climate change. And over there, in the massive tank, is my albino boa – she's a big girl, it'll take a couple of us to hold her.'

The thought of sitting beside such a huge snake made Nell want to be literally anywhere else. But a buzz told them that Erin had arrived, so she mustered another polite smile.

Sharing none of Nell's fears, Erin gazed around the lounge, open-mouthed, then peered into each tank.

Nell felt clammy, hoping Amir would start the training refresher soon. The sooner he began, the sooner it would be over.

'OK, first things first, please wash your hands, in case you have anything on them that might smell like food to these snakes.' He chuckled. 'Believe me, we don't want that.'

Nell and Erin filed downstairs to the loo and washed their hands, with Nell feeling increasingly less keen about the encounter. When they returned, Amir was keen to start.

'Right. I'm sure you both know the basics. Never go to handle a snake from above, because that's how their predators approach. Here, and in the wild, I'll use a snake hook, because that's much less stressful for reptiles – it's not warm like your hand so they don't react defensively to it. You can both practise on the corn snakes in a sec.'

'Who's this, Amir?' Erin peered in the largest vivarium.

'That's Blondie.'

'She's *massive*! Can we hold her?' Erin looked hopeful.

'Sure. She's about ten feet long and,' Amir sized Erin up, 'probably weighs more than you do. So we'll have to work together to make sure that we support her in several places and don't stress her spine or put pressure on any internal organs. And keep calm – if she thinks you're food, or if she's scared, Blondie could kill you. No problem.'

Nell had never hated Erin's enthusiasm more. Amir opened the levered front door of the vast tank and a yellowy-white head reared up from the pool, flickering a long, black forked tongue.

'Her tongue's so sensitive,' Amir murmured. 'She's using it to detect her surroundings. She can discern heat and slight temperature changes with cells in her lips and labial pits. Amazing creature. Right, give me a hand here, Erin. I'll take her head and body, you support her lower half and tail.'

'Got it.' Erin hefted her gently. 'Oh, wow, she's really heavy.' Adjusting her grip, she said, 'Her skin feels almost baggy around that core of muscle. You can feel it flexing when she moves. She's *so* powerful. Uh-oh . . . she's . . . she's getting a bit friendly.' Erin struggled to swap hands so she could unwind the tail.

'Here,' Amir thrust the head of the snake towards Nell.

She took the upper body, trying to exude calm and not to shudder, certain that Blondie could sense the vibration of her erratic pulse. Blondie's head pushed up Nell's chest and onto her shoulder, where she rested. Nell stayed stock-still. A bead of sweat trickled down her forehead.

'There you go, Erin,' Amir said. 'Oh, you look quite at home there, Nell.'

'Mmm.'

'OK, good, if you're worried, best not to move, keep still and calm.'

His unwitting echo of Rav's words, when they'd trained together, stung Nell.

'OK, let's leave Blondie in peace. Now you've handled her, Queenie will be a breeze.'

Heaving Blondie back into her enclosure, Nell watched as she scaled the glass while Amir closed the vivarium. Her long belly scales undulated against the window, pushing her upwards.

'So, this is Queenie. She's much more manageable, but that same advice applies, even though she can't eat you for breakfast.' He unwound the mottled bronze-and-black python from the tree branch inside the enclosure, and she pushed firmly up one arm and across his chest to his shoulder. 'She likes to look around. She's curious. Erin?' He held Queenie out.

Erin eagerly took her and then froze, with a grin on her face, as the snake whipped up across her shoulders. 'Keep hold of her,' Amir said. 'Imagine if we were on the heath, in the rain, and you had to measure her.'

'I don't think the adders there are this rowdy,' Erin muttered. 'Or this *big*.'

'No, but also remember that there, you'll be wearing gauntlets to translocate the adders, which makes things a little less wieldy. It may be overkill, but better safe than sorry with poisonous snakes. We'll practise wearing them with the corn snakes, then we can move on to Cleopatra – and you really mustn't get it wrong with a cobra.'

Tuesday 12th July – 6 p.m.

'James? I've got something!' Hesha crackled with purpose as she strode into the incident room.

'Great! I'm all ears.'

'The notes for Amanda Richards, the first victim, are as you know pretty . . . sparse. We have the statement from her little boy, where he said he'd been out playing at the time and hadn't seen or heard anything at all. Then we have the statement from her neighbour, which seemed to be the nail in the coffin, as far as the investigation was concerned. As soon as she put on record that Amanda was a drug user and a prostitute, the case was pretty much closed.'

She didn't repeat her criticism of the investigation, but James still agreed with her.

'Apparently, Amanda's husband, Andy, was, in their neighbour's words, "a good-for-nothing layabout, either on benefits or in prison". She'd tried to get Amanda a job with her at the supermarket, but on the morning of her interview, Amanda's son was poorly, so she didn't show up. She was always in debt, and eventually she slid into prostitution, then one of her clients got her hooked on heroin.'

'Right.' James waited for the tipping point that Hesha had found. 'So where did you look next?'

'I followed up with social services to find out what happened to her son. And they came up with the goods. He was also called Andy, after his dad. He had some turbulent months in care, then he was adopted by a family in the next county. The Deacons.'

'Have you spoken to them?'

Hesha nodded. 'Yes, they said he was quite troubled to begin with. Nightmares, bed-wetting, trouble settling in at school, all of which they expected. But, as time went on, he became a bit more secure. Made friends at school quite easily, did well academically and went on to college. Did an MBA at Edinburgh Uni, which led straight into a steady career.'

'Do we know where he is now?'

'Oh yes,' Hesha said. '*And* I've had to speak to Ashley about an appropriate interview technique. Because, in about thirty minutes, he'll be in our interview room.'

James spent that half hour reading Hesha's interview notes. He modified her plan a little, and included a request for a DNA sample, feeling as ready as he could for the delicate conversation.

But he hadn't been prepared for the jolt of recognition when he saw the man. He'd last seen him sitting next to Nell in the Coach Inn, with her laughing along at something he'd said. Now, the man in the suit was frowning at him, and James knew the recognition was mutual. His stomach churned, but he forced his best disarming smile.

'Thanks for coming in, Mr Deacon. I'm DI James Clark, this is DC Hesha Patel. May I call you Andrew?'

The man leaned over and shook their hands. 'Nice to meet you both. Call me Drew.'

'Thanks, Drew. As you know, this interview is entirely voluntary, to help us with our enquiries. We record it just for procedure.'

'Sure. I just want to help however I can.' Drew's glance flicked between them.

'We're currently going back through our files, looking at any cold cases where new technology might help to solve a formerly unsolved investigation.'

'Oh?' Drew shifted in his seat. 'Yeah, I thought so. So this is . . . this is about . . . Amanda.'

James noted he referred to his biological mother by her first name. A natural adaptation? Loyalty to the woman who raised him? Or disassociation?

'Yes,' Hesha confirmed.

She and James left a silence, watching Drew sip his water before he spoke. 'You know, the officer who asked me questions back then must have been about your age. Yet he looked ancient to me then. And now you look, well . . . *young*. Funny, isn't it?'

'Do you mind helping us with our enquiry?' Hesha asked gently.

'No, of course not. Assuming I *can* help. But if I can, of course I want to.'

'Can you tell us what you remember from that day?'

Drew's forehead creased. 'It was a hot summer. I remember the heat. It was stuffy in that flat. She never opened the windows. There was always this . . . *sour* smell hanging in the air. So that day, what I remember most was a burning need to get out. I was hungry. We'd had no tea the night before. She'd been, well, high, I realise now. It frightened me, because it looked like she'd passed out. I didn't like being around her like that, yet I was frightened to leave her. That morning, she was up, but in a foul mood. I suppose the term is rattling, withdrawal. She would scratch herself. Scratch her arms until they bled. And she'd say mean things, awful things. About me, about my dad. So I'd always try to make sure I was out.'

He stopped abruptly, took a breath, then continued, 'Dad wasn't around much. I could understand why, to be honest. Plenty of other men were, though.' He glanced up at Hesha, his brow crumpled. 'Now, of course, I know why. But, on that morning, I got dressed and tiptoed around Amanda, because I knew that if I made any noise, I'd get whacked. I checked if there was any cereal, and there was, but the milk was off. So I ate a handful of dry cornflakes straight out of the packet. I usually played with my friend, Nicky. Her mum wasn't . . . like Amanda. I thought I'd see her and try to get something to eat.'

James and Hesha let the pause breathe, without barrelling in with questions, giving Drew time to recall what he could.

'When I got to Nicky's, across the estate, she was cleaning out her hamster's cage and her mum gave me a cheese sandwich. Nicky and I went down to the playground, but we didn't play there much. There were always older kids hanging around, so we ran around on the heath. We had a little den there. She had to go back, but I stayed out. I wasn't really doing anything. Just killing time, just staying out as long as I could. It got dark, it started to get cold, and when I went back, there was a policeman standing outside and a couple of officers inside. They . . . they told me what had happened. They asked if I saw anything or heard anything. I wish I had, but I hadn't. Nothing at all.'

He took another sip of water, his hand trembling. 'I was shocked, upset. I felt responsible.' Tears fell, but he didn't seem to notice. 'I thought, if I'd stayed, it wouldn't have happened. I felt selfish for going out. And I felt selfish because . . . I was *relieved*.'

Chapter 10

Nell had to hand it to Elliot and Sylvia: they'd put together a great anniversary celebration.

Earlier, they'd invited their key clients to a catered brunch. Ensuring that every stakeholder present was included in anecdotes, Elliot and the senior team had presented key achievements, interesting projects and funny stories from the company's past thirty years.

Erin's hilarious montage of survey mishaps had been a great icebreaker. But one photo of her – soaked, muddy and draped in pond weed – had made a lump catch in Nell's throat. Rav had taken that photo less than a year ago – then had to lend Erin his spare trousers. A rush of memories flooded her mind: of them surveying and laughing together, looking out for each other on site.

While Nell had studied her hands in her lap, trying to keep her composure, their new client, Rufus, had stood up to make an unexpectedly passionate tribute. He held a copy of the local paper, with the front-page article that Sylvia had sweet-talked the editor into, showing how Brandt's redesigned development of Furze Heath would protect the valuable species and habitats on site. A delighted Rufus described how this had got a major project for his business back on track, and was already a great case study for his firm to use to win future work. And he'd given Nell a nod, saying the council had called him that very morning, ready to green-light the proposals. Across the table, Amir had flashed his eyebrows at Nell.

Around her, enthusiastic discussion had broken out between clients, as they shared their own experiences. Knowing how to leave things on a high, Elliot had concluded the conversation with a summary of EcoLogical's growth and new capabilities to support their clients with upcoming work. After inviting the clients to

Pendlebury's Nature Fest, the team headed down the High Street and across the meadow, to the river.

Sylvia's partnership with the local council and businesses to create the event had exploded with ideas. Stalls celebrating nature and wildlife were brimming with beautiful or intriguing sights. In the crowd milling amongst them were associates they'd worked with over the years – engineers, architects, landscapers – as well as local councillors and the general public, out with their families to enjoy the day.

The eco-homes section was at the far end of the field, tempting crowds over with the glorious eco-garden, planted like it was a slice of the Chelsea Flower Show. From afar, it was interesting to see the effect: everyone slowed down, pausing to drink in the scent from the blooms, pointing at the dragonflies drifting over the reed-fringed pond and leaning on the wooden bridge to enjoy the view.

The partnership responsible – advisors from the local garden centre and a local landscape architecture firm – enjoyed the reactions from the crowd. They shared their range of pre-prepared ecological garden designs: free kits containing plans, instructions, planting lists with vouchers for the garden centre, wildflower seeds and advice for maintenance.

Their gardening tips directed the crowds to the relevant local wildlife group – and, for extra 'aww' factor, encouraged folk to consider species under threat.

So the tip to leave a gap under a garden fence for hedgehogs to wuggle under, to expand their territories to a feasible size for survival, was matched with the Mammal Society's habitat enhancements, like the arched hedgehog hibernaculum. And the carefully located Tiggywinkles' stand, with a rescued snuffle-nosed, blinking hedgehog, curling into protective spikes, made hearts melt and interest soar.

As Nell walked through the field, she passed stands representing every protected species and habitat – Badger Group, Amphibian and Reptile Group, the Wildlife Trust, the local British Trust for Ornithology Group, Barn Owl Trust, Moth and Butterfly Group, RSPB, Woodland Trust, Wetland Trust and Bat Conservation Trust.

Along the way, she spoke to the volunteers hosting the stalls, most of whom she worked with often.

Families tackled the treasure hunt that wound through the castle ruins, the crumbling honey-coloured stones glowing in the afternoon sun. Beside the wildflower meadow, two food trucks offered stone-baked pizza and ice cream. And banners bearing EcoLogical's name and logo fluttered over stalls showcasing the team's skills, where the eco-themed challenges prompted laughter between competitive family and friends.

Curious about what their new recruits had organised, Nell checked out their stands.

Drew and Elliot had paired up with the local council, and were offering troubleshooting advice on planning matters. Those clustered around their stand were soaking up Elliot's advice, while Drew nodded sagely.

Amir had got Simon to blow up ten glossy photos of various types of undergrowth, to create a test of how many reptiles, and how many species, people could identify. Whenever Nell glanced over, there was always a small crowd leaning slightly forward, studying pictures intently. Amir was delighted that no one ever managed to spot all twenty serpents, and that most people couldn't name all six reptile species in the UK and the level of protection they had. Every so often, Amir would gently lift the bronze, coiled python out of the black holdall to show interested families. He described Queenie's flickering tongue, what she'd be sensing, and answered questions.

Simon's stall was lined with stunning photographs, breathtakingly crisp and detailed, printed on aluminium. His test was to ask people to match the pictured birds with numbered recordings of calls, along with guessing whether they were specially protected, beyond the general protection during the breeding season. He'd also laid out different types of feathers to identify.

When an enquiring, sticky-fingered child picked up two long speckled feathers and waved them at Simon, he snatched them back and returned them to the table. 'Those are the primary remiges of a *Circus cyaneus*.'

The child gave a solemn nod and, when his breathless mother

caught up with him, said knowingly, 'You can't touch those. They're from the circus.'

Catching Nell's eye, and the encouraging gesture she was trying to make, Simon had turned back to the little kid. 'These longer feathers are primary flight feathers. They're designed to make the bird aerodynamic, so it can fly as fast as possible. And a *Circus cyaneus* is a hen harrier.'

He pointed at a photo of the bird's magnificent wingspan. 'She can fly at about forty miles per hour. She's a terrific hunter, who predates rabbits, amphibians and other birds. She can catch larger birds, too. Like ducks. But she has to drown those.'

As the child backed away, towards Amir's stall, Simon called out, 'Don't forget, when you're looking at *his* creatures, that *this* raptor would have them all for breakfast.'

For her stand, Nell had used a section of castle ruins to stage evidence used in an inspection of a building for roosting bats. Small toys – life-size bats – had been tucked into tiny crevices where pointing had crumbled away between the stones. She'd sprinkled tiny bat droppings on the ground and even got a few to stick to the wall itself. And she'd left a single wing of a moth as evidence of feeding remains. No one trying out her quiz had found all four clues yet.

In white-gloved hands, Nell held up the tiny common pipistrelle bat so that a little girl could get a closer look.

'Wow. Is it a baby?'

'No, she's fully grown. She looks bigger with her wings out, see?' Nell gently unfurled one wing, the delicate bones visible through the thin membrane. 'These wings, and her tail membrane, which helps her steer, make her fly really fast, so she can catch mosquitos in the air. Amazing, isn't she?'

Wide-eyed, the little girl nodded, and her father asked, 'So how come you've got this bat? Is it a rescue bat?'

Nell nodded. 'I have one at home at the moment who's injured, but recovering well. With luck, I'll release her into the wild in a few days. But our local bat group, just there,' she pointed at the stand next door, 'has some bats who can't be released, due to their injuries. If those bats aren't stressed by being handled, they become our education bats, like this one. Take a look: they have a very placid noctule, which is one of our largest bats.'

Behind the man, Erin rolled her eyes and turned to Amir, Drew and Simon. 'Nell's inseparable from her bats.'

Nell tucked the pipistrelle away, smiling at the little girl as she and her dad left, trying to ignore Erin's comment.

'What do you do if there's no chance of recovery?' Simon asked Nell. 'Do you . . . ?' He drew a line across his throat.

Nell nodded. 'I hate having to do it. The most peaceful way is chloroform. But it's difficult to get, even with a licence.'

'One of my colleagues was a rescuer.' Amir peered into the enclosure to see the bat. 'Quite the commitment. How do you manage if you're away for surveys?'

'I ask someone in the bat group to help. And, actually, Sylvia's become more interested lately. She's popped in a few times to feed them.'

'I can't imagine Sylvia doling out mealworms!' Simon laughed.

'No, I couldn't, either. I think she wears about three pairs of gloves and uses tweezers!' Nell laughed, noticing Erin scowl. 'But . . . let's just say she has a good reason to have a soft spot for bats.'

Drew tilted his head. 'Oh? That's unexpected. Let me guess: an article about some rare species won her a cover story for *National Geographic*?'

Nell wished she hadn't referred to the case involving Sylvia. 'Something like that.'

'Shall we ditch the bats and get a cocktail?' Erin tugged Simon's arm. 'Come on.'

As the event progressed into the evening, some of the team's families or partners joined them for celebratory drinks to round out the day. Erin steered them towards the newly arrived converted Airstream trailer, where a liveried bartender was spinning a cocktail shaker, as twenties jazz music drifted across the meadow. As they walked over, Nell spied a group of newcomers with Sylvia and Elliot.

Simon twitched his arm away from Erin's grasp – a few seconds too late.

'Hello?' One of the women left Elliot and came over, her sharp gaze fixed on Erin. 'I don't think we've met.' As she tilted her head enquiringly, pushing glossy chestnut hair over her shoulders, Nell realised this was Simon's partner. She was wearing a white summer dress and heels, to walk around a fair that was held on a field. It made Nell wonder if she ever shared Simon's extreme outdoor expeditions.

Erin frowned. 'No. I'm Erin.'

'Ah.' Her frown cleared. '*You're* Erin.' She glanced at Simon, appraising and expectant. After a second of silence, with a huff, she said, 'I'm Lisa. Simon's *girlfriend*.'

'Oh, nice to meet you,' Erin said. She half turned, as if to include the rest of the group, putting more distance between herself and Simon.

As introductions were made, Nell saw that another woman hesitated on the fringes. She'd been with Lisa and Sylvia when they'd walked over. Sylvia had gestured towards the cocktails, but the woman had shaken her head. Raising her hand, she gave a tiny wave, more a wiggle of her fingers, at Drew.

Drew answered with a small smile. 'Everyone, this is Nicky, my partner. Nicky, you get to meet my team at last! This is Amir, Simon, Erin, Nell.'

Nicky's eyes were wide when she shook Nell's hand, her voice a little breathless when she said, 'Nice to meet you.'

She looked nervous, and Nell smiled warmly. But Nicky was tugging the edge of her floral blouse, stopping it from blowing up in the breeze again and showing that her skirt was hanging off thin hips.

'Have you had a chance to look around the stands?' Nell tried to set her at ease.

'Yeah.' Her face brightened. 'I loved the renewable energy section – they've set up a wind turbine which sends a little train around a track. The kids loved it.'

Tom joined them, steering an unsteady, gurgling toddler, with a young blonde woman following close behind. 'We've just had a go at the treasure hunt,' he said. 'I've won a year's membership to the RSPB, so that's my next few weekends sorted! A few quiet hours in a hide on a beautiful reserve. Just what I need!'

'You wish!' His partner lunged forward with a steadying hand as their little one staggered and then clutched Simon's leg with sticky hands, making Simon stare at the boy, then Tom, with the awkwardness of someone who didn't know how to wrangle kids. 'Sorry. Come here, you little monster.' She disentangled the little boy and passed him to Tom. '*I'll* lie in until 6 a.m. and then *I'll* spend a day,' her fingers made air quotes, '*bird watching*. I could do with a few days tucked up in a cosy hide, a flask full of pinot grig, quietly falling asleep all afternoon. Who'd know? I'm Anna, by the way.'

As everyone introduced themselves, Simon glanced warily at the child. Erin laughed at him, and moved to stand between them like a human shield. Simon's caution was amplified by Amir's amusement, and Lisa's daggered looks at Erin.

Drew's lip curled, but then Nicky nudged his arm. Nell hadn't even noticed her slip away. She'd brought him back a drink. 'Here you go. Dark and stormy.'

Drew stared at the glass, crammed with ice and lime, and then at her.

'It's rum. You like rum, yes?'

'Don't they have any wine?' Drew asked.

Nicky shook her head. 'Only cocktails. The guy's great. He makes a right show of creating them.'

'I bet.'

Anna nudged him. 'I was hoping for a cheeky glass of something. Don't fancy a cocktail, though.' She grinned at Drew. 'We should raid the local offy and bring a bottle or three back.'

Drew stared at her, as if she was talking out of turn. Nell wondered if it was a status thing, and he felt that his rank – as Financial Director compared to Tom's lowly intern level – was being disrespected. Finally, he lifted his glass. 'No, I'm fine with this.' He shot Nicky an approving gaze. 'Thanks, love.'

Nicky's face shone, like storm clouds parting to reveal sunshine on a summer's day. She glanced down, a small smile tugging at her lips.

'Are we *all* having a drink then?' Erin asked, but she only looked at Simon. Apparently, an answer was unnecessary, and the group drifted towards the cocktail bar, just as Conor arrived.

'Nell! How did today go? This is all Sylvia's been talking about for weeks.'

'Sylvia's worked wonders. The stalls looked brilliant, we had loads of interest.'

Letting the group walk on, he turned, appraising her. 'It isn't *all* she's been talking about. How are you?'

'Oh, you know.'

'Sure I do. How's Rav?'

Nell began to give her stock answer, then stopped. The despair she'd grown accustomed to wasn't there. Something had lifted since Rav had taken her letter. She still itched to see him – more than ever – but that bleak, desolate black hole wasn't swamping her. 'I'm feeling a little more hopeful. Thanks to Sylvia's advice.'

'Ah, yes, never shy, that one.'

Nell grinned. As she introduced him to the group, Drew's eyes narrowed, while Simon and Amir looked at him warily. Nell wasn't surprised. His self-assured manner and authoritative bearing – biceps and broad shoulders encased in a black shirt and a black suit – made people notice him.

Conor passed Nell a glass of Pimm's and took the other to Sylvia, who was chatting with Elliot. Turning back to the group, Nell saw that Simon and Lisa had moved away a little, muttering. Amir watched them, trying to hide his chuckle by taking a long sip of his Manhattan.

Simon threw his hands up, nearly making Lisa spill her drink. 'Seriously? Here?'

'Yeah, well, where am I supposed to *talk* to you? You're never bloody *home*.'

'Why would I want to be?'

'I can't answer that. You'd rather be creeping around on your precious heath. Bloody weirdo.' Lisa gave a short laugh. 'But I'm a fool, aren't I? You're not doing that at all. You're with her, aren't you?' Lisa gestured at Erin with her glass, the carefully crafted cocktail sloshing.

Erin stood up, open-mouthed, looking a little bit shocked . . . and a little bit delighted.

'*Hardly*! She's a colleague, Lisa. And about half my age!'

'Yeah, I've had enough of being lied to. About where you are.

And when. And now *who with*. I haven't come here to have my face rubbed in it. Let's face facts, Si. We're over.'

Wednesday 13th July – 5 p.m.

Rav craned his head for the millionth time, wondering when Nell would arrive. He knew she'd come today. The usual apprehensive nausea of 'what ifs?' still churned, but today, optimism was blossoming. He'd even had a shower, finally pushing aside the embarrassment of needing assistance, and that alone had made him feel better.

Hearing footsteps along the corridor, he looked up. His heart leaped as he spied Nell.

Her face lit up. 'You're looking better. Did you . . .' She hesitated, looking suddenly uncertain. 'Did you read my note?'

Rav nodded. 'I did.'

She sat beside him, her eyes fixed on his. 'I've been so worried about you. But the thing that's worried me more than anything is that you won't confide in me. And you don't have to, I know.' She held her hands up, as if trying to show she had no expectations, and the gesture nearly made his heart break. 'But I feel like you're afraid to trust me, like I might not be able to cope with how things are. Or that I may not want to stay with you. When the *one* thing you *should* be totally sure of is that I love you.'

He swallowed back tears but managed to nod.

'But . . .' That uncertain look flickered again. 'Has that changed for you?'

'No. Not a bit.' His voice sounded raspy, as fierce love surged through him. 'I've just been . . .' He looked at her and knew he didn't need to spell his every last fear out. 'I've been an idiot.' He managed a smile and reached for her hand.

Nell leaned in – but she paused, her fingers stroking his face, lacing into his hair, gazing into his eyes. And when she kissed him, it was ardent, deep with desire. Not the pity he'd feared. Relief spilled out in tears, and she pulled away.

'Sorry,' he managed. 'I've just missed you. I'm so sorry I pushed you away.'

Gripping his hands, she shook her head. 'I think I owe Conor and Sylvia something epic for their intervention.'

As he wiped his face, Rav managed a smile. 'Well, after their pincer movement, and my mum's blunt approach, I guess there are no secrets now.' He hoped his shrug hid his embarrassment.

'No. But Google deprived you of those long ago, anyway.' Nell's lips twitched, kind and impish.

'Oh, great.' He rolled his eyes, but smiled with her.

She took a breath. 'So can we talk about everything now? Properly?'

When he nodded, she asked, 'OK. So how are you doing? And what's worrying you?'

He exhaled. *This is it.* 'I asked about my prognosis this morning.' He looked at her. 'It's not great, Nell. There's such a small chance of recovery. Of . . . anything.'

Nell squeezed his hand. 'Rav, even if the chance was one per cent, *someone* would have to be that one per cent. Why *wouldn't* it be you? You're young. Ish. Fit. Ish.' She shot him a smile. 'What will it take? Surgery? PT?'

'No. And yes. And a lot of hard work—'

'And since when has that been a problem?'

'It's fine for you. You're not the one who has to do it.'

'True,' Nell said, contrite for a second. 'But I do *know* you. And I *know* you have it in you, Rav.'

'No. I don't think you're listening.' Desperation doused his optimism. This was the problem. Her expectations that everything would somehow be OK were overwhelming, and they resurrected the fear that she was with him with the vision of a normal future together, instead of how things were.

'Nell. Please – take this in. Take it seriously. Let's say I *do* work hard, and I give it everything I've got. What if it's not enough? What if I never recover beyond this? I need you to really think about that. What that would mean. For both of us.'

Nell nodded. 'I have. I didn't mean to sound glib about any of this. I'm not here in blind hope, Rav. I've researched. I understand.'

'But we haven't had those conversations. About what we might have wanted for the future. And what we might need to adapt to.'

'Like?'

He took a deep breath, braced himself and blurted out the words before fear paralysed his tongue. 'What if our sex life is affected? Or we can't even have one? What about kids? What if we can't have a family of our own?'

He gazed at her, trying to read her reaction, to see if she shared those fears.

But she just shrugged. 'Yes, I've been wondering about all those things, too. But those are ifs, not certainties. And, even in a worst-case scenario, there are options.' She lowered her voice. 'Like sex. We'll just have to navigate that with some imagination, won't we?' Her eyebrows twitched as she shot him a wicked grin.

He shook his head, still afraid she wasn't getting it.

Her tone grew serious. 'Do you want a family?' she asked.

'I don't know.' Rav shrugged. 'I don't mind being a favourite uncle. But right now I'm not sure I feel, I don't know, *responsible* enough for parenthood.' He shot her an anxious look. 'What about you, though? Don't you need an heir, for the Ward-Beaumont estate?'

'Well, I know *your mum* thinks I do! And she's probably right that my parents think the same. But the biological clock is ticking and no particular inclination has kicked in yet. And, if it does, there are *still* options, Rav. All we have to do is be honest about how we feel. It's not complicated. Not really.'

'But it might be! What if I put in all this work and it *still* doesn't get us back to having a normal life? What if I let you down?'

Nell shook her head. 'Impossible.' But her chin trembled, and he didn't dare trust her words. 'You seem to think I want what you can *give* me. When, actually, all I want is *you*.'

When the surgeon knocked on Rav's door, Nell could have cried. *Just as we're getting somewhere.* With heavy reluctance, she left Rav's room and went to make coffee for them both. By the time she returned, the surgeon was leaving, a frown on his face, and she hurried back to Rav.

'What did he say?'

Rav shook his head. 'Not enough progress. I have to buck up.'

'Right. So how can I help motivate you into action? I've said you don't need to worry—'

'Yeah, I know. Why don't you take my mind off things? What's going on with you?'

Nell blinked at the change of tack. 'Busy with work. We have a big project on Furze Heath. I'm covering the reptiles, thanks to your training. We've got three new recruits—'

'Furze Heath? Wasn't that in the news?'

Nell nodded. 'A woman was found there.' She swallowed.

Rav pushed himself up in bed. He fished around on his bedside table amongst the pile of papers and magazines. 'Yes, look, here. *Heath Hunter Claims Fourth Victim*.' He glanced at Nell as he rifled through the rest of the papers. Finding no other reports, he stared at the one article again. 'This was from *last week*. And you've been *working* there?'

As she shifted in her seat, Rav's eyes fixed on hers. 'What?'

'I . . . I found her, actually,' she admitted.

'*Jesus*, Nell!'

'Shush!' She glanced over her shoulder at the doorway. 'I also found this.' She showed Rav the photo of the Craghoppers button. 'Where the killer dumped the victim's phone and wallet.'

'Please don't tell me you're trying to play detective again,' Rav said. 'The article says it's the work of a *serial killer*, Nell.'

'I'm not, but . . . maybe we could deduce something together, you and me? We usually do.'

'Don't be ridiculous!' Rav looked panicked. 'We both know what happens when we get involved. Somewhere along the line, you'll get hurt. And I'm . . .' He gestured at his legs with impatience. '*Please*, Nell.'

Nell chewed her lip.

Rav stared at her. 'What aren't you telling me?'

'Nothing . . .' She grimaced. 'Well . . .'

'What?'

She sighed. 'When the police were called to the scene, James . . .'

Another wince made Rav's heart thud. '*What*?'

'James thought it was *me*, because there's a strong resemblance between us – me and the victim on the heath. And then . . . after he and Val spoke to a Behavioural Investigative Advisor, he gave me an official warning. The killer has a physical type, and I . . . well, I seem to match it.'

In a heartbeat, Rav's expression switched from helpless to something she recognised. Resolve.

'Right.' He shifted himself up, just as they both heard footsteps coming towards the room.

'Mr Rennie,' Rav called, and Nell turned to see his surgeon back in the doorway.

'Everything OK?' Mr Rennie stepped in and stood at the foot of Rav's bed.

'Yes,' Rav said, with a decisiveness that Nell hadn't heard for a while. 'I'd like to start my PT.' He glanced at Nell. 'Right *now*, if possible?'

Chapter 11

Thursday 14th July – 10 a.m.

James spoke into his mouthpiece, raising his voice above the helicopter's clatter. 'This is incredible! We can target the exact buildings to search. This may give us the lead we need.'

Beside him, DS Wade Ezra – his point of liaison from the Serious and Organised Crime Unit – hefted the screen he held, showing black-and-white infrared images of the houses of Pendlebury below them.

'We can compare heat signatures through this, to our home-ownership lists and our persons of interest. And when we get a *match*,' the muscular, black officer shot James an irrepressible grin, 'my team gets a *warrant*.'

'Do you find much?' James asked.

'Every so often. I have to be honest, the local suppliers are less trouble than the county line suppliers, bringing gear out of London. But the locals know the territories. Know where to avoid, and who to avoid. That intel is worth its weight in gold to us.'

He curled his lip. 'The county line scene supports a really nasty trade. A lot of violent abuse, grooming little kids. I saw a lot of it growing up. I was one of the lucky ones. One too many stop and searches, if you know what I mean.' Another irreverent grin. 'Gave the local coppers the right runaround. But I got taken under one of their wings. Landed here. Gotta say, I like stamping it out. There's nothing like a raid, mate. When you know you've cut out some of the rot.'

His words made James focus on the task. As he studied the screen, one house nestled amongst the streets glowed bright white.

'Here we go. Look at that heat signature!' Wade rubbed his hands. 'Just bear in mind that it could be an older couple with the heating on full whack, even in the summer, with poor loft insulation. Or it could be a cannabis farm, and our lucky day.'

'Do you know who lives there?' James asked.

Checking his iPad, Wade looked up the address. 'Yep. One Mr Amir Massoud.'

Ten minutes later, James was knocking on Amir's door. Wade had confirmed he wasn't on any lists the Serious and Organised Crime Unit had that would trigger a warrant. But James could still pop round to ask a few questions. He'd use the thermal imaging data to ask about cannabis growing, rather than about the murders, giving him the chance to weigh Amir up without showing that hand, just yet.

The smart terrace of Georgian town houses curved through the up-and-coming part of Pendlebury. Most of the terraces had been converted to flats, but there were no multiple buzzers and name tags at this address; Amir had all three storeys.

Amir answered. He frowned, recognition flickering. 'Oh. You're Nell's friend? What do—'

'Mr Amir Massoud?' James showed his badge. 'I wonder if I can take a moment of your time to ask about a couple of our enquiries?'

Amir folded his arms, his hands jammed into his armpits. 'What enquiries?'

'Can I come in?' James gestured.

'What enquiries?' Amir didn't move.

James looked at him, sensing the impasse.

'I don't know if I can help you, if I don't know what the enquiries are, do I?'

'Let's talk in private.' James gestured towards the hall again.

Amir shrugged. 'No. I've got nothing to hide.'

'So there'll be no problem with me coming in, then,' James reasoned.

'It's not exactly convenient. But I'm happy to talk here. And that's all you want, isn't it?'

'We've identified a distinct heat signature from the roof of your house. These are typically indicative of a cannabis farm.'

'A *what*?' Amir held back stuttering laughter. 'Or, maybe, poor insulation, surely?'

'Yes, perhaps. That's why I'd like to take a look.'

'Well, I can take it upon myself to improve the insulation. Being honest, as an ecologist, I should be preserving energy, shouldn't I? But I've never really looked up there.'

'Do you mind if I do? Now?'

'Yes.'

'Why?'

'Because I'd have thought worrying about how well insulated my house is, is probably a waste of police time.'

'It won't be a waste of time if it removes you from our persons of interest list relating to cannabis production, will it? So may I take a look?' James tilted his head. 'Or do I need to spend my valuable police time – and *thank* you for being so considerate about it – getting a search warrant?'

'On the grounds of poor insulation?'

James didn't dignify that with an answer. He just looked at him, holding the silence.

With a sigh, Amir pushed the door open. But as James passed him, he thought he caught a flicker of a smile.

James scanned the open-plan kitchen-diner that filled the first floor, with what looked like a utility room beyond. The door under the stairs presumably led to a cloakroom. James pointed. 'Let's head upstairs.'

As James left the brightness of the kitchen, the low light in the living room felt eerie.

The sudden warmth, and the silence, made James move with more care, placing his feet on the wooden stairs quietly. Then he heard it: slow, deliberate rustling. It shot pure, primeval *fight or flight* through him.

As he pressed up, towards the top of the stairs, he gazed around at the walls lined with tanks and had to fight the urge to recoil. He'd known Amir had a python and was knowledgeable about breeding. But he hadn't expected *this*.

'So why, exactly, are you so bothered about my loft insulation?' Amir was asking.

James felt like a fool for saying it now. It seemed bloody obvious why Amir's house would have such a high heat signature.

Opposite him, a python was wrapped around a branch inside its vivarium. The unblinking eyes seemed to be fixed on him.

'Are all your snakes securely away?'

'Yes. No need to worry. I take security very seriously. Well, I take the stress of my beautiful creatures very seriously. They're all locked up in their vivaria.' A wicked smile. 'Even the cobra.'

As James twisted round to scan the tanks, Amir said, 'Look, you know I work with Nell Ward. I'm a herpetologist. I have full licences for all of these. I keep them and breed them. I'll get all the licences for you, and you can take copies if you like?'

At James's nod, Amir opened a desk and rifled through the paperwork. Turning, he held out several sheets of paper. James read them, then photographed them. 'Thanks, this all seems to be in order.' He handed the paperwork back to Amir.

'You're welcome to look where you like,' Amir said. 'But, if it's OK, I'd like to make one request. Upstairs is where I have my breeding females and youngsters. They're very sensitive and vulnerable to disturbance. So I'd prefer to accompany you, if you search there. Around their young, the females can be a little bit more . . . *aggressive*.'

Thursday 14th July – 10.15 p.m.

He couldn't help searching for details about her. Hadn't Erin called her something unusual this week? *Lady Beaumont*. Probably nothing in it. *Even so . . .*

He found himself reaching for his phone, typing the name along with local villages. Cookingdean village and Finchmere both returned results. Shock seized him in a silent grip as he registered the articles, the pictures filling the screen.

It's her. It felt like the world slid sideways. *This changes . . . everything . . .*

The raised stakes made his pulse thud. He held his head in his hands, trying to *think*. Needing noise, he punched the remote, sparking the TV into noisy, prime-time action. The chaos soothed and he sank back into the sofa, staring at the screen until the programme changed. His thoughts whirled around the same nucleus: could he leverage something *more*?

Ideas streaked through his brain – but then someone said the name he was thinking out loud. He shook himself, sat up. On the screen, on the *Question Time* panel, was one Lady Ward-Beaumont. He recognised her from the photos he'd just clicked through: Nell's mother. Imelda.

Intrigued, he leaned forward, noting her clipped cut-glass accent and the banner across the screen, bearing her name and the fact she was a Tory MP.

For the first segment, she had very little to say. Then a question made his lip curl. 'With violence against women and girls higher than ever, what realistic steps can those on the panel with influence commit to, to make actual and urgent changes?'

The question was immediately passed to Imelda. She nodded at the woman in the audience.

'Thanks for your question. I think this is something we should *all* be acting on and answering. Because this is half our population we're talking about, with most of those crimes committed by the other half. The evidence shows us that these crimes are incremental – that tolerance of a low-level crime simply creates a gateway to increasingly more serious ones. So there's a strong argument for nipping this kind of behaviour in the bud. There's an obvious imperative that we need to be tougher. My reform act proposes harsher sentences for flashing, stalking—' Boos broke out across some of the audience, with other listeners applauding.

'The thing with cosseted people like Lady Beaumont,' the male panellist beside her asserted, 'is that they have *no* idea what it's like in prison. And no common sense. Increasing sentencing for crimes like this will be a nightmare for prison staff. It's totally impractical.'

Imelda bore no hint of apology. 'Oh, I don't intend to only make it *easier* to get *into* prison with my reform act, I *also* intend for it to be an awful lot *harder* for criminals to *leave*, through my proposed parole act.'

The man beside her gaped, so she continued. 'Please bear in mind that these bills are aimed specifically at those guilty of violence against women and girls. And I appreciate that this good gentleman here believes I've had no involvement with prison, but he's wrong to assume that. I wonder if he has read any of the parole notes and, along with that, the original crimes that those newly liberated individuals have committed before being sent back into the community?'

'If they're remorseful and they've served their time, then fair enough.'

'That's *precisely* my point. With parole, they *don't* serve their time. Reading those parole briefings is depressing indeed for the paltry price we place on life.'

'We're a society that believes in rehabilitation, madam.'

'We're a society that *wants* to believe in it, but that doesn't make it true, or certainly not true a hundred per cent of the time. And anything less than that means people get killed. It's an unacceptable risk that – currently – we *knowingly* impose on the society we're supposed to *protect*.'

'Pfff. It's a calculated risk.'

'And if that calculation is so measured, so successful, then tell me, what percentage of offenders reoffend after *supposed* remorse and rehabilitation – and then *actual* release?'

She held his gaze until he shook his head.

'I can tell you, since you don't know. Recent records quote that percentage, over only three months, as being just under *twenty-five per cent* of murderers committing more *murders* when they're released.' She turned her hands up. 'What on earth are we, as *policymakers*, as *protectors* of the people, *doing* by allowing, *enabling*, convicted criminals to reoffend? We know the statistics – *well* . . .' she glanced at her male detractor, 'we *should*. So we're *fully* aware of the likelihood of it happening. It's unconscionable gross negligence. And yet, for some bizarre reason, we place the burden on the innocent, as if it's right to endanger people, instead of keeping those who – may I remind you – have *already* committed *murder*, in prison.'

As another cacophony of boos and cheers erupted from his TV, he looked up the two pieces of legislation she referred to.

It was true. She was lobbying for two acts: one to increase sentences, and a second to make it significantly harder to make parole.

Rage set fire to his gut. He grabbed his coat, his keys, and strode out into the night, despite the rain.

I'm in control here. There has to be a way.

The cool night air helped to crystallise his thoughts. *Oh, yes . . . of course . . .*

Nell nearly choked on her coffee at the sight of her mother on *Question Time*. She'd known Imelda's stance had become more and more assertive over the past few months. With a wave of guilt, Nell realised how many brushes with murder she'd had in that same amount of time. Mum had been working on this for long enough that Nell knew her critique of the system would be objective, but *now* it was also laced with a good dollop of very subjective and personal protective instincts.

But Nell hadn't known that Lady Ward-Beaumont, MP, would be out in force in her professional capacity, presenting those views on TV tonight. She realised, suddenly, how out of touch she was. Today had felt like a breakthrough, seeing Rav in the therapy unit, working so hard, despite the pain. But she had no idea what was going on with anyone else.

As if making the point, her phone buzzed. A text from her mother flashed on top of her web search for PT exercises. *QT has caused ructions. Conor's stepping up my security for tomorrow night. Hope you haven't forgotten – seven thirty. Play nice.* The text that followed gave her the address of Shannon's South Bank gallery.

Nell groaned. She'd completely forgotten that she'd agreed to support Shannon's grand opening and the debut of her first artist.

As Nell contemplated an excuse, a text from Percy, her best friend, popped up: *Ugh. Just had to let Shannon know that I can't make tomorrow. Estate issues. Can't avoid it. I've offered a venue up here next month so her artist can take her exhibition on tour. Hoping that will make up for it . . . In the meantime, can you dazzle for both of us?*

With a sigh, Nell sank back against the sofa. The recent understanding she and Percy had reached about why Shannon had such a chip on her shoulder had caused them to make a pact to support her.

And Shannon also seemed to be trying. She was less spiky; she'd stopped calling herself Percy's poor relation, the cousin with no castle, having regarded her Thames-side penthouse and annual allowance as a pittance. True, it wasn't Glencoille Castle, which Percy would inherit – but Shannon had conveniently overlooked the fact that she *also* wouldn't inherit all the work required to run it. Nell wondered if James had anything to do with the recent shift in Shannon's mindset . . . assuming they were still dating? They made an unlikely couple: Nell's nemesis and her ex.

So she'd have to go. Depending on the temperature tomorrow afternoon, she might be able to squeeze in the first reptile translocation and make it to the gallery for eight o'clock.

Nell sent a quick text, confirming she'd be there. She realised that if she, Shannon and Percy really did make up, they would be resolving three generations of conflict.

Friday 15th July – 2.30 p.m.

'And we are *live* on the BBC Wildlife website!' Simon announced. As everyone clustered round, he handed his iPad to Sylvia. 'Erin's idea for an article has generated a load of interest and some great comments already.'

'Front-page headline!' Sylvia practically purred with delighted approval. 'And doesn't your cover photo look *terrific*, Simon!' She scanned the article, scrolling past two more stunning images. 'Not bad, Erin, not bad at all!'

She passed the iPad around so everyone could admire it. 'Don't forget it was in the local paper earlier this week – to great acclaim, may I say – and I also sent it out to the local parish magazines and some industry publications, so it'll be popping up all over the place. As well as on our website. So please add the link to the article to your email signatures. I want to squeeze all the juice out of this one!'

'Great! And yes, congratulations, Erin, for the brilliant suggestion,' Elliot enthused. 'And I gather you wrote it, Tom? Rufus *will* be pleased with this.'

Drew nodded as the iPad reached him. But as he handed it to Nell, she spotted that his face looked thunderous.

'Thanks, Elliot.' Erin shot a sidelong, dimpled grin at Simon. He flashed his eyebrows, and Erin blushed and smiled again.

'Why didn't I get any notification that it was going up today?' Sylvia patted the pockets of her palazzo pants, then checked her desk and rummaged in her bag. With a sigh, she dashed upstairs to the kitchen and came down, reading something on her phone. As she passed Nell, she tutted at herself. 'Must have left it there since this morning's coffee. Got a hundred emails.' She smiled as she found the message she was looking for. 'Ah, good, yes, they love the story. I'll send a lovely thank you for the prime placement.'

As the gathering dissipated, Nell finished her coffee, dashed to the kitchen to shove the mug in the dishwasher, then handed her site risk assessment to Sylvia, detailing where and at what time she'd be surveying.

'Oh, sweetie, you're not surveying in this, are you?' Sylvia tilted her head at the rain hammering on the window.

'It might be chucking it down, but it's the right temperature for reptiles to be using the refugia.' Nell *had* wanted to see Rav. But he'd texted to say that he was having an extended PT session today, so she'd had to content herself with sending a string of encouraging emojis.

And it was just as well, really. Now that the heath development was back on track and permissions had been agreed, Erin, Tom and Simon had spent yesterday overseeing the planting across different areas of the heath to strengthen habitat links and improve the site's capacity to support a growing reptile population. And Amir had joined them, supervising the reptile fence installation, which encompassed the construction zone and an area to create a pond and a south-facing bank for reptiles to hunt in and bask on.

So, today was the first day that translocations could begin. And Nell was keen to get started – July and August were suboptimal months, so extra survey effort would be needed to ensure they moved all the individuals in the working area. Given the tight timeframes of the development, that would mean working at weekends, too.

'I'll keep an eye on you.' Sylvia tapped her phone to life, seeing Nell's location blinking on the map. 'Yes, I see you. Text me when you're done.'

In Furze Heath's car park, Nell pulled her waterproofs on against the downpour and hurried across to check the reptile refugia. It had been kind of Amir to head off mid-morning to cover the afternoon survey further afield, at Upper Thwaltam, so she could survey the heath and then head straight for London. And carving up the work, as they had, meant that as much as possible could get done around this lousy rain.

An hour and a half later, Nell's short hair was plastered to her forehead and she was soaked to the skin. Her boots squelched as she approached the last trap. Her gloved hand lifted the corner of the square.

Hunkered low, one female adder absorbed the heat from the corrugated iron, for energy to hunt. She raised her head, orange eyes glowing in shadow. As Nell caught her and placed her in the bucket, she estimated the viper was forty-five centimetres long. Nell noted the information, along with the refugia number, the survey end-time and temperature.

At the car, Nell shed her non-waterproof waterproofs, and pulled on dry socks and shoes. She drove to the release site, freed her captive snakes under suitable cover, and texted Sylvia: *First translocation done.* Her saturated jeans and top steamed up the car windows as she raced home to transform herself into something civilised enough for a gallery opening.

Peeling off her clothes, she dumped them in the washing machine and dashed upstairs for a shower. She dressed hurriedly in a ruby cocktail dress and heels, smudged on some eyeliner and ruffled her pixie-cut hair into something that could be considered stylish.

Before she went, she put food out for Jezebel and locked the cat flap, then checked on Pipsqueak. The tiny bat was as feisty as ever, chattering with indignation.

'OK, poppet, you'll be ready to go tomorrow. We're just waiting for good weather now, so you'll be able to get your bearings and find some food.' Nell placed her back in the enclosure, topping up the mealworm supply and refreshing her water.

Short on time, she rushed out to the car and sped to London. Arriving just after seven thirty, she spotted her mother's damson

Bentley Mulsanne pull up in front of Shannon's gallery. Emerging from the back seats, Imelda and Hugo were visions of elegance, smiling at the gaggle of photographers – right before they began goading:

'Imelda! What do you think about the responses to your *Question Time* statement?'

'Lady Beaumont? Is it true you're out of touch with what prison is really like?'

'Is your daughter responsible for your biased views?'

'Aren't you getting too old for politics?'

But Imelda smiled and waved serenely, not giving the desired reaction, before walking gracefully inside. Nell braced herself to do the same. She grimaced at the timing when James bounded up the steps to greet her with a kiss on one cheek.

'Nell, are you getting cosy with DI Clark after his involvement in those murders at your family estate a few months ago?'

'Or are you getting closer because of your mother's views on policing?'

'Do you agree with Imelda's politics, DI Clark? Has she influenced you?'

With a smile and wave at the cameras, Nell slipped her arm through James's and steered him inside.

'I wasn't expecting the reception committee,' he whispered.

'No.' Nell glanced at her mother, who looked unsurprisingly jubilant.

'At least the work I'm doing is gathering momentum.' Imelda gleamed. 'Nice to see you, James.'

'Nice to see you too. And I wouldn't dare miss this. Even though I won't be able to afford anything. I'm just here to support our illustrious host.'

Inside, on stark white walls, huge oil portraits glowed with life. The artist, Saima Jamil, had obvious talent. Knots of guests, in various styles of dress – from street cool to high glamour – sipped champagne, grazed on canapés and rhapsodised about the art.

But Nell was busy raising her eyebrows at James's comment. 'Shannon's still keen, then?' she teased.

'Ha! Maybe.' James fiddled with the button on his jacket. 'Well, she wants bodies in the room, a buzz. And I'm all about supporting new artists.'

'Yes, I thought so.' Nell saw his smile. 'This must be a dating *record* for Shannon.'

'I'll take that as the compliment I'm sure you mean it to be.' James grinned. 'If you're happier, can I ask, does that mean Rav's doing better?'

Nell gave a small nod. 'He's trying.'

'Oh, that's *great* to hear. Send him my best, will you?' He glanced over his shoulder, then leaned in. 'Look, Nell, can I talk to you about something serious?'

'Sure.' She frowned. 'What is it?'

Across the room, Shannon raised her champagne flute at them and steered a woman in black leggings, black turtleneck and a drapey gold sequinned duster coat – Saima, the artist – right over to them.

'Oh.' James winced. 'I . . . It'll have to wait. But I need to speak to you, before you leave. OK?'

Chapter 12

James was torn between worry over Nell – with two of her colleagues on his radar as persons of interest – and delight, as Shannon made a beeline for him. He accepted the drink offered by the passing waiter and took a long sip of the mocktail mojito. The waiter might have called it something groan-worthy, like a *no-*jito, but he was too busy to notice as he said thank you, tried to reassure Nell, and attempted to look cool and collected as Shannon approached.

'Nell! So glad you could join.' Shannon leaned in to air-kiss her, wrapping them all in her seductive oud and amber scent. 'Saima, this is Lady Eleanor. One of my *closest* family friends. Huge advocate for artists.'

'I'm Nell, lovely to meet you.'

'And this is *James*, avid aficionado and supporter of the arts.'

He tried not to choke on his drink.

Saima beamed and leaned in to air-kiss them both. 'Are you collectors?'

'Well, I . . . Not yet . . .' James spluttered, making Shannon's eyes narrow.

'My family has a modest collection.' Nell swooped in. *Thank God.* 'Local artists, mainly, with one or two known names. And I *love* these, Saima.'

Shannon slid an arm around Saima's waist. 'Nell's our secret weapon. She'll slink up to guests, praise your work and name-drop comparisons in her family's collection. She'll encourage new buyers to take the plunge, and old buyers to beat them to it.'

'She's outrageous, isn't she?' Saima grinned at Nell.

She sounded sweet, full of excitement and slight disbelief at her work being displayed, and James warmed to her instantly. He shot Shannon a sidelong glance. This looked pretty impressive to his inexperienced eye.

And Nell was on the case. 'Tell me all about your technique and inspiration, so I can advocate for you.'

'I love traditional styles and methods. But I wanted to paint seemingly candid pictures. Un-posed, full of humour or pathos. I like the juxtaposition of the closeness of painting a sitter, with the intense attention and deep understanding to really *get* them – yet painting them as if they haven't noticed. Like I'm a stalker with oil paint.'

Shannon pointed at the nearest canvas: a woman's face in extreme close-up, laughing, a fleeting moment captured in paint. 'I love the intimacy. And *energy*. In both mood *and* brushstrokes. It's truly masterful, Saima.'

Absorbing the details, James had to agree. Shannon had an unerring eye for art. She was happier since she'd found her niche, doing something she loved and was good at. It had given her that vital sense of purpose. Maybe it was nothing to do with dating him . . .

Before he knew it, Nell was circulating, gesturing at the paintings as she spoke to fellow admirers. Shannon introduced Saima to everyone in the room. He milled about on the fringes, feeling like an interloper in this high-value world.

As Nell moved from group to group, red dots appeared on the paintings' title cards like a spreading rash, until most pieces were claimed. By nine o'clock, Nell circled back to him. 'Enjoying the evening?'

'Yes.' He tilted his drink at the nearest sold painting. 'You've worked some magic.'

Saima rushed over, her face bright, excited. 'I've just sold the last one! I can't believe it! I didn't expect this exhibition to really happen, let alone sell out!' She held up a bottle of champagne. 'I'm going to down this immediately!'

Shannon joined them, saying, 'Thanks, Nell. Most of the people you spoke to bought a piece.'

Nell shook her head. 'Nothing to do with me. Not one buyer needed any persuading. These are all genuine admirers. Congratulations! It's a terrific first exhibition. This has been a great launch. For both of you.'

'Thanks.' Shannon looked surprised – then worried. 'So sorry. I haven't asked about Rav.'

'He's . . .' Nell hesitated and James could see she wasn't sure what to say.

'Understood.' With surprising empathy, Shannon squeezed Nell's hand. 'Send my love, won't you.' She turned to James. 'Everyone will leave now. I'm sure Saima will want to go on somewhere to celebrate. Want to join?'

Yes, yes! He wanted to, very much. But he had to speak to Nell. Something was nagging him, making him feel unsettled. And taking tonight off meant he'd have to start early tomorrow. 'I'd love to, but not tonight. Enjoy your evening with Saima. Maybe we could do something together at the—'

He was going to say 'weekend', but Shannon said, 'At the end of your case?'

It was a more accurate suggestion. He gave her a rueful smile. 'This one's a tough one.'

'Lucky that you're worth the wait, then, isn't it, Detective?' She kissed him softly.

His heart soared at the unexpected line, and the kiss.

'Keep me posted. I'll be busy. I'll be buzzing the collectors in New York and Europe, so if I don't reply immediately, I may just be in a different time zone.'

That was Shannon all over. She wasn't one to hang around. As James turned to leave, he saw that Nell had been intercepted by her parents, Hugo and Imelda.

Attempting to skirt around them, he tried to catch Nell's eye, so he could take her aside and warn her about her colleagues being suspects. Then he saw her stricken face, and heard her father saying, 'There have been several emails, Nell, I can't think how you missed it. Motorsport UK are giving their verdict on Rav's accident tomorrow morning. It was problematic finding a suitable date, apparently. Hence the weekend meeting. But we *must* attend. If they decide the fault lies with us, we must be there to accept it. And Rav's parents will be there. It will be disrespectful if we aren't.'

It looked like Nell swayed on her feet. 'I just . . . I just didn't expect it to be so soon. And Rav's *only* just started his PT. What if this sets him back all over again?'

Friday 15th July – 9.30 p.m.

Nell stumbled away from her parents and found her car. She dreaded hearing the official dissection of Rav's accident – their professional assessment of how it happened, who was culpable, if there were any issues with her family's racetrack, and her father's car, if the health and safety measures had been satisfactory. Nothing in the report would change things for Rav, though. And that was all that mattered.

But she'd led aspects of the racing event, so now it was her responsibility to see it through. That meant listening to the findings of the committee. Even if they were going to describe in painstaking detail all the things she should have done better to prevent the accident that had changed Rav's life.

Just as we're finally talking. Just as he's starting his treatment . . . Her stomach twisted at the thought of him returning to that state of despondency.

She couldn't dam the tsunami of tears. By the time she reached her car, she knew mascara had already streaked down her face. Driving was at least something to focus on.

Arriving home, waiting for her gates to slide open, worry crowded in again. She parked, then trudged inside, her heart even heavier than her feet. Turning off the alarm on autopilot, she flicked on the lamp on the counter and went to check on Pipsqueak.

She froze as she saw she'd left the bat's enclosure open, the unzipped mesh gaping. With more than enough room to let Pipsqueak escape.

Oh, God. Nell tried to quell her panic. The utility room door had been open. *Pipsqueak could be anywhere. Or have injured herself in her bid for freedom . . .* Nell winced. *She was ready for release. She'll starve if I can't find her.*

She took a breath. *Be methodical.*

She checked between the folds of the tea towel inside the enclosure, just in case. Finding nothing, her heart sinking, she closed the door and readied herself for the meticulous scrutiny for droppings on the floor or stuck to the wall that might indicate Pipsqueak's activity. Reaching the light, she switched it on and turned, scanning the room. She caught something dark in her peripheral vision, on the wall opposite Pipsqueak's enclosure. Snapping her head round, she stared, then staggered back against the counter. She couldn't register what she saw.

A black and scarlet smear streaked across the tiles. Nell moved towards it, trepidation thumping in her stomach.

Half a bat wing was stuck to the wall, with blood clots seeped from the delicate elbow and knuckle joints. The ulna had splintered and pierced the fine wing membrane like an ivory needle. The bat's body was a corruption. The crushed head and torso were smudged across the tiles. Brown fur matted with black, sticky blood and something pinker, like pulverised internal organs. One tiny foot was splayed out, preserved like a pressed flower.

'Oh, God.' Even as her sobs erupted, Nell couldn't take in what had happened. She looked around blankly. *What the hell could have caused this?*

For a horrible moment, she wondered if Jezebel had hunted Pipsqueak. Launched herself at the little bat. But the position was high on the wall, away from the counter. Jezebel might be acrobatic, but she couldn't have managed a move like that.

Nell scanned the area carefully. Directly below the remains of her bat was the radiator. Avoiding getting too close, Nell pressed her forehead against the wall and peered behind the heater.

Parts of the other wing had lodged behind it. Nell's instinct was to find something to recover the body parts, put the tiny bat back together like a tragic jigsaw puzzle. But something stopped her. She stared at the remains again, considered the pressure it would have taken to crush the body until it stuck to the wall. Hot, rancid vomit fired up from her belly to her throat and she ran to the sink. The bile burned the back of her nose as she was violently sick. She wiped her mouth and stared at the scene in horror, as realisation dawned.

A person had done this.

Panic spiked through Nell. She stared at the closed door. *Are they still here?* Her legs jellified and she gripped the sink. One hand moved involuntarily to her phone and she called James's number. He answered almost immediately and she whispered urgently, 'James? It's Nell. I need help. Or . . . Well, I need to report a crime. Please could you come to my place?'

'I'll be there in ten. Keep safe. Are you alone?' James said. Nell could hear the background sounds of him driving. 'Keep talking to me, Nell. What's going on?'

'Nothing. At the moment. But I'm going to look around, just in case.' Nell opened the utility door a crack and peered out, worried that if anyone was there, her heartbeat *had* to be audible. She dragged a deep breath slowly through her lungs, trying to slow her pulse, calm the feverish fear slicking over her body. Her cocktail dress stuck to her back. She felt vulnerable. She'd never longed to be encased in pond-scented camos so much in her life.

The downstairs loo was empty. Nell pushed the door back against the wall to make sure no one could hide behind it, then pulled the door closed again.

The kitchen seemed empty. Creeping towards it, the wooden beams threw shadows around, the dim light playing tricks, making Nell second-guess herself. Opening a cupboard, Nell extracted the cast-iron griddle pan, wincing at the shrill metallic scrape against the shelf. She held it high with her free hand, biceps trembling, as she scanned under the dining table, then searched the living room.

She glanced left and right, as if crossing a busy road, squinted behind the sofas and under the coffee table, even though it was too low for even Jezebel to get under. Nell suddenly realised her cat was mysteriously absent and another wave of sickness rose. Continuing the search with more urgency, she checked under her large desk. No one was lurking down here.

'So far, so good,' Nell whispered into the phone. 'Still looking.'

She crept upstairs and pushed open the bathroom door. It was easy to check with a sweeping glance: the small cupboards, lack of a bath and the clear-glass shower wall offered nowhere to hide. Nell moved on to the spare bedroom. She could see from the doorway that no one loitered under the high bed. But she had to creep in and open the wardrobe doors, flinching at the sound. Finding it empty, she moved to her room.

Convinced someone was hiding under the wooden-framed bed, hidden by draped linens – ready to grab her ankle, pull her over – Nell gave it a wide berth while she checked around it, then gingerly lifted the duvet to peer beneath the frame. She stood, breathing heavily, as if it had been a huge exertion. Nell turned to the dressing room, the only room left, her heart thumping.

Nell opened the door slowly, eyes adjusting to the pitch blackness, raising the griddle pan to her shoulder. Her arm tremored with the weight; the square handle cut into her palm.

A shape loomed in the darkness. Nell's hand went clammy. She dropped her phone and gripped the pan with both hands as she lunged, pivoting sideways. She caught a flash of movement and smashed the pan downwards with all her strength.

She struck the target. But felt no resistance and stumbled forward. Nell froze. In the silence, she heard a tinny noise and held her breath as she tried to decipher it. She realised the noise was James yelling through her dropped phone, then became aware that she was sitting beside a tangle of clothes and a dislodged hanger. She stood, shaking, realising her adversary had been a jacket hanging on a hook, and the movement had been her own shadowy reflection in the mirror beyond.

Picking up the phone, Nell tried to speak through ragged breathing. 'Hi, I'm here. It's OK.' From under the bed, Jezebel slunk over, her belly low to the ground, her ears back. She looked terrified.

Nell sank to the ground, reaching out one hand in encouragement. With a tentative sniff, Jezebel moved closer, until her body pressed against Nell's bent knees, her tail shimmering against her. Nell's arm curved around her cat, hugging her close.

Through the phone, James's words made her feel weak with relief. 'I'm around the corner. Be ready to buzz me in.'

James directed the forensic team to the bathroom while Nell packed. He was glad she was moving to Finchmere. And glad that it coincided with Imelda's security increasing.

He stared at the remains on the wall, struggling to understand it. The bat was so tiny, so defenceless. It was such an unnecessarily violent act. He swallowed, then moved aside so a SOCO could take photographs and process the scene.

'I'm sorry,' Nell said to the officer. 'I was sick. I rinsed the sink but I didn't wash it. I thought that if someone had done that,' she pointed at the bat's body, 'they might have washed their hands in the sink. I didn't want to clean up in case there was any evidence.'

The officer nodded. 'Good. And don't worry. We've seen worse than a bit of puke.'

'Who knew you were out tonight?' James asked Nell, steering her into the living room.

She shrugged. 'Only other people who were there. My folks, Shannon. That's all.'

'No one else? You're sure?' he asked, steering her out to the dining area.

'No.'

'Did you speak to anyone at work about it?' James persisted.

'No,' Nell said. 'And tonight's one of the few nights I haven't been out surveying, because of the weather. And everyone at work would have known that. So, if it *was* anyone there, this would have been the worst night to choose. They'd have expected me to be home.'

Did you see anyone hanging around when you left tonight? Or any other time?'

Nell shook her head. 'No, and anyone doing that would be obvious, on this lane.'

James sighed. 'OK, if you think of anything, let me know. And in the meantime, think about taking some time off work. You've got a lot on your plate. Stepping back won't do any harm—'

'No, no way.' Nell looked aghast.

'Nell, you can't tell me who's managed to get close enough to you that they know when you're out, they can override your extensive security system, *and* they know how to get to you and hurt you. This is a message, Nell. A *dangerous* message. And you can't even narrow down who it might be from.'

His mind raced. If this was their killer, this wasn't part of his MO. No other victim had reported any threatening behaviour or break-ins.

So either something had triggered this new line of attack, or they were dealing with something – some*one* – separate.

'So you think someone's, what? Trying to threaten me, frighten me? Won't they think they've succeeded, if I stop working or change things?' Nell retorted. 'I'm not having that. And I don't see how me getting on with my job stops you getting on with yours.'

'I don't care what that someone *thinks*, Nell, as long as you're safe.'

His tone made her hackles die down. She bit her lip. When she frowned, he knew she was thinking seriously, wondering who might have had access to do this.

When she groaned and sank onto a chair, he knew he was about to get a lead. But Nell had turned ghost white. Apprehension prickled.

'*Oh, no . . . Oh, no.*' She was shaking her head slowly, staring at the wall, then her gaze gradually turned to him. 'It *is* someone from work. It must be. No one – except Rav, my parents, their estate manager and Sylvia – has my security code. And none of them would tell anyone. But Sylvia mislaid her phone earlier today. At work.'

Nell leaned forward, wrapping her arms around her stomach. 'She's always making notes or sending emails from her phone in meetings. Anyone could have spied her passcode.'

'But you've just said that none of your colleagues knew you were going out tonight,' James countered.

Nell shook her head. 'I wouldn't have needed to.' Her nervous swallow sounded like a gulp. 'Because of the surveys I'm doing, I'm sharing my location. I'm not used to doing that, so I keep forgetting to turn it off.'

James reeled. On the one hand, that was a help. *On the other—*

But Nell had jumped up. She strode into the kitchen and he turned, following as she opened the copper fridge.

'*Oh, God.*' She stared at James, her face stricken. 'He's taken my chloroform.'

Chapter 13

Friday 15th July – midnight

James knocked on the door of the detached, Huf Haus-style home – a dramatic A-frame, all monochrome timber, glass and angles. Val answered – still working, in her suit and holding a folder – and ushered him into the sleek open-plan space, as he apologised for the late call.

'I've heard the news. I was expecting you.' Val invited James to sit, poured him a coffee from the cafetière on the glass table and sat back to listen to his summary, before saying, 'You realise this could be totally unrelated to the case, James, don't you? As far as we know, this is *well* outside the usual MO. No one's reported anything like this happening.'

James nodded. 'Of course. But equally, something could have triggered this different—'

'Sure,' Val interrupted. 'I just want to make the point that we keep the wide view on the investigation, and not get tunnel vision on this.'

'There have been four new recruits recently at Nell's work, who could have accessed her home security code and shared her location via their phones, so would have known she was in London: Amir Massoud, Simon Slaker and Tom Davenport – plus, one already known to us and related to the first victim: Drew Deacon.'

Val nodded. 'Don't misunderstand me – if this *does* narrow our search down to Nell's colleagues, that's a massive step forward. But what I *don't* want to do is show our hand too early, and warn the killer. It was enough of a coup to get the press to agree to a reporting embargo – they had the good grace to be sheepish over the one gratuitous headline they managed to get in, and they've agreed not to report while we're investigating. But we need to make sure they continue to cooperate. Especially with Imelda's TV appearance bringing a sharp focus on this type of crime right now.'

James gave a tight smile. 'Good. Well, Hesha and Ed are on the case already. And we should inform Nell of her risk level, tell her about the case and get her out of her work environment.'

With a sigh, Val agreed. 'Call Nell in tomorrow morning to give her statement, and I'll speak to her then. Tell Hesha she's scored a stay in a spa hotel for the foreseeable, and get her to Finchmere Hotel, on Nell's parents' estate, tonight if you can. Then she'll be close at hand for instant backup. And chase forensics for a prelim report on Nell's flat. What we need *now* is a case for arrest.'

Saturday 16th July – 10.55 a.m.

After packing the previous night, Nell had moved, with Jezebel, to Finchmere House to stay with her parents. The conversation with her parents and Conor about the break-in had been difficult, but they'd all been relieved she'd asked to stay.

Despite not wanting fuss, after the sickening horror of what Nell had found, the cosseting – hot chocolate on the terrace, in her pyjamas, with the night-scented gardenia around them, and hugs on tap – had been a real comfort.

When she'd gone to say goodnight to Conor, though, she'd been alarmed to see him sitting with his security team, surrounded by stacks of letters, all to her mother. On pressing him, Conor had revealed that though some applauded her stance, others responded with threats. A brief search showed Nell that online responses were even more polarised. There, the anonymous threats were off the charts. The posts that argued for the proposed reform only inflamed the opposition.

With all this going on, Nell didn't want to add to Conor's already huge task, or distract the team from protecting her mother.

But Conor had been an oasis of calm. He'd had to liaise with the government company, who'd insisted on assessing estate security, as well as Imelda's personal protection and travel security arrangements. He'd drafted in another team for reinforcements, briefed everyone, assigned prioritised tasks and planned for every eventuality.

Nell knew the operation would be breathtakingly expensive, *and* that her mother would prefer to fund it herself. And she wondered how the irony – this incredible amount of effort being necessary to keep herself safe, for daring to raise the issue of the safety of women – was making Imelda feel. Determined, Nell guessed. Doubly so.

Conor had told Nell to keep vigilant. He'd made sure Nell was discreetly escorted when she'd gone to Pendlebury Police Station first thing in the morning to make her statement. Despite the gesture, Nell had felt like she was making a fuss over nothing.

Val turning up to speak to her had lanced concern through Nell, but the news that she was at risk from a killer wasn't the revelation that James and Val thought it would be. Nell realised the general underlying concern had always been there, ever since she found Amy's body, and James had warned her about the killer's type. But any worry about that had been drowned out by her concerns over Rav.

And now, her concern about him was skyrocketing, as she waited to see the officials of Motorsport UK for their official verdict. Sitting in the meeting room of the red-brick building, set in a leafy Oxford suburb, Nell's heart was thumping, her stomach in knots.

Rakesh opened the door, holding it for Neeta. Then he pulled out a chair for his wife. Both of Rav's parents glanced at Nell, then looked away, chins raised. Neeta was rigid with tension, her face fierce as her glittering eyes took in the company. Rakesh looked somehow sunken, and so much older than when Nell had last properly looked at him.

Chief Constable Trent stood to the side, in dress uniform. He nodded, almost reverently, at Rav's parents. Aanya sat beside her father, her wide eyes darting about. She tilted her head at Nell.

Her parents, Imelda and Hugo, had both dressed in navy suits. Sombre and respectful, but not too funereal. Nell saw her mother begin to reach for Neeta, in welcome or comfort, before Neeta's rigid expression told her just how unwelcome such a gesture would be.

Finchmere's ice-blonde young Race Manager, Birgitta Liefgrün, looked up from her open laptop to nod once, before returning to her screen.

At the head of the table, only the head and shoulders of the Secretary of State's representative were visible above a wall of files. Between his thinning hair and considerable chins were kind eyes, which he kept tactfully on his notes.

The clock on the wall ticked through the laden silence. Rakesh squeezed Neeta's arm, but Neeta's sharp shake of her head rejected any solace that might make her veneer crack.

At exactly 11 a.m., the door opened and a thin man in a grey suit walked in. Glancing around, he placed a folder on the table. 'Welcome to our office. Thank you all for attending, especially on a Saturday. This seemed most expedient for all concerned, and none of us want this to take longer than necessary. I'm Mr Dodson. I led the official investigation which was submitted for review.'

The balding man at the head of the table cleared his throat and peered over his stacked files. 'I'm Richard Houghton-Browne, acting for the Secretary of State to clarify and deliver the verdict of the investigation into the crash at Finchmere track on Monday 22nd April, where Dr Aravindan, or Rav, Kashyap incurred potentially life-changing injuries. This is a difficult time, so I intend to make this as brief, yet clear, as I can. However, if any of you have any questions, please don't feel hurried on my account. Today is about making sure that everyone affected by the crash at Finchmere understands the outcome of the investigation.'

Richard looked steadily around the room, then patted the files. 'I can see from the volume of work that has been carried out, and the level of detail *in* that work, that a great deal of investigative care has been put into practice to ensure an accurate and fair conclusion. I extend my thanks to the local police force and Motorsport UK for that, as well as Finchmere estate, for their cooperation.'

Neeta visibly bristled at thanks being given to Finchmere. Hugo's automatic murmur, 'Of course,' only inflamed her further. She crossed her arms and stared at Richard.

'Again, as you're aware, the investigation sought to establish the cause of the crash, which happened when Dr Kashyap participated in a parade lap of classic cars. In particular, the investigation is obliged to determine if the crash was due to any negligence on Finchmere's behalf. To that end, three strands of enquiry were investigated. One, to determine if the track was physically safe; two, to establish if the car driven was fit for purpose . . .'

Nell noticed Hugo drop his gaze to the table. She knew her father was eaten up with guilt for suggesting that Rav drive his prized racing Alfa.

'And three, to verify if any organisational aspects contributed to the crash.'

On Nell's other side, she felt Birgitta stiffen. The young woman raised her head and looked directly at Richard, as if inviting the challenge to her professionalism.

'I'll go through each of these investigations in turn,' Richard continued. 'But first—'

'First,' Neeta interrupted, standing. Her hand shook as she raised the stapled pages of the Kashyaps' copy of the report, dog-eared from re-reading. 'What happens if these assessments are inaccurate? You are all basing your opinions on these reviewing outcomes. But errors happen. How do you account for those errors?'

Richard leaned on the table, looking at Neeta. 'That's a good question, and one we take great care over. To ensure all investigations are robust, they have to follow procedures and guidelines, before being verified and reviewed. It's a rigorous process precisely to ensure it's accurate. And fair.'

He waited until Neeta met his eyes, nodded and sat down, then Richard looked at Trent. 'First I'd like Chief Constable Trent to describe how the crash occurred.'

Trent cleared his throat. 'The police Road Traffic Accident team are acknowledged experts in crash investigation. My team took measurements from the site and watched footage of the crash to build an accurate picture of what happened. The crash occurred on a straight opening out from a tight bend, initiated when the lead car, a Lotus Cortina, had a blowout, causing the driver to spin out and hit a Mini Cooper.

'Race wardens immediately deployed safety signals, but as they did so, three other cars became involved in the collision, meaning vehicles were scattered across the track. Subsequent cars followed the warnings, slowing down and keeping to the right-hand side of the track.'

Pausing, Trent took a breath, before reading the account of Rav's crash. 'There was a long gap before Dr Kashyap's car approached. He'd dropped behind and footage shows him accelerating to catch up. He entered the bend at speed, took a tight racing line and accelerated out of the turn, into the obstacle of cars. He braked and swerved left. This caused the back of the car to slide out and skid sideways across the track. His front wheel hit some debris from the crashed cars, causing the car to flip over and roll three times before coming to a stop on its roof.' Trent sat down.

Nell fought to keep the bile down. That scene played out vividly in her mind every day. She clenched her hands in her lap, driving her nails into her palms.

'Thank you.' Richard nodded at Trent. 'Your department has worked with Motorsport UK on the first avenue of investigation, that of track safety. Would you or Mr Dodson outline your findings?'

'Yes,' Mr Dodson said. 'Chief Constable Trent's department and a team from Motorsport UK independently measured the bend and the camber on the track, taking account of racing lines. These are all within optimal levels for race safety. Motorsport UK looked at the maintenance record of the track and conducted a number of tests to establish the condition of the surface and subbase. It was found to be in good repair, recently resurfaced, with no substrate issues.'

'Thank you,' Richard said. 'The review of your tests agreed that no fault lies with Finchmere's track design or maintenance. It is satisfactorily concluded that track safety was not a contributing factor in this crash. That brings us to point two, the safety of the car.'

Mr Dodson turned a page in his file. 'The condition of the car, immediately before the event, had been recorded through the numerous pre-event checks. Three such checks had been undertaken that morning. Each one of them showed the car to be in good racing order and the repetition of details between the three separate checks, conducted by different mechanics, demonstrated a high degree of meticulous accuracy.'

Trent stood up. 'The car was impounded and tested by my team after the crash. Accounting for the damage that occurred during the collision, nothing was found to indicate the car had been unfit for purpose prior to it. It was clearly a well-maintained vehicle.'

Richard nodded. 'And I can confirm that the independent review of your collective data concurred that no fault was found with the safety of the car.'

Beside her, Hugo let out a held breath. He glanced at Richard, then at Imelda as she squeezed his hand.

'So that leaves the organisation of the event,' Richard said. His eyes locked with Birgitta's. 'It is *highly* unusual for a member of the public to be invited to drive a car in the event. Drivers are typically professional or retired racers, or well-practised amateurs with racing experience and credentials. Those drivers know the track well and are familiar with their vehicles. Dr Kashyap had no such racing experience and credentials, and familiarity with neither track nor car.'

Neeta's hawk-sharp eyes, avid with accusation, burned across the table.

Hugo leaned forward into Richard's gaze. 'If I may clarify, the event was a parade lap, not a race. You're right that no inexperienced amateur would be permitted to race, but a parade lap is very different. It's a genteel display of the classic machines, where cars remain in their line-up and follow around the track. Not a race where cars speed and change position. I must emphasise that, while Ms Liefgrün is our Race Manager, Dr Kashyap was driving at *my* invitation, not hers, and I extended that invitation after Ra . . . Dr Kashyap had driven the Alfa a few laps around the track when the event was closed.' Hugo sat back. The purple tinge creeping up his neck betrayed his anxiety, but Nell was pleased he'd spoken up and not let Richard direct the fire at Birgitta.

Richard nodded. 'Yes, all this is taken into account.' His lips set into a thin line.

Neeta leaned forward, her eyes fixed on Richard. It looked like she was holding her breath.

'Ms Liefgrün,' Richard asked, 'would you outline your experience, both in coordinating events on racetracks and in dealing with inexperienced members of the public, and relate that to the steps taken at Finchmere on this occasion?'

'Most certainly.' Birgitta's German accent made her sound slightly dispassionate, but her blazing eyes and raised chin showed how deeply she cared. 'I am Birgitta Liefgrün, Race Manager for Finchmere estate. I have managed race events here for three years. Each event is over four days, with each day averaging eighteen races. This makes 216 races during my tenure at Finchmere. Each race or parade lap has a log, and I have submitted the relevant one to this enquiry. I sometimes have to make changes to the programme, which means reorganising races. This particular weekend was especially difficult for this. A race driver had been killed – off-track and unrelated to my races – and I had to keep moving events and laps around to accommodate impacts to the schedule.' The matter-of-fact words hung in the air. Neeta looked shocked at the apparent lack of empathy.

'Before Finchmere, I coordinated events at the Nürburgring. This is a world-famous track which attracts members of the public to various types of driving events. Despite many rules and conditions, crashes are not unusual. People have blowouts, spin off the track, have collisions or engine problems. At the Nürburgring, each year we would see between two and twelve fatalities. The challenge was to make the driving events as safe as possible for participants who seek a thrill. These measures included safety training, which had both a theory and a practical element, with demonstrations and even licensing in some instances.

'At Finchmere, the events are scaled down, but still closely regulated. All event participants must wear safety clothing – a helmet and a fire-retardant suit – and these were issued to, worn by and checked to fit Dr Kashyap prior to the event. Participants must also undergo a detailed safety briefing, so that they reliably understand signals from a race warden and know the appropriate track protocols. Each participant must sign a waiver to confirm this.'

When Neeta sat up straight and stared at Richard, Nell's heart sank.

'He signed a waiver?' Neeta questioned.

In unison, Richard and Birgitta extracted a document from their files.

'He did,' Birgitta confirmed, holding up the original.

'Here's a copy.' Richard slid his document across the table. Rakesh reached for it and read it, then handed it to Neeta.

Her trembling hand made the paper shiver. She blinked, as if her eyes couldn't take in what was written, then shook her head. 'No. No.'

Richard waited a few minutes, allowing Neeta to absorb the news. Around the table, everyone present seemed compelled to take a quiet moment, eyes downcast, as if giving Neeta as much privacy as possible to process. The pain of another extinguished hope was evident. Neeta needed someone to blame, someone to direct her fury at. Nell's heart twisted in her chest. The guilt weighed heavy on her shoulders, whatever today's outcome would be.

Richard asked, 'Ms Liefgrün, could you confirm what measures are in place when a crash occurs, such as this one, and other drivers on the track need to be warned?'

'Yes. Wardens will signal to drivers with flags. In some areas of the track, we may also use lights to signal to drivers. In this case, drivers were flagged to slow down and move to the right.'

Richard turned to Mr Dodson. 'Mr Dodson, would you outline Motorsport UK's findings, both regarding the protocol and the actions actually carried out on the day?'

Mr Dodson nodded. 'Yes. Professional, properly trained race wardens were operational, and their actions were captured in recorded footage. It's clear they made the correct signals, and that they did so in a timely manner, to Dr Kashyap ahead of the straight. These signals warned him to slow down at a point where, had he done so, he would have avoided the crash.'

Richard looked levelly at Mr Dodson. 'Yet Dr Kashyap did not slow down.'

'No.' Mr Dodson checked his notes. 'I've watched the footage several times. It seems Dr Kashyap didn't see the warden or, if he did, he didn't heed the warning.' Mr Dodson looked at Richard, then Trent. They each gave a sorrowful nod.

'The review of this evidence agrees with this finding,' Richard said, looking at Rav's parents. He spoke slowly and clearly. 'The conclusion of this enquiry finds that Dr Kashyap's crash at Finchmere occurred as a result of driver error.'

'No!' Neeta tried to stand but sagged back in her seat, wheezing like she was winded. Rakesh threw a protective arm around his wife's shoulders and stared at Richard, his face stunned with shock. 'How do we appeal?'

'There's no appeal to this process,' Richard said gently. 'Two independent organisations have assessed the case, and a further independent review of the data has been conducted. As I explained, it's designed to be scrupulously fair—'

'Fair?' Rakesh asked. '*Fair*?' He shook his head in disbelief. 'While my boy . . . ?' Unable to hold back the tide of grief any longer, his cheeks trembled and he buried his face in Neeta's hair, as aching sobs wrenched from him.

Hugo stood, holding his hands out. 'Mr Kashyap, please let us pay for the very best care for Rav. Any rehabilitation. Any adaptations. We'll do anything you need . . .'

Neeta straightened up, an arm around her husband. 'We do not require your charity.' Her eyes glittered with held-back tears as she cast a proud glare at Nell and her family.

Aanya slipped an arm around her father's waist and pulled him away from the table. 'Come on.' She tugged her mother's hand, drawing her towards the door. 'Let's go home.'

Nell looked at Aanya, hoping for a glance before they left. But Aanya kept her eyes down as she closed the door behind them.

Neeta's keening cries and Rakesh's deep, broken sobs echoed from the hall, leaking into the room.

Nell squeezed her eyes shut and held her head in her hands. The result didn't make her any less guilty. If Rav hadn't been trying to impress her – or her dad hadn't been trying so hard to make Rav feel part of the family on Nell's account – he would never have got into that car in the first place.

All this verdict had done was double the heartache for Rav's family – and make it even more impossible for hers to help.

Chapter 14

'Yes, I'm looking for just four vehicles, between 5 p.m. and 11 p.m.'
James tried to make his ANPR search sound minor.

It wouldn't be conclusive, because anyone driving to Nell's would use unmonitored country roads. But, as far as he was aware, none of their suspects had any routine reason to travel west or south on the A-roads leading to the country lanes towards Nell's house on the evening when her little bat was killed. They didn't live in those directions from Pendlebury, and Nell had confirmed that their suspects didn't have any evening work that would have taken them in that direction.

So, if any of them had driven that way, he'd have reason to ask why. He looked at the officer's screen, willing the search on, secretly hoping that Drew's car would make an appearance.

'Ah! Got one! The silver Lexus IS, registered to Andrew Deacon. On the A-road camera near Tesco, south of Pendlebury at 7.20 p.m.'

James leaped up. 'Brilliant!'

Nell would have been almost at the gallery in London by then. So if Drew had been watching her location, he would have known he'd have at least an hour and a half to access her house. He couldn't believe it. It was never this easy.

'Hold on, that's not all . . . Here's the 2001 white Kia Sportage, heading west out of Pendlebury at 8.26 p.m.'

Huh. Simon, too.

'And now I've got another hit for that Lexus, heading back at 9.05 p.m.'

Allowing for an hour round trip, that would have given Drew about forty-five minutes near Nell's house. Easily enough time for him to break in.

'And just one more, before 11 p.m. Blue Toyota Supra, heading west at 10.07 p.m.'

James exhaled. So Amir had also headed towards Nell's place.

'That's it until 11 p.m. I can keep going, see when the other two cars return?'

'Yeah, would you?'

'OK, here's the Toyota, back at 11.23 p.m.'

Nodding, James realised that gave Amir about fifteen minutes around Nell's place. Still time enough. His finger hovered over the iPad, ready to add Simon's return time. But the officer shrugged.

'Nothing for the Kia. I'm scrolling. We're up to 3 a.m. now. He doesn't return.'

Saturday 16th July – 3 p.m.

Reaching Rav's room, Nell heard his mother, Neeta, talking to him. She sounded upset, but like she was trying to put on a brave face for her son.

Nell's heart sank. It had been agony to wait until the afternoon to see Rav, but she'd forced herself to give the family time to discuss the official findings of the accident. She turned to hurry away, but Aanya stomped out to the corridor.

'Nell?' she hissed.

Turning back, Nell held her hands up. 'I'm sorry, I won't intrude. I know today's verdict upset everyone. And if they see me, I know it will make things worse.'

As Aanya nodded, Nell jerked her head towards Rav's room. 'Has he been exercising?'

'Yes, yesterday he had a good session, apparently. Today, though, he's just been like this. In bed. All day. He's wrung out.'

From inside his room, they heard Rav speaking. 'Now the verdict's finished with, can we put it behind us? If you need to blame anyone, you now know that that person is me. No one else. Just me. And if that isn't the answer you want, then I'm asking you now to put it aside. Because I need you rooting for me, looking forward, not back. I don't have the energy to cope with my therapy *and* all the upset around the accident. Please.'

'Yes . . . yes. OK.'

To give Neeta credit, her agreement with her son was immediate. Even if her voice shook. But Nell became even more aware that she'd need to make a rapid retreat, so his parents wouldn't know she'd overheard this.

'That isn't all I need.'

Nell glimpsed Rav pushing himself up, as if gaining strength. She was so delighted to see him looking determined, that she paused.

'I know that, after today, it will be hard. But please could you be more welcoming towards Nell when she's here? You were right, Mum. I did need to talk to her, and trust her.'

Nell held her breath, then had to hold back the flood of tears that had built up over the past few months.

'Especially as *she's* giving me the motivation to do my therapy.'

Nell winced, knowing that would be a stab in the heart to his mother, who'd come every day and tried to encourage Rav, just like she had.

But Neeta was clearly more generous than she gave her credit for. 'I don't care *why* you are doing your therapy, *Beta*. I'm just glad you are.'

Saturday 16th July – 4 p.m.

Hearing the result of the race's investigation felt like a weight rolling off his shoulders. Rav hoped it would mean Nell would stop blaming herself – and that his parents would, too. They'd been quiet since he'd spoken up. But he could understand their anger and frustrations, and their fear.

That's what *he'd* be focusing on, too – if he didn't have Nell's case to think about.

He itched to see her. Even now, as he heard footsteps, he craned his head to see if it was her, but it was Aanya in the doorway.

'Look who I found in the café upstairs.' She stepped aside to let Nell in the room.

Rav sat up. 'Hi.' His beam was irrepressible. 'It's *so* good to see you! Come in.'

Her gaze darted around, and Neeta and Rakesh both made eye contact with her for a moment, before Neeta swallowed and managed a smile.

'Hello, Nell,' she said, then glanced at her husband, before adding, 'perhaps . . . you and Rav would like some time together.'

Neeta nudged Rakesh, who nodded, standing up, and bent to kiss Rav's cheek. 'Persevere with your PT, *Beta*. Nell, we are relying on you to help keep his motivation up.'

'I'll try,' Nell said, grateful to Neeta.

Once his family had left, Rav said, 'I heard the verdict. So we can draw a line under all that. Not that I ever doubted it, but now we know officially that no one was to blame but me, and no one's going to make it awkward for you to visit.' He reached for her hand. 'Thank you for coming. I want you to be here.'

Nell nodded, then took a breath. 'OK. But I meant what I said to your mum. I'm going to keep your motivation up. I'm not coming here just to sit by your bed. I'm going to be visiting you often, and that means you'll be getting up and we'll be going out.'

'Yes, ma'am.' Rav gave her a mock salute.

Together, and with the help of the duty nurse, they worked out how to get Rav out of bed and moving. And soon Nell was pushing Rav in his wheelchair to the training unit.

'Rav?' His trainer looked up. He was tightening up the stability bars, flanking a narrow path that someone could walk along with support each side. He gave one a wobble, checking that it held steady, before leaping to his feet.

Rav hated those bars. Being between them, trying to move his legs, having his trainer move them for him, wasn't just excruciating, it was humiliating. A massive demonstration of what he couldn't do.

'Good to see you, mate. You want a session? I have time.'

Rav gestured at Nell, shaking his head, 'We're going—'

'Yes,' Nell interrupted him firmly.

Brilliant. Now I'm going to look pathetic at everything, in front of her, before I've even built anything up.

'And let me know how I can help and what we can practise in between sessions,' Nell added.

The trainer grinned at Nell. 'I can see we're going to get along! So how are you feeling today, Rav? Pain anywhere?'

Rav nodded, and when he didn't say where, the trainer clarified, 'Everywhere?'

'Yeah, so let's ignore it,' Rav said. 'It'll hurt whether I work or not.'

Nell squeezed his hand.

As the trainer began with standard exercises, Rav saw Nell making mental notes, and he knew she was going to push him to do these every day. Several times.

Pain flared through his body. He felt like an idiot, lying on the mat, trying to tilt his pelvis, the movement pitifully small.

'That's good, hold that position for a little longer if you can.'

Sweating, Rav clenched his teeth, maintaining the stretch as long as he could bear it, sweat stinging his eyes.

Nell leaned forward, eyes shining, and kissed him. 'I can see how hard you're trying. You're a total superhero.'

For a moment, the glow in his heart blotted out the fiery pain everywhere else. He nodded at his trainer. 'Shall we have another go at the bars?'

Twenty minutes later, exhausted from standing while the physical therapist assessed his weakened quads, Nell pushed him out of the lift, into the café on the top floor.

She selected a salad for dinner. But, suddenly conscious of his neglected muscles, Rav chose a turkey sandwich and a protein shake.

As Nell pushed him through the French windows out to the roof garden, the fresh air and sun on his face made Rav give a deep, peaceful sigh. His shoulders relaxed for what felt like the first time in months.

They were the only ones there, but Nell took him to the far corner, for the maximum effect of the view. As he gathered her into a hug, he was conscious that Nell had to reach over the wheelchair arms, angling herself, taut and rigid rather than sinking into his embrace. She pulled a chair over and sat, twisting towards him.

'We'll have to work this out somehow,' Rav said. But he pulled her to him, holding her tenderly, inhaling her familiar scent – orange blossom and warmth – that he'd missed so much. Finally, he kissed her with all the longing that had burned inside him all these wasted weeks.

When they finally stopped to eat, Rav noted that the view northwards gave them a glimpse of the demolition site of Heath Rise, as well as the distant Furze Heath. Copses of birches and conifers dotted the habitat, glinting with gorse sunbursts over bronzing bracken. The tree line at the northern side hid the tunnel he knew of, from hibernating bat surveys.

'The heath's huge, Nell. Are you all working round the clock?'

She shivered, and he wondered if she was cold or if the heath bothered her more than she liked to admit. 'It's better now a group of us are on site together. And at least Erin is pitching in at last. She was a bit creeped out.'

'Yeah, that does sound like the sensible reaction, to murder.'

Nell scrunched her nose at him. But she didn't offer a reason why she was so attached to the heath. The unusual convenience of a working site so close by wasn't lost on Rav. Neither was the fact that Nell couldn't possibly want to work where she'd found a dead body. A twinge of guilt hit him. *Was she working there because of him? Because it made it easier to visit?*

But Nell didn't *need* a job to make it easier to visit. Hell, if that was her aim, not working at all would be the obvious answer. The thought was accompanied by another sharp stab of guilt. *She shouldn't have to give up her work for him.* But then again, the obvious solution would be the rewilding work on Finchmere estate. She'd be her own boss, she could manage her own time, doing work she loved, and *still* be close by. Nell's choice didn't make sense to him.

Unless she's playing detective again?

He glanced at her. 'I did some research. On the past victims. Are you aware just how much the murders centre around the heath?' He stretched to point at the site of the now-demolished Heath Rise estate. 'Amanda Richards, mum to a young boy, was found dead in a flat there. And the playground,' his finger moved past the fenced-off site to the park between the former estate and the heath, 'is where Julia Beckett was killed while her toddler was playing. Then Kelly Granger, who was pregnant, was found on the edge of the industrial estate by the heath.' He pointed to the south of the estate, below the heath. 'And now Amy's been found on the heath itself. *Exactly* where you've been working.'

Hoping that would be enough of a deterrent to stop her going back, he waited for her reaction. But she just nodded.

Clamping down on his exasperation, he pushed the point. '*Please* tell me you're going to stop working there? And that you're not going to try to find clues? Can't you see it's not a game? Can you keep out of things? For once?'

Nell hesitated, and immediately his senses fired on full alert. 'What?'

She side-eyed him. 'Promise not to overreact.'

'Oh, perfect. I'm not worried at *all* now. What *is* it?'

'It looks like the . . . the killer . . . may have broken into my house—'

'*What?*'

'And killed Pipsqueak.'

'*What? Why?*'

'And taken my chloroform.'

Rav stared at her. '*Please* tell me you're not serious?'

She bit her lip.

'And all you have on him is a button that may be his, or might belong to any one of the hundreds of other walkers.'

Nell nodded.

'Anything else?'

Nell swallowed, and Rav knew there was.

'Tell me.'

She looked at him, like she wanted to hold something back.

'If you tell me, I'll spend all day tomorrow working at those sodding bars.'

She narrowed her eyes. 'You promised you'd do that anyway.'

'All right. All week. Whatever you want.'

'I know it was a colleague.'

He couldn't have heard right. 'Wha—'

'We've had three new recruits. Four, if you include our intern. All male. They're the only people – who I don't know well enough yet to trust – who could have got hold of my security code *and* known where I was.'

Rav closed his eyes as nausea rolled up his chest. 'You're not working anymore, are you? Tell me you're back at Finchmere. Speak to Conor. Does James know?'

'Yes. And Conor and James are on the case. Horribly, actually. Because Mum needs extra protection right now, and this is just a distraction.'

'Don't be an *idiot*! This is *serious*, Nell. And breaking in – did that happen to the recent victim, Amy?'

Nell shrugged. 'I don't think so, judging from James's reaction.'

Staring at her, Rav's heart sank. 'I know what you're going to say. You reckon you can work out who it is before something happens to you, don't you?'

As Nell started to justify her point of view, he held his hands up. 'You reckon you're invincible because we've managed it before, right? But there was a decent amount of *luck* involved then, Nell. And I wasn't stuck like *this*.'

He punched the arm of his wheelchair. He felt so hideously helpless.

'*Please* don't put yourself in danger. On your own. Because I'm *terrified* about what could happen to you. And I . . . I can't help you this time.' He hated saying it out loud. But he couldn't deny it.

Nell couldn't meet his eyes. *Why* did she have to be so damn stubborn?

With a grunt, he pushed himself back to the lift.

'Where are you going?'

'Back to the PT room. If you're not going to let this lie, I can't either, can I?'

Saturday 16th July – 5 p.m.

'I have some info,' Ashley said. 'Tech have unlocked Amy Fallon's computer. I've got some printouts of her recent searches and emails and backed-up photos.'

'Oh? What do they tell us?' James asked.

'She's an avid runner – anywhere and everywhere. Furze Heath was a favourite spot. What *is* horrific is that her Apple watch was monitoring her during the attack. We can see her running, with her heart rate the same as for other runs she'd recorded, so it was elevated. Then it falls, as if she's paused. Then a major spike, which must be the attack. The GPS tells us the attack happened where we found her, in that sheltered part of the heath, so she wasn't moved, just dragged into the ditch. It looks like the killer approached her, then struck.'

It was awful, seeing the heart rate on the graph go from such healthy vitality to that fearful spike – then to zero.

'It means we have a pinpoint-accurate time of death: 2.03 p.m.' James grimaced.

Ashley nodded. 'Yes. I needed a moment, after seeing that. Tech said that her web searches were pretty standard. Things for work, shopping. One of her friends was getting married, so she'd been searching a lot for wedding gifts and outfits. Nothing out of the ordinary. *But* one thing that did catch our attention was that – because she couldn't make the hen do, which was going to be in Amsterdam – she and the bride-to-be did a survival weekend together. It was on 2nd and 3rd July – just a few days before she was killed.'

'Where?'

'Local. In fact – get this – at Furze Wood, just beyond the heath. With a survival expert called Simon Slaker.'

Chapter 15

Sunday 17th July – 8.30 a.m.

'Oh, it was brilliant,' Erin enthused as she sat next to Rav while he ate breakfast.

Glad that his new regimen meant he was already showered, dressed and sitting at the table rather than lying in bed, he was now trying valiantly to smile through the chit-chat. He wanted to get to the important bits. *What were her new colleagues like? And how had they been on the Saturday nightjar walk – the day after Nell's place had been broken into? And which one of them had done it? And why?*

'We had a great day. Simon and I got there in the morning, to do one translocation, and went for lunch in town. Then, the whole team met us on site in the afternoon. We watched the demolition of the Heath Rise tower blocks from up there. There was this massive *BOOM!* Then the columns sort of shivered to the ground and disappeared into great clouds of dust. It was quite emotional, actually.'

'Had you planned to be there to see that?' Rav asked. 'Or was it a coincidence?'

'A bit of both. We knew they were coming down sometime around then, and we thought it would be interesting to see it if we could. After the old tower blocks had been destroyed right in front of us, we wanted to focus on the regeneration. So I took everyone on a tour, showing them all the planting, and the reptile fencing. Then Simon, Amir, Tom and I did the world's fastest reptile translocation, before the evening nightjar walk.'

'How did everyone seem?' Rav asked.

'Sylvia took some photos. She was especially happy with one she got of Amir with a smooth snake. She said that would be our next national article. Drew and Colette were politely interested, but didn't get involved.'

'And how was the nightjar hunt?'

'Brilliant! Simon knew exactly where the nest was, and where we could watch for the best view, without disturbing them! Look!' With obvious eagerness, she showed him the photos.

Blurry images of the ecotone between scattered gorse over bracken and conifer copse were not helpful. Rav squinted. 'Where?'

'Yeah, exactly!' Erin laughed. 'Basically invisible, isn't she? She's there.' Erin pointed under a tree on the edge of the copse. 'Nestled on the ground between the gorse and that log. See?'

Amongst the leaf litter and tangle of low scrub, Rav could just about make out some cryptic camouflage. 'Wow.'

'Listen.' She played a video of the bird fluffing up her feathers, then calling. 'Sounds like something mechanical, doesn't it?' She shook her head in amazement. 'I can't imagine how long it took Simon to find them.'

'What's he like?' Rav shoehorned the question in before she could steer the conversation to something else.

'Simon? He's . . . well. He's a bit of a funny one to get to know. But he's really nice once you *do* get to know him. He's pretty direct, so you know where you stand. He spends so long having to keep still and silent, in hiding to get the perfect shot, that I think he's more used to that than socialising.'

'Right.' Dread thumped in the pit of Rav's stomach. *Pretty handy skills for a killer.*

'I think a lot of people don't really understand him.'

'Oh?' Rav's head snapped up. It sounded like Erin was about to say that *she* did, implying that made her feel special. His skin prickled. 'So what do *you* think of him?'

'He's super-talented. His pictures are epic. I'm not surprised he's in demand by *National Geographic*.'

Rav made a mental note to look them up later. 'What about the other new team members?'

'Ugh. That Drew is a right pompous arse. The type who takes credit for other people's work.'

'Uh-huh.'

'I *know* my article idea wasn't earth-shattering. But it's one of those things that can make a difference for the client and the project—'

'And I hear it *did*,' Rav said. '*And* I hear Nell helped you to get the rightful credit—'

'Yeah, I think that was *Simon*, actually. So Elliot said, anyway, after they'd all had a pally-pally lunch together. But someone like Drew shouldn't need to tread on other people to get ahead. He's already a Director.'

'Maybe that's how he got there.'

'*Yes!*' Erin shuffled forward, as if delighted someone else saw what she believed was obvious. 'That's *exactly* what I think. Doesn't have any ideas of his own, a bit threatened by people who do. Like he's hanging onto that position by the skin of his teeth. Useless arse. Nell doesn't like him either. He interferes with all her projects, even though he can't add anything.'

Good. Hopefully that meant she'd steer clear of him. 'He wouldn't go out on site, though, would he?'

'No way. He's not the type to get his hands dirty.' She shrugged. 'Although Elliot *did* say we need all hands on deck now that the translocation is starting.'

Great. Perfect timing. Nell wouldn't ignore a call to help.

'Personally, I'd love it if he came to site and fell in one of the ponds.'

'That's *your* speciality, isn't it?'

Erin pretended to punch his arm. 'Well, Drew did turn up for the nightjar walk. He was all kitted up like some country gent. Barbour and tweed all the way. And *wellies!*'

'Did he look like he knew the place well?'

Erin shrugged. 'No idea. He followed along, chatting like the rest of us. Sylvia had bought some new walking boots and kept complaining about getting blisters. Simon wanted to give her a second pair of socks to wear, but they were so rigid, I don't think they could have been washed in the last century, so she declined, and then had to hobble along, wincing in silence. Drew and Amir were being very attentive.'

'How did everyone seem on the walk?' Rav asked.

'Fine. Why?'

'Well, Saturday nights are sacred, aren't they? Given we . . . you . . . *ecologists* can't socialise during the week in survey season.'

'Everyone seemed happy to be there. Simon was pleased with the response and how everyone was excited to see the birds. We all took his advice very seriously, following closely and keeping quiet. Well, fairly quiet. Drew was pretty chatty.' She pulled a face.

'Yeah, I gather you don't think much of Drew.' Rav grinned as Erin shook her head in firm confirmation. 'What about Amir?'

'Pff. He thinks a lot of himself.'

'Ah.' Rav grinned again.

'Yeah, *you* can talk. You think everyone's swooning over you. Talk about ego.'

Erin's face flamed, and Rav had a flashback to the awkward chat he'd been unable to avoid, when she'd been particularly flirtatious and he'd had to make it clear that nothing would happen between them.

'So what gives you that impression about Amir?'

'He's got a bit of a swagger. Never hurries for anyone. Like he expects people to run around *him*. I reckon his snake charmer thing is some kind of USP. I can imagine him being a bit awks as a teen. Maybe getting his python out was his signature move.' She sniggered.

Rav almost joined in with her, but unease crackled. 'Seriously?'

'Yeah, that's not all he's got. Massive boa, corn snakes and a cobra.'

'Oh . . . Wow.'

'Got an amazing set-up with huge vivaria at his house. It's like his lounge was built for all his reptiles, rather than a human. Nell didn't like it much.'

'Nell's *been* there? To his *house*?'

'Oh, yes.' Erin's face flickered with a sly smile. 'Maybe she's falling for his charms now. And they have been working closely together. Amir got the mitigation licence for the development, since there are smooth snakes and sand lizards there.'

'Right.' Rav sank back into his seat. Despite his better judgement, he couldn't help a flash of insecurity. *Is that why Nell's so reluctant to step back from work?*

Erin, seemingly content to leave on that note, stood up. 'Anyway—'

'I'm totally impressed with how much you got done yesterday,' Rav gabbled, feeling there was still something else to find out. 'Firing on all fronts!' He tried to smile. 'Didn't Simon mind giving up a whole Saturday?'

'No.' A faint blush crept up Erin's olive complexion. 'He was fine about it. We both were.'

Despite knowing that Erin had been trying to stir, Rav didn't want her to put herself in harm's way. 'Is there something going on with you two?'

Erin's shake of her head was too vigorous. '*No!*' She picked up her backpack, ready to flounce. 'And even if there *was*, it's no one else's business!'

Sunday 17th July – 8.30 a.m.

James completed the introductions with the guy in head-to-toe camo and stated that the interview was being recorded. With a nod, he signalled to Hesha to start the questions.

'Thank you for assisting us with our enquiries, Mr Slaker,' Hesha said. 'May I call you Simon?'

'Yes.'

'We're investigating the death of Amy Fallon. She and a friend recently did one of your survival weekends. We were hoping you might be able to give us some insights into how she was?'

'Death?' Simon looked at them both. 'What happened to her?'

'She was found dead. On Furze Heath,' Hesha said.

'She was the one in the news?' Simon looked shocked.

'Yes. So this is a murder enquiry. And you might be able to give us your ideas of what she was like. How was she, on your survival weekend?'

Simon shrugged, blinking as he regained his composure. 'Seemed pretty normal to me.'

'What did she do, as part of your survival training?'

'Well, the *idea* is that people learn general skills. First, finding a suitable place to build a camp. We went to Furze Wood. I got them to cut branches and bracken to make a shelter. Next, they had to find different grades of wood to lay and light a fire. Then find and purify some water. There's a lake, so that's easy. Next was foraging.

And then I usually teach people how to make a trap to catch a rabbit, so we can skin and cook it, but she and her friend wouldn't do that.' He pulled a face. 'I thought they were a squeamish pair. And it messed up my plan for the activities to provide meals. So we made nettle soup, instead, and then I set an orienteering challenge, which led to a cache of supplies. Usually those are surplus, in case the traps don't catch anything. But this time it was necessary, otherwise they wouldn't have had an evening meal.' He groaned, and added, 'They'd snuck in a bottle of vodka, so the astronavigation didn't go to plan, *either*. They spent the *whole* night gassing and giggling, not savouring the peace and quiet. I didn't sleep a wink. Next day, we were supposed to check the traps and cook, but as they'd refused to set any traps, they worked their way through the supplies, and went wild swimming. Idiots.'

'What did you make of them?' James asked, despite having a pretty good idea.

Simon sighed. 'Look, I'm sorry about what happened to her. But I'll be honest. I thought they were townies having a laugh. No respect for the countryside. Ignorant about reading the landscape. Lazy. I didn't like them, and I was glad when the weekend was over.'

'Does your work still take you in the area of the wood and the heath?' James asked.

'Oh yes, I'm often there.'

'Did you see anything on the afternoon and evening of 6th July? Or hear anything?'

He shook his head.

Hesha leaned forward. 'Surely, someone as well attuned as you to reading the landscape, to noticing things, would have spotted *something*?'

'Yes, I saw your tent. I saw the search team. But I didn't see anything before that.'

'What about on the evening of 15th July? Did you drive anywhere?' James asked.

'Just between the office and the heath, and home.'

'Nothing took you westwards?' James pressed.

Simon shrugged. 'Nope.'

'Are you the only one who drives your car?' James clarified. 'Your 2001 white Kia Sportage.' He read out the registration number.

Simon shifted on his seat. 'What's this all about?'

'Your car was recorded driving out of Pendlebury on that evening.'

'So? That's not a crime, is it?'

'No,' Hesha said. 'But we asked you if you went anywhere, and your answer contradicts our evidence. So you can understand why we want to get that straight, Simon.'

'Well, I probably saw a mate.'

'Who was that?' Hesha leaned forward, ready to note down the name.

'I'd . . . need to check. I can't recall.'

'It was only two nights ago. Have a think.' Hesha's tone was encouraging.

'Well, I probably went to the heath and stopped there. Camping.'

'So which was it?' James pressed. 'A mate, or the heath? Could anyone help refresh your memory? Do you live with anyone who might know? A partner?'

Simon's gaze snapped to James.

'No. No. They won't help. And no need. You can call my mate. I'll give you his number. He'll confirm I saw him on Friday night.' He opened his Contacts page on his phone, then passed it to Hesha.

As she made a note, James asked, 'Why so cagey? If you saw a friend?'

Simon shrugged. 'It's bad enough there's been a murder in the area. You don't want friends thinking you had anything to do with it.'

'Oh.' James turned his palms up. 'Your friends wouldn't just think that you were being excluded from our enquiries, then? Given how often you're at the heath?'

Simon glared at him.

'And given how well you *know* the heath, if anything does come to mind, about the day of the murder, please let us know. However minor or irrelevant it may seem. We rely on good citizens, like yourself, who notice things.' With a flash of inspiration, he nodded at the camera case by Simon's rucksack, at his feet. 'Keen photographer? Any of the heath?'

Simon gripped the strap of the camera case. 'Yeah, a few. Obviously.'

'Any chance we could take a look? Just in case they have something useful? You might have captured something without knowing.'

'Don't you need a search warrant for that?'

'Only if you refuse,' James said. '*Are* you refusing? Or will you let us take a look?'

'No! Of course not! I can't risk you taking custody of my photos! These are my main livelihood. I've got contracts with a few stock agencies to send the best ones to them. That's good money I can't afford to lose before they're safely backed up. I couldn't risk any of you accidentally leaking them, or even deliberately selling them if a copper wanted to make a few hundred quid.'

James nodded. 'Understood. Those are all valid concerns. We deal with sensitive data and things that impact people's livelihoods all the time. You'd get a full receipt of anything we take, and my personal assurance of the integrity of my team.'

'Assurances aren't guarantees.'

'Fine. In that case we can go down the warrant route. It's no problem for us.'

With a disgruntled sigh, Simon took his camera from the case, handling it with familiar dexterity. 'Here. You can take the memory card.'

As James went to take it, Simon moved it back an inch, holding it up in the air. 'Just remember that I haven't had a chance to back everything up. So be bloody careful. And I want a receipt.'

'Great, thank you. I'll organise that,' James said.

'And I'll get the card straight to tech.' Hesha whisked it away before Simon could change his mind.

'You're welcome to wait here for it, out in reception, or we can return it to your place when we're done,' James said.

'I'll wait.' He checked his watch and suppressed a groan.

Sensing advantage, James said, 'It might take several hours. I can't guarantee the tech team can start on this straightaway.'

With a huff, Simon glared at James. 'Fine. I can't stay here that long. I've got to work today.'

'Then I'll call you when we're ready to return it.'

Ten minutes later, James and Hesha were looking over the shoulder of the officer in the tech lab as he scrolled through Simon's pictures. Endless birds, and copious shrubbery bushes where James presumed there were supposed to *be* birds – then the weekend of 2nd and 3rd July. James jumped as a large close-up of Amy Fallon appeared. She was laughing, her eyes rolling back into her head a little, and he realised she must be drunk. Then, photos of her swimming in the lake: close-ups of her laughing, hair slicked back, then wading out of the waist-deep water, her back to him. She was topless, and possibly naked.

The tech officer pointed at the screen. 'You can see by the depth of field that this was taken with a powerful telephoto lens. See how the background is more blurred, while the subject is crisper? Not perfectly crisp, so probably taken in a hurry.'

James shifted uncomfortably, imagining Simon camped out on the other side of the lake, taking intrusively intimate shots. But he couldn't look away and risk missing any vital evidence.

The officer kept scrolling.

And now he was looking at several close-ups of Nell.

Sunday 17th July – 9 a.m.

Rav cleared the email alert from Nell from his phone's screen so he could finish reading Simon's photography blog.

He had to admit, the photos were amazing. Well framed, sharp, great composition, but something else . . . the pictures seemed to capture the character of the species: little terns wheeled over craggy cliffs; majestic white-tailed eagles soared over a tumultuous sea; and comic puffins had indignant stand-offs, their bright beaks crammed with sand eels. Rav could well imagine the lonely, silent hours of observation that would take.

He turned to Nell's email: 'Please don't ever say you can't help. It's not true. And, since you ask, Elliot wondered if you'd mind going through the files – all our photos and survey data sheets – to help us write up the reports and licences for Furze Heath.'

Rav groaned. That hadn't been what he'd meant, and Nell knew it. *Is she just trying to distract me?* Irritation burned. He'd wanted to be able to get out of here and *help*.

He looked out to the corridor, to see if his physical therapist was there yet. No sign.

With a huff, he opened the file. It was a mixture of photos and videos. And pretty weird ones. He sat up, frowning as he stared at the screen. He opened a few more, then realised that the dates had been used as file names, and all ended with SS. Simon Slaker.

As he scrolled through the files, the dates stretched back over the past thirteen days, to 5th July. Rav frowned again. Simon hadn't started at EcoLogical Consultancy until 11th July, had he? Five days after the murder.

Nausea roiled in his belly as Rav opened the file for 6th July, the day of the murder. The film started with Simon's camo-waterproof-clad torso filling the screen as he leaned in to adjust the wildlife camera's settings. As Simon checked the switches, Rav saw his expression. The grim face, tense and determined, sent a shiver through him. When Simon moved aside, the camera gave a view of the heath. A dense thicket of gorse stretched along a ditch to the right, and conifers scattered to the left.

A quick flash of khaki told Rav that Simon had pulled his hood up against the rain and headed off to the right.

As Rav stared at the screen, he assumed that the camera was on motion detection and would soon stop recording. But the file showed it was about eighteen minutes long. Rav soon saw why. The breeze whipping past the gorse made a bough waver almost continuously.

Rav didn't know what he expected to see, but he couldn't drag his eyes from the view of the heath. The frame, empty except for the vast habitat, was accompanied only by the unsettling sounds of pattering rain, rustling vegetation and the blustering breeze.

Listening, Rav realised he was holding his breath. At sixteen minutes, he caught a muffled sound. He took the recording back to listen again, checking the time stamp: 2.03 p.m.

A muffled cry.

His heart hammered. It could easily be a bird . . . or a fox.

But something in his gut told him it wasn't.

Chapter 16

'Has he left already?' James sprinted up the stairs from the basement tech lab to the station's waiting room.

Hesha was just ahead of him, scanning from the doorway. 'Looks like it.'

'Damn.' James stopped abruptly in the corridor, so his frustration wouldn't become a public spectacle to those waiting to see officers. He saw Hesha checking with the constable behind the desk and getting a disappointing nod of confirmation.

He thumped the wall. He didn't have enough to arrest Simon. He'd taken the pictures on public land and hadn't apparently harassed anyone to do so. But it did skate dangerously close to stalking and potentially taking intimate pictures without consent. So a friendly chat would have been entirely appropriate – *if* they'd caught him in time. *Now Simon has a chance to come up with excuses . . .*

'James?' Hesha beckoned him over. 'Simon left at least twenty minutes ago, in a camper van, apparently. A black VW Caravelle. Our officer on reception noted the registration. It may be worth doing an ANPR check on it? And, in the meantime, DS Wade Ezra from the Serious and Organised Crime Unit is looking for you. He got the evidence he needed for a warrant to search Amir Massoud's house. Wondered if you'd like to join them?'

After asking Hesha to start building a case for Simon's arrest, James hurried off. Even though Amir was no longer his main focus, he'd like to know what evidence Wade had, *and* if that would mean that *one* of his suspects would be under arrest today, one way or another.

He hadn't had a chance to update Wade fully – he'd sent a quick message saying he'd visited Amir's house, but hadn't conducted a full search because it no longer seemed suspicious. The paperwork hadn't been a priority when there was a serial killer to find. Now, a rising dread made James painfully aware that his lack of detail meant they'd be running into this search unprepared.

Wade and his team were kitting up when James found them. 'Before you leave,' James asked, 'have you got a snake handler?'

'What?' Wade looked like he was about to laugh.

'I'm serious. Amir's place is full of snakes. All in those . . . vivariums, and secure. But if he wants to make life difficult, warrant or not, he could.'

'I'm sure our lads are more than up to it.'

'Even with a boa bigger than both of us? And a cobra?'

Wade paused, mid-zipping up his flak jacket. 'A *what* now?'

'Yeah, exactly. *Are* we up to it?'

'Let me phone a friend. *Then* we will be.' Wade flashed James his trademark grin as he clapped his arm, and then sprinted to his office, calling over his shoulder, 'Love a challenge, me. Good intel, James.'

Half an hour later, Wade gestured to one of his team, who hammered on Amir's door. 'Police. Open up.'

Around James, the officers and their newly recruited snake handler braced themselves. It seemed slightly overkill when Amir answered the door in gym gear.

As the officers dashed past Amir, spreading out to cover the house, Wade handed him a copy of the warrant. 'We have a warrant under the Misuse of Drugs Act to search these premises, as we have evidence there may be drugs here.'

As James wondered what the evidence was, Wade handed Amir a copy of his electricity bill, saying, 'Pretty high heating bill, mate. You can see how it raises questions.'

James's heart plummeted. That would be down to the vivariums. But Wade was already walking inside. And this was an opportunity to have a proper look around, and see if there was anything here to link him with the murders.

As he went inside, he texted Dr Saunders, asking for a SOCO team. He may as well capitalise on the warrant and gather as much information as possible, without mentioning his investigation.

The officer in the kitchen was searching every drawer, cupboard, packet of food and appliance. He heard movement upstairs and followed, while Wade kept Amir occupied.

Hurrying upstairs, James saw the snake handler placing the python into a soft cloth bag, securing it so that another officer could search the tank. The handler moved towards the cobra, pulled on a pair of thick gauntlets and readied his metal snake hook.

Opening the levered door on one side, he scooped and lifted the cobra, placing it into its own bag and drawing it closed. He nodded at another officer. Glancing around, James saw that all the snakes were bagged, except the boa, and wondered how they'd tackle it.

The handler must have been wondering the same thing. Their eyes met, and James asked, 'Do you want to check upstairs next? Amir said that's where he keeps his breeding snakes.'

The handler raised his eyebrows. 'Right. I'll go first.'

As he ascended the stairs, the handler opened the fire door.

The one room, plus a bathroom, took up the entire top floor. James imagined this would be the master suite, *if* the owner wasn't a snake breeder. Instead, the room was taken up with two massive tables, each holding a vast enclosure.

'Blimey.' The handler peered into both vivaria, checking they were secure. 'This is quite the set-up.'

One housed a substantial, rippling python, with creamy, leathery eggs visible between her coils; in the other, a vibrant red-and-white corn snake was wrapped around off-white pebble-like eggs.

The scent of warm vegetation made James look around. More tanks lined the walls, with shrubbery under hot lamps, like mini-greenhouses. Checking them, James saw the same plants that filled the tanks downstairs, minus the snakes. It looked like Amir cultivated the plants, as well as the reptiles.

Another officer joined them, recoiled from the breeding snakes in their enclosures and passed James to check the bathroom.

It was then that James spotted the stepladder leaning against the wall. Glancing up, he saw the loft hatch directly overhead. He set up the ladder just as the officer rejoined him and, with a nod, headed straight up the rungs. As the officer opened the hatch, heat and bright light spilled out, and an overwhelming odour hit them. A heavy, pungent, sweet, herby aroma. Unmistakably cannabis.

'Bingo,' the officer said. Leaning towards the stairs, he yelled, 'Oi! We've got something up here.'

Blinking, James climbed up and peered around.

The centre of the loft bristled with a miniature jungle of cannabis plants under glowing lamps. Beside the hatch, a table was taken up with metal drying shelves, racks and equipment. Under the sloping edges were lines of plants draped over clothes hangers, drying out and ready for processing.

The officer whistled. 'Quite an operation for someone flying under our radar. What d'you reckon? About three hundred and fifty plants? We're probably looking at a value of about a hundred and fifty grand.'

James didn't care about the estimate. He just cared that this might be one way to get one of his suspects off the street.

He hurried down the ladder, down the stairs, past the rustling cloth bags, to the kitchen, just in time to hear Wade, who'd heard the confirmation his officer had yelled, say the words, 'Amir Massoud, you're under arrest . . .'

Sunday 17th July – 9.30 a.m.

Nell swore under her breath. *This wasn't the bloody deal.* Since the incident with Pipsqueak, and the suspicions she now had about her new colleagues, she'd decided to *only* work on the heath if there were three of them going together. But where the hell were Erin and Simon this morning?

Despite her annoyance, and her unease at being there alone, she needed to approach the reptile refugia quietly. Her footsteps had to be gentle enough not to send warning vibrations to the sensitive snakes under the shelter of the corrugated iron.

Reaching the next one, Nell crouched and lifted back the metal sheet with her gloved hand. A tangle of squashed stems and roots, bleached after being denied sunlight, all looked like knots of snakes, and Nell checked carefully before replacing the trap and moving on to the next.

She could already see the common lizard on top of the black-painted square. Holding her breath, she inched forward. These were fast little blighters. So easy to miss or – worse – to grab only by the tail, which would fall off and allow the lizard to escape. It was a life-saving manoeuvre – but only *sometimes*: precious fat stores in the tail meant that losing it could cause starvation.

And Nell, especially, didn't want to make this inquisitive little beast starve to death. The female lizard was clearly gravid, her leathery body swollen with eggs. Nell estimated she was the standard fifteen centimetres from the tip of her proud slim head to the tip of her tail, held high in the air as she posed on the corner. Her scales glowed bronze in the golden morning sun.

Holding her breath, Nell tiptoed towards her, hunkering low on protesting thighs. She always needed to do more yoga. She aimed for a grip at the lizard's shoulders, hoping to keep well clear of her tail and delicate body.

When she was close enough to reach, her hand darted out sideways. The lizard was way too fast, despite being pregnant. But at least this was a species that would dart away when it was time to clear this part of the site, unlike slow-worms or grass snakes, who would play dead. Which wasn't an effective defence against a digger.

Having disturbed the lizard, Nell didn't expect to see the brown zigzag markings of an adder, curled around a squashed bracken stem, as she peeled back the rigid sheet.

She let go of the square, blocking it from falling on the snake with her body. It slapped against her side, making a snail stuck to the metal's underside catapult through the air and land, with a gooey squelch, on Nell's face. Grimacing, she gently unfurled the snake from the fern and placed it in her bucket, securing the air-holed lid.

Returning the snail to its residence and replacing the trap, Nell stood up, stretching, and scanned the heath.

As she turned slowly, she couldn't believe there was still no sign of either Erin or Simon. *This is really taking the bloody—*

'Hi.'

Nell wheeled round at the voice.

'Oh!' She tried to laugh away her surprise. 'At last! Good to see you, Simon. I made a start. So we don't have many to finish.'

He held his hand out for one of her buckets.

'Haven't you brought your own? So we can split the work up between us?' It wasn't a good idea to overload the buckets with animals. And Nell hadn't expected to need to share hers out.

'Oh.' Simon scratched his head and looked a bit lost for a moment. 'I've had a bit of a . . . a bit of a weird morning.'

Something in his manner set Nell a little on edge. He had an air of jerky agitation that made him seem a bit . . . unpredictable. And where was Erin?

'Fine. Why don't you check the next one?' Nell offered a bucket and pointed at the distant refugia, partly to get him away from her, and partly so that she wouldn't be the one to turn her back.

Grabbing the bucket, he marched off.

With a relieved sigh, Nell checked her phone. One bar of signal. Not great, but the best she'd get out here.

She started to find Erin's number, but a call flashed. Rav.

'Hi.' Her voice was a little breathless.

'Nell? Can . . . talk?' The line crackled. Nell had to concentrate on what he said.

'Yes, of course—'

'I . . . gone through . . . files. Simon *was* there on . . . day of the murder. And not . . . that . . . He walk . . . in the directi . . . of . . . murder, not long before it happen . . . I think . . . *heard* it. Just . . . just make sure . . . not alone with him.'

Sunday 17th July – 11.30 a.m.

Back at the station, James searched for Hesha, hoping she'd have an update on Simon.

He found her by the evidence board. She was just staring at it, not moving. Nothing about her suggested any *urgency*. He tried not to feel aggravated.

'Hesha, are you about to tell me Simon's in an interview room?'

'What?' Hesha barely dragged her eyes from the board. Then she glanced at him. 'Oh, hi. Sorry, what?'

'How are you getting on with Simon? Are we in danger of bringing him in, yet?'

'Oh. Oh yeah, no, I haven't got any further.'

'Right.' James huffed a long exhale. 'Only, that was the urgent task of the day, Hesha.'

'Yeah, I know. I'll get on it. Sorry. Only . . .'

'Only what?'

'We've had something else come in. Bit of a curveball.'

Trepidation crawled across James's stomach. 'What?'

The door opened and Dr Saunders walked in, holding a folder. 'Found it, Hesh. Ah, are you bringing James up to speed?'

'Up to speed on *what*?'

Dr Saunders took a breath. 'I just had a thought that perhaps it might be worthwhile running a few more tests. And it turns out, it was.'

'Oh?' James said.

'We know that the perpetrator is very forensically aware. He's been careful to leave no trace at all. Ashley spoke to me about the large gaps between victims. So I wondered if, maybe, there were more. And *that* made me wonder how I could determine that.'

James gaped as he caught on. 'You mean—?'

'*Exactly*! Apart from a physical resemblance, the thing all the victims definitely had in common was this strangely marked ligature. So I'm hypothesising it wasn't just the same *type*, but the same *one*. And, if that's the case, even if he thought to clean it – which he may well overlook – then there's a small chance some DNA of a previous victim might have transferred to Amy.'

'And?' James didn't know why he was pressing; the Doc wouldn't be going through all of this if there'd been no result.

But Hesha stole the punchline. 'The Doc didn't only find DNA, James. She found DNA which doesn't match any of our victims.'

James held his breath. 'So we've got—'

'Yes. Another victim.' Dr Saunders handed over the folder. 'I've found her details. Shirley McGuinness. Killed in 2006, sixteen years ago, near Aberdeen.'

Chapter 17

Sunday 17th July – 11.30 a.m.

Hanging up the phone to Rav, Nell stared at Simon, a few yards ahead of her, as apprehension prickled the back of her neck.

Erin arrived, waving at Nell from a distance, presumably to avoid explaining why she was late. But she had at least brought a bucket and fell into step with Simon, to work along one section. Nell watched as Erin finished her area and caught up with him, nudging him with the side of her body. He turned, laughing, and pointed at her bucket, which Erin hefted as she answered. He pointed at the next section of traps and they parted to check two parallel rows of refugia.

Their body language made Nell even more uneasy. They probably wouldn't care if she made up some excuse and left. But as Simon stood up from looking under the first metal square, and turned to gaze at Erin – with that long, unwavering, silent stare of his – Nell was determined not to leave her alone with him either.

She tried to decide what to do. She needed a viable excuse to abandon the trapping. She saw Erin catch two snakes, then move to the next trap. She'd already caught another one by the time Nell walked over, making her stance assertive.

'How are you getting on?'

Erin replaced the last trap of that section. 'Good, caught five here in all.' She stretched, her eyes straying to Simon. 'We're about halfway through, aren't we?'

'No – this is the last one. I varied the route this morning. So let's release them before they get agitated. It's a warm morning. I don't want them getting overheated in the car.'

'Oh. Great.' Simon glanced at Erin. 'So we're done here for the day?'

Nell nodded. At least none of them were doing the afternoon shift.

On the way back to the car park, Simon nudged Erin. 'Fancy getting lunch?'

157

'Erin, I'll need to show you the new release site,' Nell said, a little too loud, too bright. 'It won't take long, and it'll set you up for future surveys.'

Erin's face scrunched. 'Really? Now? Can't we just release them like normal and go?'

Nell bit back her wince. 'I can keep the work stuff to a minimum, so I don't eat into your lunchtime, but I *do* need to show you, Erin.' The made-up reason sounded lame, and Erin wasn't biting.

'It's OK, I'll join you,' Simon suggested. 'I'll need to know if we're taking them somewhere different. We've got time before lunch, Erin.'

No, no, no! Nell turned to him and forced a smile. 'Sorry, Simon. I want a bit of one-to-one time with Erin. She's my mentee, and I've got a couple of other points to discuss, so today, I need time with just her.'

'Yeah, but *I* don't want one-to-one time,' Erin protested. 'Not *today*. It *is* my bloody *weekend*. You can't commandeer me for work stuff now we've done the survey.'

Biting back her irritation at Erin's customary attitude, and pre-empting Simon giving another reason to gatecrash, Nell added, 'Simon could even head into town *now* to find a table somewhere nice, and you won't be long joining him.'

Then, hopefully, I can convince Erin to text him an excuse.

'Oh, done,' Simon announced.

'What?' Nell glanced at him, her heart sinking.

'I've already booked a table. It'll be ready in half an hour's time.' He flashed his eyebrows at Erin. 'So I *can* join you, and then you and I can head into town together.'

Nell forced a smile. *Maybe I can drive Erin to the release site. That might give me enough time to say something.*

But Erin dumped her bucket in the boot of the site car, then backed off towards Simon's camper van, with a hint of a pout. 'We'll follow you.'

'How about you drive with me, Erin, then I can talk over the issue without taking any extra time up on your weekend. Win-win?' She tried to make her tone warm, hoping to encourage Erin. 'And maybe you could keep an eye on the buckets? Don't want them accidentally falling over!' Nell tried to laugh. 'Imagine what a disaster that would be!'

Erin hesitated. Nell beckoned her, then got into the car, holding her breath as she turned the ignition. In the mirror, she saw Erin roll her eyes at Simon, then stomp to Nell's car. Nell let out a long exhale of relief, which she covered with a smile when Erin got in.

Driving out of the car park, she glanced at Erin. 'I needed to get you alone, to tell you something about Simon.'

Erin's head jerked round. 'What?'

'Rav went through the files for Furze Heath, to help us write up the report. This morning he checked Simon's files. They go back to before the date he started working with us. They go back to the day of the murder.'

Turning into the road around the heath, Nell's eyes flicked to the rear-view mirror. Simon was tight on her tail.

'So? I know that he's there all the time. Tracking the wildlife and wild camping.'

'Yes, but his video is *right* at the *time* of the murder, and *near* it. And Rav reckoned he heard it. After Simon walked in that direction.' Saying the words out loud made Nell feel sick.

'Oh, for God's sake. You and Rav are total murder tourists. You really need to stop seeing suspicion in everyone.'

'Erin, I'm serious. Even if my assumption is wrong, there's no harm done. Give him a reasonable excuse to head straight home, or go to see a friend so you're not alone. All that will have happened is that you'll have missed a lunch. You can make it up. But if I'm *right . . .*'

'Yeah. I can just see Simon strangling someone, stabbing them and leaving them naked, can't you?'

'Well, under the circumstances, I don't want to take any chances, Erin. Not when it's easily avoided. I know you and I have had our differences, but you *are* my colleague, and I do *care* about you.'

Erin looked even more irritated. Shaking her head, she stared out of her window, and they drove the rest of the way in infuriated silence.

Reaching the release site, in Furze Wood, Nell sent a text to Sylvia to say where they were. Then she sent one to Rav, saying she'd tried to dissuade Erin from going off with Simon. She stared as the texts didn't send, and a 'Message failure' notification appeared.

'Are we going to sit here all day?' Erin huffed. 'You said this wouldn't take long.' She got out to join Simon, who was already loitering by their car.

Taking the buckets from the boot, Nell shivered as she glanced around the dense conifer wood. Remembering the murderer had taken her chloroform, she asked Simon to carry the buckets, so he'd have his hands full, and she'd have a warning if he put them down while they were walking to a suitable place.

Not wanting to stray far from the car park, Nell pointed at a sunny patch of scrub on the fringe of the wood and the heath. 'This is a good spot. Why don't you release them here? Tuck them under the vegetation so that they're hidden, then they can get accustomed to their new surroundings without being stressed that they're exposed.'

It took a few moments for Simon and Erin to gently transfer the captured snakes.

'You told us we'd be releasing the snakes somewhere different, Nell. This is exactly the same location. So what's different?' Simon asked.

'We want to make sure the released snakes aren't all bundled under the same bushes. We need to make sure we're evening out their distribution when we release them, to help their dispersal into the habitat.'

'Oh, right.'

As Nell leaned in to check that the reptiles were being placed under cover, Simon's loosely rolled shirtsleeve caught on a bramble. Standing up, he fiddled with it, unrolling it so he could tuck it up again.

Nell stared at his cuff. The khaki Craghoppers shirt was missing its button.

Simon might spend a lot of time here. But what are the odds that his button would turn up exactly where Amy's phone and wallet had been dropped in the bushes?

Her heart thundered but she tried to keep calm. 'OK, thank you. Perfect job. Erin, you wanted to keep it short and sweet, so we're done. Can I drop you off anywhere?'

Sunday 17th July – 1 p.m.

'We know that Andrew Deacon went to university in Edinburgh,' Ashley confirmed. 'Which isn't far from Aberdeen. *And* that the timing of his university course overlaps with the date Shirley was killed.'

James was reading through her interview plan. 'Looks good. Has Ed brought him in?'

Ashley nodded.

'You happy to take the lead?' James wished he could sit in, but he knew he felt too involved. His concern about Nell would affect his ability to stay calm and conduct the questioning. So he'd watch, while Ashley and Ed tackled Drew.

Through the screen, he saw Drew sipping his water, making cordial small talk with the man James assumed was his lawyer, and Ed.

Ed chatted as he calmly set out their notes, and smiled when Ashley joined them. She instantly took command, making the formal introductions. Drew's body language changed. His relaxed posture became stiffer, and he shot micro-glares at Ashley when everyone looked down to take notes.

James leaned forward, noting Drew's reaction to a woman taking charge.

'Can you tell us where you were on the evening of Friday 15th July? You weren't at home then. Or at work. Where were you, Drew?'

'No comment,' the lawyer interjected. 'You don't have to answer any questions.'

'No, no, no, I have no problem saying where I was. Happy to help. But I'll have to think . . .' His disarming smile also vanished when the audience looked away. 'I was at the pub, probably? Can I check my phone?'

'By all means.'

'Oh, here we are. I finished work a bit late, so Nicky and I decided to get a takeaway for dinner. I prefer the place in Cookingdean. Great tandoori. So I suggested that. Offering to get the shopping in from Tesco on the way was the clincher.'

His smile was too secure, too languid, for James's liking.

'By the time I'd done the shopping and got to the takeaway, it would probably have been around eight thirty? Quarter to nine? Something like that.'

'You'd kept your wife waiting that long for dinner?' Ashley arched an eyebrow. 'Didn't she mind?'

Drew looked completely confounded. 'Mind? Why would she? I was bringing dinner home.' He smiled again. 'It was fine. I bought her some flowers.'

'She must be very accommodating. Did you stop off or do anything else on the way?'

James realised that Ashley's maths had been quick enough to realise that Drew had either driven unexpectedly slowly along the country lanes from Tesco to Cookingdean – or he'd *raced* to Nell's, and very swiftly attacked the bat and taken the chloroform.

'No.' Drew met Ashley's searching gaze calmly.

'What about another date, going back to 2006 – 16th December? A long while ago, I realise. It would have been a Saturday. You'd have been at . . .' Ashley made a show of consulting the notes. 'Oh yes, Edinburgh University.'

'That's, what, sixteen years ago! How the hell would I know?' Drew laughed. 'I can go and see if I have anything, I don't know, archived in my emails or something, to give me a clue. But otherwise, I've no idea.'

'Yes, would you mind checking? And if you recall, please let us know.' Ashley played the question down with a shrug. 'It might be nothing, but we have a duty to follow up anything that might be related to our investigation, however slight the chance.'

They knew Drew had been at Edinburgh Uni, near where their unexpected extra victim had been killed. James had wanted to check his reaction, without telling him why. But Drew just looked amused at the idea he could remember with any accuracy what he'd been doing on a specific day nearly twenty years ago.

'So how about a more recent date?' Ashley persevered. 'Where were you at 2 p.m. on Wednesday, 6th July?'

Drew shrugged. 'A couple of weeks ago, mid week, I'd have been working.'

'Where?' Ed asked, even though the team had read his LinkedIn profile.

'At that time, I was working from home, as an Independent Financial Advisor.'

'What made you move from that to working at EcoLogical Solutions?' Ed asked.

'A new challenge.' Drew shrugged. 'The IFA work is interesting enough. You meet a few high net worth individuals, work out the best solution for them. But I heard through my contacts that there was some financial challenge related to this local development. And that intrigued me. Who *wouldn't* want to put their skills to good use, and contribute to some local regeneration?'

'Did you happen to go out for a walk that day?' Ashley asked. 'Anything like that?'

'Highly unlikely. Bit of a workaholic.' He gave a self-deprecating chuckle that only lasted as long as it took for the people around the table to look at him.

'OK, now I want to ask you if you've ever met this woman.' Ashley laid a photo of Amy on the table.

Drew studied it, then shrugged and shook his head. 'No.'

'Are you sure?' Ashley confirmed. 'Take another look. Not a friend, or a colleague, or extended family?'

'Sorry, who are you saying this is?' Drew asked.

'I'm asking *you* if you know who she is, Drew.'

'I *don't* know her. I've never met her.'

'That's Amy Fallon,' Ashley said.

'Oh?' Drew's brow crinkled.

'Is her name familiar?' Ashley pressed.

Through the screen, James watched Drew like a hawk for any tells. But Drew shook his head. 'Should it be?'

'Yes.' Ashley didn't elaborate. She sat, waiting. The clock ticked through the silence.

Finally, Ashley said, 'She was one of your clients. A few months ago. You met her three times to give her personal financial advice, wrote several emails and an investment plan. And you're now trying to convince me that not only do you *not* recognise her photograph, but that you *also* don't recognise her name.'

Drew gaped. 'What?'

Ed slid a plastic bag containing a page of typing towards him. 'Can you tell me what's written on that page?'

Scanning it, Drew nodded. 'That looks like one of my emails. Standard message to a client. Yes, it's entirely possible she was a client of mine.'

'So now you suddenly remember her?' Ashley said.

'I have a lot of clients. I can't remember them all. She was relatively small fry.'

'Ah, so now you suddenly not only recollect *her*, but you recollect the work you did for her in *detail*? You've been withholding information from us.' Ashley sat back, and gave Ed a brief nod.

As Drew threw up his hands in exasperation, Ed removed the handcuffs from his belt and began to read Drew his rights.

Chapter 18

Sunday 17th July – 3 p.m.

With Drew in custody, James had asked Ed to apply for a warrant to search his house and his computer. Meanwhile, James was preparing to interview Amir, now that the questions from the Serious and Organised Crime Unit had concluded – for the moment.

He could surmise that Amir was Amy's dealer. But that was *all* he had on Amir right now. Maybe tech would come back with some more information soon. In the meantime, he'd have to rely on skilful questioning. He just hoped he wouldn't blow this chance to see if there was any other connection.

He ordered the pages of his interview plan into the folder, stood up – and nearly ran into Dr Saunders at the door.

'Now, I'm not suggesting that you owe me cake, or wine, or anything but, if you're interested, my favourites are carrot and merlot. Because I *am* fast-tracking everything for you on this case,' she said. 'And I had a tip this might be quite timely.'

'Oh?' Instantly riveted, James put the folder down.

'The SOCO team you sent in this morning prioritised a few samples. Amir has dark black hair. But they found a brown hair on the sofa.'

'OK.' He didn't get his hopes up. That could be from a mate.

'It was Nell's.'

'Nell's?' James spluttered. *Oh, no. What was she doing there?* They were . . . *colleagues,* he reasoned. But if she'd gone to his *house* . . . What was she *thinking*?

'And we found another brown hair in the bedroom.'

Oh, no.

But Dr Saunders was nodding. 'I know what you're thinking – and you're right.'

'Not Nell, surely? She didn't . . . go into his . . . *bedroom*?' There could be any number of explanations. It didn't have to mean . . . *that.*

'No! Not Nell! *Amy*!'

James sat down again and looked at his interview plan. Now that he had more ammunition, there was more at stake.

Thirty minutes later, he sat opposite Amir and the Legal Aid lawyer. Once the introductions were concluded, James took a deep breath and gave Amir a smile.

'You must be fed up of questions by now. But I do need to ask a few more.'

Amir shrugged. 'Ask away.'

'I'm not interested in the cannabis. I want to talk to you about another case, Amir. I think you could be a witness.'

'Oh?'

'We know that you met this woman,' James slid the photo of Amy across the table, 'at the Copperhead pub.'

'I thought you weren't going to ask about that.'

'So you *were* dealing? To her?'

Amir shrugged again.

'This woman was murdered, Amir. A few days after she saw you. Can you tell me what you knew about her?'

'What?' Amir looked shocked. 'I heard about the murder, but I didn't realise it was *her*.' He paused for a moment, before continuing. 'I didn't know her well. I saw her in the pub. She came to speak to me.'

'With your icebreaker reptile?'

Amir frowned.

'Your snakes are a good cover, I admit. For the whole operation, actually: a collection of snakes in heated tanks is ideal cover for your place having a whopping heat signature. *And* it's a perfect distraction in the pub – people are looking at the snake while drugs and money swap hands. And, *again*, it's the perfect way to deter an officer from searching your bag.'

'I *thought* you weren't asking about that,' Amir repeated.

James noted that Amir's belligerence was masking his fear. When he reached for his water, his hand shook. The raid would have been unexpected; he'd obviously assumed he'd got every angle sewn up. And James's recent visit may have made him feel even more secure.

'What did Amy speak to you about?' James asked.

'Not much. She thought Queenie was pretty cool. We got talking about that. She knew I was an ecologist. She was an architect, so we'd both worked with each other's disciplines on developments. We felt like we had some common ground there. And she was quite funny, quite sweet.'

'You liked her, then?'

Another shrug. 'She seemed nice. Yeah.'

'Did you see her outside of the pub?'

He shifted on his seat, 'No.'

'Sure about that?' James tilted his head.

'Hmm.' Amir's eyes flicked to his lawyer, who was making a note.

'This is a murder enquiry, Amir. And any information you have could shed some light on something that gets us closer to finding the killer.'

'Yeah, I wish I could help.'

'Did you ever go to her place?'

'I've said no.'

'Did she ever go to your place?'

He shifted on his seat again, and glared at his lawyer. 'Aren't you supposed to be saying "no comment", or something?'

The lawyer leaned over and murmured something. James looked at his desk as if giving them privacy, while he tried to catch what she said. 'Agreed to cooperate . . . more lenient . . .'

When Amir sat up straight again, he looked at James. 'Yeah, she came back to mine. It was a one-time thing.'

'What happened?'

'She came back, we had a couple of drinks, then . . . you know.'

'So you'd have got to know each other a bit, then. What else did you know about her?'

'Honestly, not a lot. We talked about work, hobbies. Mine were . . . obvious. She didn't have much free time. She talked a lot about her ex's wedding coming up. She wouldn't have gone, but he was marrying a good friend. I thought that sounded a bit questionable. She kept going on and on about how she wanted to get a knockout outfit. She kind of swung from being totally insecure about it, to being completely done with men. One minute, all her friends are

167

married, settling down, having kids, and she's the odd one out. Next minute, she's endlessly fishing for compliments. Made her a bit of an easy target. So, you know, I . . .' he spread his hands, 'obliged.'

'Easy target. Interesting description.'

'It's honest, though. That's what you asked for.' He gave a slight chin jut.

'So how did you leave things between you?'

'Oh, she didn't stay. She got an Uber home. Said she had a big weekend. I didn't ask what she was doing. By that point, I was finding her a bit full-on.'

James made a note. Tech could check that on Amy's phone.

'So, what were you doing on Wednesday 6th July, around two o'clock?'

'Is that when . . . ?' Amir exhaled. 'Working, probably. I was on a contract before I moved to EcoLogical. I can check and let you know. But . . . you know.'

Amir's phone was with the tech team, so they'd all know before Amir did. James just nodded. 'Please do. And I need to know if anyone can verify where you were. It's just to count you out of our enquiries. Just a formality.' He delivered the lie with an easy smile.

'OK.'

'What about the evening of Friday 15th July?'

Amir shrugged. 'Probably out at the pub.'

'Until what time?'

'Till closing, probably.'

'Did you have any reason to drive out of town?'

'Oh, on the 15th? Yeah. I sold my last corn snake from the last breeding round to a bloke out in the sticks. We met at some country pub. The Foresters Arms, I think. Got there not long before closing. I thought it was deliberate, so he only had time to buy me one drink.'

'And he'll corroborate this, of course?'

'Yeah, I'll give you his name.' Amir reached in his pocket. 'Ah. When I get my phone back.'

James nodded. Amir's alibi, and hopefully recollections from others in the pub, would tell him if he had the opportunity to break into Nell's.

'Thanks, Amir. We appreciate your cooperation.'

'Good. You can let DS Ezra's team know, then. It's important they know that. What happens next?'

'That's up to them. But I can at least put in a good word, now.'

'And how long will this disrupt my work for? And my social life?'

'Honestly, I don't know, Amir. I will say that any cooperation will obviously help.'

'This is perfect bloody timing.' Amir tutted. 'I don't even know what their bail conditions will be yet. Let alone if I'll meet them. Or when you'll be finished with me.' He shot James a pained look. '*You* probably think this is the worst of it. But your interrogation will be nothing compared to the grilling I'll get from my aunts. Once they realise I'm not turning up this weekend.' He huffed. 'Now they've taken my phone off me, I can't even call them with a feasible excuse.'

'Ah. Over-invested relatives?' James feigned empathy. 'Would it help if you could call someone now?'

'I thought I only got one phone call?' Amir said. 'I had to use it to get my mate to look after the snakes.'

'Leave it with me,' James said. 'I'll make sure you get a phone call.'

'Thanks.'

'What's the occasion you're missing?'

'Parents' golden wedding anniversary. Bit of a faux pas, isn't it? My absence won't go unnoticed.'

James winced. 'Yeah, I can imagine the heat I'd get for that.' James shot him a rueful smile. 'Are you a close family?'

'Kind of. I was brought up by my grandparents. For . . . various reasons. I've tried to build bridges with my parents now I'm older. When they retired a few years ago, they moved away. The distance takes the pressure off, because a visit takes some organisation. Which has helped.'

'Oh. Where did they move to?'

'Scotland. Cairngorms. Stunning place. Near Dundee.'

Sunday 17th July – 9 p.m.

Nell could see there was little point arguing with Rav. He was on a mission.

'Strained muscles are *good*! That means I'm working them hard. This is at least a pain I understand.'

'*Working* your muscles is good. *Straining* them isn't. Don't set yourself back because you're overdoing it. You know you need to build up gradually. It's going to take time.'

'Pff. I'll be fine. It's you I'm worried about.'

'I promise, I'm being careful. I didn't hang around with Simon after your call. And I tried to persuade Erin to give him a wide berth, too.'

'And did she?' Rav looked worried.

'Yeah. Eventually. She told him she'd got a call from her housemate and had to help with an emergency at home. Even then, he offered to help, and when she said no, he offered to drive her home. But she said I was passing her place, so she'd get a lift with me. Then she spent the whole trip moaning.'

'Good. Not about the moaning. About not being alone with him.'

'What did James say about it?' Nell asked.

Rav frowned. 'About what?'

'The file! The sound you heard! Simon being right *there*!'

The creases on Rav's forehead deepened. 'I thought you'd tell him.'

'But you've got the file! You could send it to him!'

'Yeah, so have you. And you're on . . . friendlier terms with him.'

'Oh, like that matters. Why didn't you contact him?' Nell wanted to blurt out that Rav had the time. And spending one hour fewer in the PT suite today would have been a good idea, as it turned out.

'Well. You know.' Rav gestured. 'He's your ex. He hates me.'

'He doesn't, actually, he sent his best wishes.'

'OK, then it's me being the—'

'OK, stop that. Stop with the "I can't do anything" attitude. Yes, there are some things that are *limited*. But that isn't stopping you doing *everything*. And if you start thinking like that, it'll become a self-fulfilling prophecy. You're the least helpless person I know.'

'Fine. I'll send it to him now.' Rav huffed and typed a rapid email, following it up with a text. He shot Nell a glare. 'I don't think I'm helpless. I thought you'd done it. Given that you're supposed to have stepped back from work. You know, to avoid a murderer and be a bit sensible and safe. *And* less busy. Only you haven't, have you?'

Nell felt her face flame. 'I didn't make any promises.'

'Well, I think you need to, Nell.' He held her gaze. His dark eyes were full of love and worry.

With a sigh, Nell relented. 'Fine.'

'*Thank you!*' Rav sagged, like a rag doll, with relief.

'Only because I think I should be here, making sure you're not overdoing it.'

They looked at each other, their gazes fierce, and Nell had to lean in and kiss him. 'I'll head home now, but I'll call Elliot, and I'll see you bright and early.'

'Good.'

But as Nell walked along the corridor, guilt at letting Elliot down, and abandoning the project, nagged. At least there was more of a team to help now. And maybe Rav would let her help with finances directly, so she wouldn't need to entangle Elliot in an unnecessarily complicated plan. Walking into the crisp air and fast-fading light, she took a deep breath. Now her focus should be on Rav.

She walked through the car park, to the overflow one on uneven ground, and reached for her phone for the light. A text from James was on the home screen.

Nell, sure you already know but I've got info from Rav on one of your colleagues. I hope you've stopped work. If you haven't, do so immediately.

She texted a quick reply: *Yes, I will, and I'll call my boss on Monday to confirm.* Then she used the torch app to light her way, tripping on the rutted ground, the dark surroundings melting into blackness beyond.

Without warning, some kind of bag was jerked down over her entire head, plunging her into total, airless darkness. Panic spiked. A cord pulled around her neck. The attacker's arms pinned her own arms to her sides, as pressure crushed against her throat.

Nell tried to punch back with her elbows, but couldn't free her arms. She kicked behind her, whacking the attacker's calf, then their knee. But the grip around her tightened. Her ragged inhale drew in a mouthful of synthetic, foul-tasting material.

She lowered her chin to her chest, then flung her head back with all the force she could muster. The headbutt made her head *ring* with pain. But the attacker staggered back with a grunt. The movement made the cord tug around her exposed throat with so much force that she thought it would break her windpipe.

Unable to breathe, Nell jabbed back again with her elbows, *and* all her might. She made contact. The grip on her arms broke and Nell staggered forward, trying to rip the hood off her head.

A blow to her back winded her, making her stumble. She held her hands out blindly to break her fall, lunging sideways rather than forward. Then she desperately tried again to pull the hood off. The terror of not being able to see her attacker made her *frantic*.

The cord was tight – tied, or stuck – and she panicked, clawing at it.

Feeling vulnerable on the ground, not knowing where the assailant would come from next, she threw herself sideways, rolling, bumping over rutted ground. Her fumbling fingers found a toggle at the back of the hood. Willing her hands to stop shaking, she tried to pinch the button, slacken the cord.

Finally, it released and she tugged at the hood, frantically searching for her attacker as she gasped for lungfuls of air and scrabbled to her feet.

Chapter 19

Rav wanted to hug Nell to him, fierce with worry and fear and impotent frustration. But she wouldn't come close enough.

'No I . . . might have his DNA on me. I need to preserve any evidence . . . Just in case.' She was shaking, her voice tremoring.

He tried to push himself to standing, to reach her side, hold her, forgetting for a moment that he couldn't. He slapped the arm of the wheelchair, but inched closer.

'Are you hurt?' The lurid red marks around her throat punched fear through him. She'd been ghost white when she'd weaved in, still in shock.

She touched her throat. 'Sore. And a bit . . . winded. Shocked, more than anything.'

'Did you see anything?'

Nell shook her head. 'It was too dark, and they jumped me from behind.' She shuddered. Fragmented pictures of the struggle splintered through her mind.

'How did you get away?' Rav asked.

Nell shrugged. 'I don't know. Maybe they gave up because I fought back? I headbutted them. Bloody hurt, so I hope it did some damage. I fell over. I thought it was all over then. I was trying to get out of the way of someone I couldn't even see. But when I got up, they'd gone. And they must have run to have been completely out of sight.'

'Maybe something – or someone – disturbed them?' Rav suggested.

Nell shook her head. 'I don't know what that would have been then. Maybe someone leaving, or the guard doing his rounds? I called James on my way back in. I needed to be on the phone while I walked. I asked the security guard at reception to look at the CCTV recording. But it doesn't cover the overflow car park, just the main entrance.'

Rav bit back the *I asked you to be careful!* line. As scared as he was for Nell, this wasn't about how he felt. Last time they'd argued – which felt like another lifetime ago now – he'd made Nell's horrible past experience all about him, like he'd been entitled to know about her lowest moment, because someone harming her fired up all his protective instincts. But she wasn't asking for his protection. Which was just as well, because he couldn't give that to her now.

Instead, he asked, 'What do you want to do about this? How can I help?'

She turned to him, her face trembling. 'I'm really afraid . . .' She swallowed, and he wanted to hold her again. But he didn't expect what she said next. 'Because if they attacked me *here*, then they know about *you.*'

Blinking rapidly, she stared at the ceiling. 'Oh, great. I don't want to dilute any DNA with tears.' After a moment, she looked at him again. 'I couldn't bear anything else happening to you.'

'I couldn't bear anything happening to you, either.' Good. He'd said it. 'So, what do we do?'

Sunday 17th July – 9.45 p.m.

James parked badly at the entrance to Pendlebury's Spinal Unit and sprinted inside, with Ashley and a SOCO hurrying in his wake, while Dr Underwood followed sedately.

Nell and Rav were waiting just inside the entrance. As much as Nell must have needed a hug, she wasn't having one. In fact, she was sitting some distance from Rav. James knew she was preserving as much evidence as she could.

He suggested the suited SOCO take the necessary samples – from her clothes, her face, under her nails – in Rav's private room first; then she could have the hug she must be aching for, and *then* they could talk.

But, once in Rav's room, with the door closed, Nell insisted that the samples should be taken while she talked to James, so they wouldn't lose any time. The SOCO began by clipping her nails into a plastic bag.

'I was so certain things were safer,' James lamented. 'We had three suspects: Amir, who's been arrested and hopefully won't meet his bail; and Drew, who was arrested at lunchtime today—'

'Then it must be Simon,' Rav concluded. 'Did you get the file I sent you?'

James nodded. 'A short while ago. I'd just watched it when Nell called. And I dashed straight here.'

'Yeah, so you saw for yourself. Simon looked pretty grim when he turned the camera on, didn't he? Although, I *did* wonder why you'd want to record yourself committing a crime. Pretty daft, surely? Unless it's, what? Voyeurism? Thinking he's too clever to get caught?'

'Perhaps,' Dr Underwood said.

'Do you know if Simon has ever been to Scotland? Specifically near Aberdeen? About sixteen years ago?'

'How would they know?' Ashley tutted.

But Nell and Rav were nodding.

'Yes. He went to the Orkneys,' Rav said. 'So not a million miles away from Aberdeen. I saw that in his blog, so you may get some dates from that.'

Nell gave James a sharp look, and he knew she was already wondering why. With a sigh and a glance at his team, he lowered his voice. 'This is highly confidential, Nell, but I can see you're going to ask. There's another victim. She hasn't been related to these murders locally. The press don't know about it. None of the suspects have been told we know about her, so this really cannot get out, understand? She was killed in Scotland. Her name was Shirley McGuinness.'

Nell's inhale told James this was what she'd assumed – yet dreaded having confirmed. She took a moment, thinking, or reflecting, and then noticed the SOCO bag containing the nylon khaki drawstring sack.

'That bag that went over my head.' Nell pointed at it. 'I've seen it before. It's Simon Slaker's. When he wild camps, that's the sack he stuffs his sleeping bag into, to compress it.' She looked at the SOCO, suddenly hopeful. 'When it was over my head, I headbutted the attacker. So there's a chance it could have their DNA on the outside. Maybe even their blood?' she suggested, a bit too cheerfully.

James frowned, turning to Ashley and Underwood. 'Are we looking at a different method of attack here? We haven't seen anything like that used before. Just strangulation and stabbing, usually afterwards. Use of a hood would leave traces on the face, surely. And it's a personal item. So far, the perpetrator has shown much greater forensic awareness.'

The SOCO swabbed Nell's face, securing the sample in a plastic jar.

'Are we looking at more than one perpetrator, then, James?' Rav asked. 'Could it be that this attack and Nell's break-in weren't carried out by the murderer? Are we limiting the investigation by assuming that?' James noticed how he was gripping his hands together.

'It's a fair question, Rav. But we *are* keeping open-minded about who and what and why. As you rightly point out, assumptions would narrow an investigation.'

'The break-in – and this attack – *could* be related to Mum's prison reform bill,' Nell said. 'It's attracting a bit of heat from some pretty . . . let's politely say, *unpredictable* characters. But with my security, honestly, I don't think the break-in could have been opportunistic. It had to be someone who knew how to get in, *and* who knew I'd be out. And that's a limited number of people.'

'And those people happen to be our suspects,' James said.

Nell shivered. Rav wrung his hands again. James saw plainly that if anything was going to get Rav to leap to his feet and sprint a marathon, it was Nell.

'OK. But if that's the case, he stole Nell's chloroform. That would be an easier way to subdue someone, surely?' Rav asked. 'And that would have shown us a link. So if they didn't use it . . . ?'

'Chloroform isn't as effective as TV would have you believe,' James said. 'It needs time to take effect. You'd also have to be able to subdue your victim for a while. And it doesn't last very long, either.'

'Perhaps this attack was spontaneous, rather than planned?' Ashley suggested. 'Maybe he's getting more desperate?'

'Yes, I agree, DS Hollis,' Dr Underwood said. 'And if desperation is setting in, then there's good news and bad news. The *good* news is the carelessness on his part. Giving us more potential for forensic evidence. Like this bag, using what was to hand instead of planning something with precision. The *bad* news is that a changing pattern reduces his predictability. But the *worse* news is that this is the most dangerous he could get. This is his endgame.'

Chapter 20

Monday 18th July – 6 a.m.

Nell heard the commotion downstairs as she dressed in her bedroom at Finchmere. She hadn't been able to sleep. Every little sound had made her tense up in rigid silence, holding her breath.

Last night, her parents had been horrified to hear about the attack. Her mother had fretted it was related to her own work. Once Nell had been able to relay the detectives' assessment that it probably wasn't, the idea that Nell was being targeted by a serial killer had raised even more alarm. Conor stepped in to say his team would take extra measures. And Nell had accepted the kind – and not unsubstantial – offer, in terms of cost and effort, with good grace.

Hugo had worried about the head injury Nell had sustained four months ago, in March, being followed this closely by a headbutt, and had tried to google warning signs. That had taken a ponderous age, with Nell having to help, while also protesting it was unnecessary.

'I have to let you sleep, then wake you up after half an hour,' her father had insisted. 'And if I can't rouse you, I have to take you to A & E.'

She'd been annoyingly unable to fall asleep on demand, after a pretty stressful evening, so eventually Imelda had told Hugo and Nell to go to bed.

Finally, Nell had dozed, but woke with a start, hearing a car nearby. It must have been one of the security team swapping in for their shift.

Having got up as soon as dawn crept in through the gap in the curtains, she'd had a shower and dressed. Sluggish from lack of sleep, she sent Elliot a text to say she wouldn't be in today. She knew that, in the grand scheme of things, it was a minor point, but she still hated letting him down. But if she got some rest, and if James arrested Simon and closed the case, she could be back on form tomorrow.

And now, the commotion made Nell grab a hoodie, dragging it

on over her T-shirt as she ran downstairs. The gathering in the hall made her slow down as she joined everyone.

Astrid, the Estate Manager, looked shaken. 'Yes, don't worry, Imelda, I sent him home. Poor lad. He was only trying to make an early start on the clearing-up after yesterday's wedding. Didn't expect to find . . .' She gulped. 'Left right in front of our church.'

'How long before the police are here?' Hugo asked.

'I called 999. Any minute, I'd hope.'

'What an utter bastard. That poor woman.' Imelda paced, pushing Hugo's arm away as he tried to console her.

'What's happened?' Nell asked.

'A woman has been *killed* . . . and left . . . *here*,' Imelda stammered.

Nell could see that her mother was shocked, despite her efforts at putting on a brave face. And she also looked torn between desperate anguish and sheer anger. Nell could imagine how horrified she must feel that another woman had been harmed, and she fought back the nauseous feeling that it was in response to her mother trying to stop women being hurt.

'So, what's going on?' Imelda tried to make sense of the senseless. 'Some sick individual has killed an innocent woman and left her here, as a message? To get me to stop pushing the bills through parliament?'

'Maybe,' Conor said. Nell noticed how stricken he looked, too. The small church was far enough from the house to not have been within the security team's purview. But it was still within their grounds, and Conor looked torn between feeling like he'd let Imelda down horribly, and being determined to go to war.

'Or are you at risk, Nell?' Imelda continued her questions. Her face trembled.

With all eyes on her, Nell shook her head. 'I don't know. How could I know?'

'Astrid.' Imelda took her hand, clearly needing to control something amidst the chaos. 'I'm so sorry for this awful shock. You and the team, anyone who needs it, can take some time off. I will ask one thing of you, and that's to please follow up with the detectives to find out who the victim is, so I can reach out to her family.'

As Astrid nodded and left, Imelda turned to Conor. 'There will probably be press.'

He shrugged. 'There will only be press if you want there to be press.'

'Then no press. Keep them away, please. I don't want anyone anywhere near the woman – no photos, no vultures. We must do everything possible to protect her.'

'Understood.' Conor stood by the door, his arms held out a little from his body in an action-ready stance. His steady eyes met Nell's for a second.

As her parents cast their eyes downwards, Nell turned to go upstairs. She sprinted to her bedroom, grabbed her binoculars from her kitbag, then ran up to the second floor and along the hall. Taking the door on to the refectory roof walkway, she sheltered behind the parapet wall and focused her lenses on the little church.

As she gazed at the enlarged view, searching for signs of what had happened, Conor cleared his throat behind her.

'Just keep low, would you? If the person who did this is still around, they could well get some sick kick out of your reaction.'

The thought made Nell feel hunted. She'd ducked low out of some instinct not to be noticed. But she hadn't considered she might be seen by the killer.

'Some of the team are searching the grounds, just in case. I can easily imagine a bastard like that getting himself a safe distance away, watching us with his own binoculars. And, frankly, I think you're in his crosshairs well enough already.'

As Nell glimpsed the body of the woman, lying before the door to Finchmere's family church, she gasped.

Carefully, she moved the lenses so she could study the hard-standing path that sliced through the long grass and vivid wildflowers wafting in the morning breeze.

The path extended around the side of the church, then curved towards the small, tarmacked car park. Nell considered the distance to her bedroom, on the far side of the house. If someone had brought the body here in a car, the closest they could have got was the church car park. And she knew she could hear cars there from her room, albeit faintly.

'I think the body was brought here about two or two thirty, something like that. I didn't sleep much, and I heard a car sometime around then. I had some water and glanced at the time, but I can't recall it exactly.'

'I'll find out what was happening with my team around then.' Conor turned away to mutter the question through his earpiece's microphone, to his active colleagues.

Nell continued scanning the ground through the binoculars, noticing the rose petals on the path. Their unique Finchmere eco-confetti – rose petals and wildflower seeds – was the reason why the lawns swathing the church were so vibrant with wildflowers.

'The eco-confetti seeds from yesterday's wedding may have attached to the killer, when they left the body here. The seeds could have transferred to their car, or inside their home ...' She pulled her gaze from the binoculars to glance at Conor. 'I can give the detectives a sample, as a comparison.'

At Conor's nod, she re-focused on the victim. With a thud of dread, Nell noticed that the woman had short brown hair. She was naked, with two stab wounds to her chest, which hadn't bled.

Fear clamoured inside Nell, but so did ferocious outrage, and anger at another woman being killed – to what? Threaten her? Frighten her? Why? Because she'd got away?

She couldn't believe this was the action of someone she'd been working alongside. Someone she knew. What had they learned about her to cause ... *this*?

Blinking away angry, hot tears, she tried to calm her shuddering breaths.

Turning to Conor, she said, 'Mum's half right, isn't she? This *is* a message. But it's not to her. It's to me. It's the killer from the heath, not a random attack in response to her bill.'

As Conor remained silent, Nell knew he agreed with her.

The wail of a siren heralded the arrival of police. They parked at the far end of the church car park. Nell folded her arms, shivering, despite the morning warming up.

James got out of the car and hurried over to the body of the woman. A pathologist – presumably Dr Saunders – joined him. They both pulled on their white hooded suits, blue booties and gloves, before crouching beside the corpse.

As Val left the two of them to it and strode towards the house, Nell and Conor headed back inside to see her. On the way, Nell went to the boot room and found a sample of confetti, folded into a sachet of recycled paper textured with more wildflower seeds.

In the hall, she handed it over to Val, explaining what it was. 'And I think the killer brought the body here at about two or two thirty in the morning.'

Conor provided Val with the name of the security detail she should speak to for more information.

Taking notes, Val glanced at Nell. 'I know you don't want to hear this, Nell, but it would be wise, at this stage, to take precautions.'

'Noted, ma'am,' Conor asserted.

Nell didn't want to get into that argument again. She acquiesced enough to escape to the kitchen for a hot drink. Anything to make her feel less chilled, less shivery.

Her mother was on the phone, gripping a huge mug of coffee.

'Yes, I completely understand your position, Prime Minister. But you're entirely wrong if you think this will deter me. In any way.'

She grimaced at Nell as she listened. 'Oh, yes, I have every certainty those are *your* genuine concerns. And while I may share them, they will not cow me into inaction. If anything, this underlines the *imperative*.'

In silent exasperation, Imelda shook her head. 'No. Let us be clear. Violence against women and girls isn't new. Women have fought this since time immemorial. From the time men wrote the Bible, claiming Eve's original sin is to blame for all that's wrong with the world – while hiding behind a religion structured to subjugate females – to incels today blaming women for not wanting to have sex with life-incompetent man-babies who are hiding behind their computers in their parents' basement. This is a problem that won't go away.'

Listening, she rolled her eyes. 'No, quite the contrary. If anything, today's actions show that it will only *escalate*. And, as you may recall from your Eton days, you don't face up to a bully by handing over what he wants – whether it be your dignity, or parliamentary inaction.'

She gave a sigh. 'I'm sorry you feel overwhelmed. And please acknowledge your fortune at having that option. It doesn't matter how weary we *women* may grow of it – we cannot retreat, because this is our daily reality. Women *have* to continue to find the wherewithal to fight. It's men like you, fresh to the battle, who should have the energy to pick up the baton and share the load. And I *do* hope you won't let *fifty-one* per cent of your voting population down. Because, at present, that's *exactly* what you're doing.'

Nell half winced, half grinned at her mother, and Imelda grimaced back, taking a slug of super-strength coffee.

'Yes, of course. I'll be there . . .' She checked the phone. 'Let's say ten o'clock to allow for traffic . . . Oh, yes, I'll be prepared.'

She rang off and heaved a sigh at Nell. 'Heaven forbid women ever get angry about our sisters being violently killed.' Leaping to her feet, she looked for Conor. 'I have to head into the House.' She grimaced at him. 'He's called a COBRA meeting. I've been asked to present.'

As Conor walked out with Imelda and prepped the travel team, another of his detail walked in. 'Nell? Conor suggested you might like to brush up on your self-defence techniques. If you like, we could—'

'Yes please! Now? In the gym?' Nell was already standing up to join him.

In the spa complex, Nell was soon sweating. Not just from the warmth infusing into the gym from the adjacent infinity pool in the atrium-style barn, but also from the intense workout this training was putting her through.

Conor's colleague was making her dodge, evade, tumble, spar, use the opponent's weight against them – and he was relentless.

Every time Nell took a minute to catch her breath or gulp some water, he'd say, 'OK, that's good, but let's try it this way now . . .'

Two hours in, Nell's reactions had sharpened, and her responses became more natural, her muscle memory gradually remembering old training. 'The killer's MO is changing, though. What do people do when they're sending messages?'

'All sorts. Depends what they're trying to achieve. Harming

someone you care about, kidnap, maybe ransom of a family member.' He shrugged. 'Conor's got extra security, and a team are installing more cameras around the place. We're trying to keep a step ahead.'

After another two hours of training, Nell was becoming exhausted. She wondered if she should ask to refresh her kidnap training, too. If Conor was trying to keep ahead, Nell just prayed James was managing to do the same.

Perhaps the killer had even been arrested by now . . .

Monday 18th July – 1 p.m.

James sat back, observing Drew across the interview room table. It was clear Drew hadn't slept, but he had a belligerent air about him. Like he was indignant at this treatment. And he'd certainly bristled at James's last question.

'It's not really anything to do with me that my father was incarcerated. He wasn't around much when I was little. And I didn't understand why he kept disappearing. I wasn't ever told. It just felt like a treat when he did come back.' He gave a small, self-deprecating smile. 'Bit of hero worship, I guess.'

'That can't have been easy for your mother,' James said. 'Coping on her own.'

'No, well, it was her fault he left.'

'How so?' James asked. 'He was imprisoned for GBH after fighting in a pub. It had nothing to do with your mother.'

'No, but she probably drove him to it.'

'How do you make that out?'

'I think she was quite a demanding woman. And she didn't work.'

'Didn't raising you count as valid work?'

Drew shrugged.

'And your dad had a decent trade, as a plumber, as I understand it. Could have earned a good wage – *if* he'd wanted to.'

'Yes, well, it seems neither of my parents really wanted to, did they? Look at what Amanda turned to, in the end.'

'Yes.' James's tone was sympathetic. 'Her addiction would have played its part in that. Do you know how that started?'

'Yeah. I saw this bloke give her something that looked odd. I knew something about it was . . . wrong. Something that made me feel sick in my stomach. He was the kind of man that made your flesh creep. The way he treated her, the way he looked at me. Now I know why he was there, what his agenda was.'

'Did you give his name to the police?' James asked. 'Did you think he'd killed her?'

'I didn't know his name. But when I described him, the officer didn't seem too surprised. Looking back on that now, I'd guess he was known to the police.'

James made a note to check the file again. With Drew's twenty-four hours in custody running out, he had to decide whether to apply to hold him for another twelve hours or release him. He didn't like his chances of the extension being granted; the warrant to search Drew's home and computer had already been denied, on the basis of insufficient evidence. And now there had been an attack while Drew had been under arrest, CPS would be even less persuadable to extend this line of investigation. James began to wonder if he was reading too much into Drew's attitude.

The rest of his team were still searching for Simon. Even a text to let him know that he could have his precious memory card back hadn't brought him racing to their door. Moving his focus from Drew to Simon would be the best way forward.

Although, at this point, James had to admit that he'd only feel happy when all three of his suspects were under arrest.

Drew folded his arms, stared at the wall. 'I don't really like revisiting that part of my life. It's like . . . all that was a horrible dream. The things I saw at that age are things you don't want to know about. What people are capable of doing to one another.'

'Yes, I can understand,' James said.

Drew looked at him, staring at him for a long while. 'You can *understand*? I suppose you're talking about what you see in your line of work?'

James nodded.

'You probably started out in the force in your twenties? Saw some serious cases a few years in?'

James didn't react. This wasn't about him.

Drew leaned across the table towards him. His tone was low, almost sorrowful. 'You think you can understand what it feels like to go through things like that, when you're detached from it, and an adult? You think you know what it's like to see a monster, do you?' He shook his head. 'You should think yourself lucky. My monster found me when I was seven.'

His hands were shaking, and Drew placed them on his lap and stared at the table. 'And the person who was supposed to *protect* me, my own *mother*, did *nothing*.'

James recalled the file on Amanda. Countless calls about domestic abuse, some of which matched the old injuries recorded in her pathology report, but not all. Systematic abuse which suggested she had no better time of it with Drew's monster – or maybe Drew's father – than he'd had.

'What about your father?' James asked.

Drew's head snapped up. 'What about him?'

'What did he do about it, when he was around?'

'It didn't happen when he was around.'

'No, but did you tell your father? Did he help you address it?'

'I couldn't tell him!' Drew said.

'Why not?' James asked.

Drew looked dumbfounded. 'It's . . . it's not as easy as that.'

'But wouldn't you expect him to do the same as your mother, if he knew? Protect you?' James suggested.

'No way.' Drew's lip curled. 'He'd have been disgusted. He'd have said I was weak, or knocked me around a bit.'

'Why couldn't you have the same expectations of your father as your mother?'

'Because your mother is *supposed* to love you. She's *supposed* to notice. *And* still care. *And* protect you.'

'Shouldn't your father do that, too?' James asked.

'He protected me just by *being* there. It was when he wasn't around that everything went wrong.'

'Is that why you visit him so often?' He'd seen the prison reports; Drew was a regular.

'Can't blame me for wanting to build bridges, can you?'

James wondered if dredging up Drew's past was really helping. If Nell's attack and the new murder hadn't happened while Drew was in their cells, he'd be wondering if he'd been traumatised by his mother's murder, and maybe copied the MO.

But he couldn't argue that case with CPS, now that the killer had struck again.

'Tell me about your adopted family.' James hoped to conclude the interview on a more positive note.

'I guess I was lucky, wasn't I? I got away. The family who took me in were my sunshine in the dark. Told me it was healthier to forgive. And it's funny, when you've got opportunities – got a roof over your head, food in your belly, a sense of purpose in the world and someone who believes in you – it's suddenly a lot bloody easier to be magnanimous.'

Monday 18th July – 2.30 p.m.

From the upstairs window, James watched Drew leave the police station, then headed to the incident room. He and the team were waiting for the pathology results from today's victim, but the Doc's caseload had been growing, and he couldn't possibly visit her yet to ask for an update. With those results out of the question, he wanted to hear that Simon was waiting to be interviewed. But when he opened the door, he was met with a row of worried faces.

'Before you ask, the answer is no,' Ashley said. 'No updates on Simon.'

'We've searched his *house*.' Ed stabbed the map on the board, emphasising the location. 'We've had a team out to search the *heath*.' Another stab. 'Nothing.'

'His ex-girlfriend has no idea where he is,' Ashley said. 'And I'm inclined to believe her.'

'He didn't turn up at work,' Hesha added. 'He hasn't been working there long but his boss said that, from what he knew of Simon, he'd be more likely to spend more time than needed at work, not less.'

'And nothing in any hospitals,' Ashley added. 'Just in case.'

'ANPR?' James asked.

'The team are on it,' Hesha said. 'I'll go up in a sec and see if they've had any matches.'

Fear bubbled through James's chest. 'If Simon's getting more unpredictable, more dangerous, we don't have the luxury of time here. Get on the case with ANPR, Hesh. *Now*! *Go*! Follow up all emergency services, Ash. If the team have finished on the heath, Ed, get them over to Finchmere, now we know that was on his radar. Draft in another team if you need to. This is a manhunt – and we're against the clock.'

Chapter 21

Monday 18th July – 3 p.m.

Nell paced along the terrace at the back of Finchmere House. The heat of the afternoon was infused with the heady perfume of the jasmine that climbed the building's flint walls. The view of the downland around her was glorious. But she was ignoring both, feeling frustrated.

After the morning's activity, the day had *dragged*. She'd watched SOCOs from a distance, collecting what evidence they could from the church and the car park. The body had been borne away by the grim-faced team.

The fresh air was helping, but the lack of something to do wasn't. She wanted to see Rav, but the attack in the hospital car park meant that Conor and James had advised against her going there. And, as much as she longed to see Rav, she wasn't sure if her assailant knew why she was at the hospital, and she didn't dare risk them following her again – and finding him and hurting him – to get to her.

So the text from Sylvia was a godsend: *Darling, so sorry to ask, but since we're down on manpower, is there any chance you could help Tom and Erin with the translocation this afternoon?*

Yes! Nell hesitated, wondering what Conor would say. He'd ask if she felt safe, if the journey there was risky, if she trusted those colleagues. With the new regime of working in threes, and the pair she'd meet being Tom and Erin, Nell decided the risk was low. But she slipped a penknife into her pocket, just in case.

She didn't want to have to explain herself to Conor, so she walked casually to her site car, checked no one was looking and drove off.

Monday 18th July – 3.30 p.m.

James found Hesha overseeing the ANPR search. 'Any joy?' He prayed his burning anxiety wasn't audible.

'Not yet, but we're still checking.'

'So, what's that telling us?' James asked. 'That he hasn't gone anywhere? Or that he's managing to keep on off-camera roads?' Like the country lanes around Finchmere.

'Hold on one second, I think we have a bite. Here. Hey! Simon's heading our way in his Kia Sportage! On the road out of Pendlebury. Towards the police station, or the hospital.'

James frowned. 'Or the *heath*.'

Monday 18th July – 4 p.m.

Waiting in the car park, Nell grew impatient. Erin was always bloody late, but Tom was usually more reliable. And, after sneaking out, she itched to get started.

Well, she was here now, so she may as well get on with it. She grabbed the stack of buckets and lids from the boot and headed off.

She climbed over the plastic wall of reptile fencing, into the area where the construction would take place, and crept towards the first trap.

As Nell lifted the corner, a tangle of adders writhed. Nell crouched, gently caught one, slithering from the knot, and transferred him into the bucket. His body thrashed against the plastic prison, trying to scale the slippery side. Nell caught another two, then the last three, and finally placed the lid on the bucket. The cargo roiled. Nell kept the bucket steady, trying to minimise the stress on the six captured animals.

She worked methodically across the area, pausing only occasionally to stretch and look around. The place was so silent, with only the buzz of insects around her, lazy in the afternoon sun.

By the time Nell had finished on the site, she had four buckets, each heavy with churning vipers. Checking the lids were secure, she carried two buckets in each hand and headed back to the car.

Monday 18th July – 5.30 p.m.

James listened over the radio to the update he didn't want to hear.

'Sorry, we've lost him. We'll keep covering the area, though. Let us know if you get any leads.'

Groaning, James leaned on his desk, sinking his head into his hands. So far, there was absolutely nothing. It seemed Simon really was a master of camouflage.

A knock on the door made him look up as Dr Saunders walked into the incident room.

'I didn't ask you for the budget, but I've doubled my team. I knew we'd need time on our side and there's only so much I can fast-track.'

'Yes, good, thank you.'

'And the results from Nell's forensic tests are back. As we thought, Simon's DNA was all over her. Especially her face.'

'Anything else?'

'Some fibres on the back of the sleeping bag sack – so it could be that the assailant wore a balaclava? They're useless without something to compare them to, though.'

'Well, with luck, we'll come up with something soon.'

'Good. I'll have a result for the other victim as soon as I can manage.' Saunders looked at James, about to say something, then thought better of it.

'What?' James asked.

'I was just going to say, Trent didn't solve this case, and neither did Val. It's just . . . This was never going to be straightforward, James. Keep at it, but don't give yourself a hard time.'

'Doc, there's *another* woman in your morgue, there's Nell in danger *again*. There can't be any more of this. We *have* to catch him. I just need . . . something.'

His phone rang and he snatched it up. 'We've found him,' the officer said.

'You've made an arrest?' James clarified, hope soaring.

'No. Sorry. We haven't got *him* but we've found his car. The Kia Sportage is parked at Pendlebury Hospital. Arrived here about thirty minutes ago, according to his ticket.'

'Right.' James's relief plummeted again. 'Get a team in there to search the hospital, while you follow the route you'd walk to Furze Heath. It's good cover if he wanted to go there but not have his car spotted in the car park. It'd only take someone, what, fifty minutes to walk the two miles there. So you may catch him en route.'

Monday 18th July – 5.30 p.m.

Nell pushed the lidded, air-holed buckets, heavy with writhing adders, into the car. They wouldn't be in there for long if she drove to the release site quickly.

On the road, she passed a police car heading towards the car park, then turned into the lane along the heath. Eventually, she reached Furze Wood. She'd hoped to find a shady patch to park in so her captured adders wouldn't get even more agitated with the heat. But the sun pitched straight into the clearing. Well, she didn't want to hang around. She'd just have to be quick as she took each bucket and freed the snakes.

Heading to the boot, she leaned in to pull the buckets nearer, planning to take the heaviest one first.

Something flashed in front of her face, yanked her neck, crushing her windpipe. She clawed at it but couldn't get under the metallic ligature sinking into her skin.

She wheezed, unable to draw air into empty lungs. Her vision sparkled, while panic lanced through her.

With her elbows pinned to her sides, she couldn't move. It was like her whole torso was being constricted, her airless lungs crushed.

The ligature tightened. Her vision swam . . .

. . . Then everything went black.

Chapter 22

Monday 18th July – 6 p.m.

The throbbing in Nell's head woke her like someone pounding on a door. Her head hung low, chin lolling against her chest, heavy on her aching neck as she sat, slumped.

Mustering *all* her self-control, she forced herself not to move. She had no idea if her attacker was there or not, and she was desperate not to alert them to the fact that she'd come round.

But her mouth and oesophagus were on *fire*, her tongue swollen, slugged against her teeth. Her face *itched* – probably from the chemical burn of the chloroform – and every breath was a raspy strain through a bruised, tender throat.

The cloying scent of chloroform clung to her. She was dying to swallow, lick her sore lips, sit up, look around, move, *escape*. Adrenaline made the urge for flight kick in. She fought to stay still.

Keeping her breathing rhythmic, she assessed.

Whatever she'd been slumped on, it was cold. Her hands were wrenched behind her back. Unyielding cable-ties bit into her wrists and ankles, crushing veins. She tried to relax, focusing calming breaths into limbs desperate to struggle.

Am I alone?

Keeping her eyes shut, she strained to hear doleful plips of water. She was somewhere cavernous, judging from the droplets' echoes – like cacophonous, out-of-synch ticking clocks, reminding her she'd no idea how long she'd been unconscious for.

Softening her eyes enough to see darkness through her lashes, Nell saw a pinprick of light to her right. The closed-in sense of a narrow space around her. Limited escape routes. Claustrophobic panic clamoured. No feet were in her peripheral vision. She moved her head a little, taking in more of the space.

Her feet were numb with cold. She flexed them. *Ugh!* Her feet were *bare*? Where were her shoes and socks? Splaying her toes, she found hard stone, grit, icy water. Her ankles were sore from the pinch of the ties.

The dank, musty smell resurrected memories of bat hibernation surveys. This had to be the tunnel on the heath.

She raised her head, wincing at the pounding thump, the reawakening pain in her neck. Worse than the world's worst hangover.

'Ah, Nell.' A disguised, distorted voice seemed to boom around her. The alien, unempathetic tone was unnerving. 'Awake at last.' A blinding white light blazed at her, bleaching out her vision, making her head pound even more. She flinched away, hating that it would look like she was cowering.

'I just need you to help me with a little home video. First, I need your mother's personal email address. I think she'd like to know how you are.'

Nell snorted, but it turned into a coughing fit. 'Don't think,' she rasped, 'for one moment this would worry her.' Words grated against her raw throat. 'It'll be a waste of time sending anything to her.'

'Well, let's see, shall we? Go ahead. I'm ready to make a note.'

As Nell dictated the address, she furtively glanced around her, at what the blazing light illuminated. To her right, a brick wall, crumbling and damp. Yes – definitely the tunnel on the heath.

She fidgeted, trying to feel if her phone was in her pocket. It wasn't. Her knife wouldn't be either, then. Panic rocketed, at the thought of having armed her attacker and losing a lifeline. She battled the rise of terror and recalled her hostage training, wishing she'd refreshed it. But she could remember it: she could plan, stay calm, focus, use her senses, *detect*.

She already knew *where* she was; she would try to work out *who* this was. And how she could get away. Her breathing steadied, even though each breath still felt like fire.

'OK, showtime. I just need you to stand up and turn all the way round, very slowly. So that your family can see no harm has come to you. Yet.'

Standing, Nell winced as glass and flint bit into her feet. She shuffled in a slow circle. Her shoulders ached and she rolled them back.

Only the sounds of her bare feet crunching into stone and the plips of water could be heard, until Nell caught the distant but distinct churring of the nightjar. Unsure if the call would be picked up, she tried to touch her ear, but with her hands tied, all she could do was nudge her shoulder up to her ear.

Behind her back, she flexed her hands, trying to get rid of the tingle of pins and needles and get blood back into them, leaving her palms splayed wide. As she slowly turned her back to the light – and where she imagined the camera to be – her thumb twitched. She stared at the space that had been behind her. The light washed everything in ice white, then faded into cavernous black, and she squinted as she turned around to face its blinding onslaught.

'How obliging,' the disguised voice echoed. 'That'll do nicely.'

Monday 18th July – 6.25 p.m.

Answering his phone, James heard the officer from the police station's reception say, 'Got someone here to see you. Drew Deacon. Says I can take a message if you're too busy . . . ?'

Dashing along the corridor, James knew he probably looked breathless, like he'd been running a marathon, his face tense. But if Drew was there, he wanted to speak to him.

Upon finding him in reception, James tried to smile. 'Thanks for coming by. How can I help?'

'It's more that I think *I* can help,' Drew said. 'You asked me earlier if I knew the man who . . .' he swallowed, 'saw Amanda. My mother.' He took a breath. 'Well, *I* didn't know anything about him. But *Nicky*, my wife, said there was a rumour at the time that the man was an *officer* . . .'

Drew emphasised the word, as though James should know exactly who the man was.

'You know . . . a *police* officer. Maybe that's why the investigation didn't go anywhere? If her dealer and her abuser – and mine – was a man of the law?'

James shot him a hard stare. Quite the accusation. 'Then I'll have to ask you to make a statement.' He beckoned Drew towards the corridor and the interview rooms.

Drew followed. He heaved a sigh. 'I'm so relieved you want to put it on record. I wasn't sure how that kind of . . . information would be received.' As he sat down opposite James, he took another breath.

As he turned on the recorder, James wondered if this was an elaborate deflection. If Drew was wasting their investigative time. But he made the introductions for the tape and invited Drew to speak.

A few minutes of waffle later, with no real substance to the accusation, James was finding it harder to hide his irritation. He concluded the interview and stood up. As he opened the door to show Drew out, his phone beeped. He glanced at it, hoping to hear news about Simon. But his heart stopped when he saw the subject line – *Hostage Video* – and, inside the body of the email, the still of Nell, with a play button over the image.

'I . . . er . . . I have to take this. If you can recall any more details, please leave a note at reception, and my team can follow it up. Thanks. Excuse me.'

The email had come from Nell's mother. She'd been sent the video only minutes ago, she said – and, despite the sender's warning not to involve the police, she'd sent it straight on to James.

In the next interview room, James slammed the door, leaned against it and played the video.

Nell was floodlit, clearly bound at her ankles, her hands secured behind her back, squinting in the blinding light. Her feet were bare, her neck was a bright lurid red. He looked closely. There was no mistaking it: her throat was blotched with new, garish red marks, not the purplish bruise that last night's injury had caused. She'd been attacked again.

He looked for signs of what had happened. Her awkward stance made him worry. Her eyes were very bloodshot, the area around her nose and face rashed with irritation. Had chloroform been used? It looked likely. Her lips were swollen and looked sore.

He scoured the frame for any clue of where she was, but the whitewashing from the light made it impossible to make anything out clearly. Her movements were stiff, her breathing laboured. When she turned, he saw her moving her shoulders, flexing her hands, like it was a relief to move, however limited the opportunity.

He sent a text to his team: *Emergency meeting, incident room, now.*

Then he hesitated for a moment and watched the video again. *Nell's smart. She's had training. What if there's a message in this?*

If there was, James knew there was only one person who would understand.

Monday 18th July – 6.30 p.m.

Rav's hand, gripping his phone, trembled as he listened to James. *Oh, God . . . Oh, God, what's happened now?*

James was warning him about the content, urging him to look carefully at it. 'Rav, listen to me. If Nell is communicating anything, you're probably the only one who will know. Try to put all the emotions aside, try to look and see if there's anything you can decode.'

With shaking hands, Rav wheeled himself to the door of his room and closed it, then, just in case, he put his earphones in. Taking a steadying breath, he stabbed the button and played the video.

Utter terror sliced through him at the sight of her being so vulnerable, at the hands of someone who wanted to do her harm.

He tried to fight his fear down, to focus in the way James had asked. As he looked at Nell, he understood why James had suggested he pay attention.

She had a new injury around her throat but she didn't look defeated. Something about the way she stood, moved her limbs, was rigid with indignation. The way she was glancing at the floor, and around her, told him she was assessing everything. It made his heart contract.

He replayed the video and watched every movement she made.

The first thing she did was roll her shoulders. Rav repeated the movement, felt the freeing of tension, the stretch in his chest. He wondered if that was just a reflex after being able to move.

Then she shrugged one shoulder, moving her head as if trying to get her right ear to meet her right shoulder. Again, Rav copied the movement. It was a quick twitch, her elbow lifting and her hands moving as far to the right as they could. He glimpsed one clenched fist, the index finger pointing.

Is she pointing at something? He couldn't make out anything in the frame. The setting was completely bleached white.

He reran the movement to watch it again and again, mystified.

Neck. Ear. Ear-neck. Neck-ear. Shoulder. Right shoulder. Right ear. Right hear? Right here? Where's here?

Was she looking at something, in some direction? He studied the frame. No, she couldn't be, her eyes were closed. For longer than a blink. So, she was trying to say . . . What? *Listen?*

But the video was totally silent.

He let the video run on. As she turned, he noticed her hands were splayed now. He took the video back to earlier, when he glimpsed her hands as she shrugged. Yes, they'd definitely been clenched.

So, the wide open-stretched palms were deliberate. Her thumb moved across her palm once, then again. As if she'd had a small itch, or her hands tingled from being bound.

He replicated the move. It could look like she was making the number four when her thumb moved across her palm.

Four . . . then four again. Four-four. Forty-four? For? Fore?

Were the splayed fingers in between part of it? He stretched his hands in the same way. *For-splay? Foreplay? Nope . . .*

Did it mean five? *For-five? Four-five? Forty-five, forty-five?*

Like the bat? The frequency a common pipistrelle echolocates at: 45 kHz.

He sat up straighter, his heart pounding. Because of exactly that: the bat connection – four-five-four-five was a code. He dredged his memory. His local bat group used it as the combination code for the local hibernation sites. They were always locked to prevent anyone without a licence accessing them and damaging the fragile, but important, habitats.

So, she was in a hibernation site. Which one?

He ran the video back to her shrug. He still couldn't hear anything. He cranked up the volume.

He only just caught it: the faintest whirring sound. It sounded like a fax machine.

But there was no doubt in Rav's mind.

Chapter 23

James's team watched the video again. 'Come *on*! What are we *looking* at here? Where *is* she?'

At the row of blank faces, he fought back panic, trying to find his professional self, rather than being the less helpful frantic ex-boyfriend.

'OK, if we can't see anything obvious, then let's try a different route. Hesha, talk to Sylvia at her work. They track locations. See where her last known location was. Ashley, ask her family if they know where she could be – perhaps somewhere at Finchmere. Ed? You've got superb local knowledge. Any ideas? Looking at this?'

As Ed shook his head slowly, James's phone rang. Rav. He answered it, not daring to let hope fly again. 'Rav?'

'Nell's in the tunnel on Furze Heath. There's a combination lock on the gate. The code's four-five-four-five. There's no doubt about it. I heard the nightjar in the background.'

James wheeled round to the screen, in time to see the gesture Nell made with her hand. He would never have realised what it meant. But relief rolled off him. Rav had just saved them hours, maybe days – maybe Nell's *life*. 'Rav, you are a *genius*.'

As Ed took the intel to the team, Dr Saunders walked in.

'James?' Her voice had a terse edge to it, like this was urgent but she was trying to keep calm.

'I said I'd have something for you on the new victim. Brace yourself. It wasn't the same MO. It looks like it – ligature strangulation and stabbing – but there are key differences. The ligature pattern, which is so distinctive on the other victims, is different. It's a rigid belt, like patent leather or plastic, judging from the clear edge-marks. And the stab wounds are universally shallower. I know the previous stabbings had some variation, but these don't. They're *all* very shallow. As if . . . reluctant. Very different to the rage-fuelled attacks we've seen before.'

Frowning, James processed the new evidence. 'So, you're saying . . . ?'

'This is a copycat kill, James. It's not the same perpetrator.'

'Oh, God.' His stomach plummeted. 'Could it be another example of him using whatever's to hand, rather than planning?'

'It's statistically different, James. I never tell you anything I'm not prepared to stake my reputation on in the dock. And I'm saying that the evidence shows me it was perpetrated by a different person.'

As Saunders left, James stared at the incident board, and the photos of their three key suspects.

With Drew and Amir both having been in custody when the murder took place, he'd been certain they were out of the frame.

But now, they were very much back in it . . . And, as Amir made bail yesterday, all three of them would have been able to kidnap Nell.

This time, the game has a twist . . .

She thought she could be the hunter. Now she knows she's the hunted. How long before she'll 'prey' for mercy?

The darkness seemed denser, more closed in, after the blinding light. The silence even eerier. Nell waited for what felt like hours, especially with those ticking water droplets plipping all around her. But it would only have been moments. She forced herself to wait, to listen, to check she was really, truly alone.

Because she had a plan; and she could only test it out once she was certain that no one else would be there.

After absolute *eons*, she stood up, shaking. Just in case, she made a pretence of stretching. Nothing happened. No one spoke, no new sound emanated from anywhere.

She knew how to free herself from cable-ties. But it took huge effort, and it *really* hurt. Standing up had made her vision swim, after the chloroform and then the blinding light. It took long, slow breaths to clear her foggy head, and she clenched her stomach to balance on bound legs and tingling, freezing feet.

Remembering what she'd been taught in her kidnap training, Nell fiddled with the cable-tie until its lock – its weakest point – was positioned between her bound wrists. Then she made one strong movement – starting by lifting her arms as high as she could behind her, she then made a forceful bend forward, as she crashed her wrists against her tailbone while trying to wrench them apart.

But the cable held, and gouged into her skin. She took a breath and repeated the movement, light-headed with the exertion of pummelling her back as she smashed the binding against her bone while trying to keep her balance. The ties on her hostage survival training course hadn't been so stubborn. And her wrists had been protectively taped.

Anxiety skewered her as the cable squeezed her veins but didn't release. Her vision blurred. Nell took a deep breath, yanked her arms again. A desperate sob welled up as the binding refused to budge, just sliced deeper and deeper.

Trying again, she lost her balance. Her icy feet found jagged slivers of rock. Or glass? Nell often counted more broken beer bottles than bats on surveys, if the disused tunnel had ever been a local hangout. But her feet didn't hurt as much as her wrists did.

She sat, feeling for a shard of glass, wondering if she could cut the tie. But even though she found something sharp, her wrists were tied too tightly for her to get the right angle to saw at the plastic. Wriggling on a ground strewn with jagged objects, she tried to get her feet close enough to her hand to cut the ties around her ankles. But she just couldn't reach.

Now she had to get to her feet again. All she could do was try again to break the tie the way she'd been trained. She managed to kneel, then cram herself against the rock she'd sat on, creeping on her toes to bring them in front of her so she could press herself up to standing.

She was exhausted, her arms and feet covered in wicked, stinging cuts.

Taking a breath, she tried again, bracing her back for impact, preparing her wrists for pain, channelling desperation into rage and positive action.

As she smashed her wrists against her spine, she lurched forward on feet that couldn't move.

But her free hands shot out to save her as, on bound feet, she toppled like a felled tree.

Nell slammed into the damp wall, winding herself. She snatched air as short, shocked laughs escaped. Relief made her tears spill down her face.

Pressing against the wall, she turned her back and slid down to the floor, then swung her legs in front of her. She patted the ground until her fingers found another shard, then lodged the improvised blade beside the lock of the tie and sawed. It slipped, cutting into her hand and nicking her ankles with vicious slices, as Nell worked in the dark.

Finally, oh God, *finally*, the binding severed. Nell pocketed both sets of cable-ties and slid a shard into each pocket.

She stood, wheezing, and staggered towards the sliver of light, cradling her gouged wrist as rubble crunched under her bare feet. The uneven ground demanded balance she didn't have. She winced at another sharp stone, slipped. On damp tunnel slime? Or her own blood? *Don't think about it.*

The light grew from a sliver to an encouraging aura, blotting out whatever lay beyond. Fear lumped in Nell's throat as she stumbled towards it. White light filled the gateway, barred with iron, the lock slung around the bars.

Nell fiddled for the combination barrel and froze, as she found a padlock instead.

Oh, God . . . She'd been so sure of escape. Sure that getting to the gate would be the hard part. And now she'd made it here, she was still trapped.

Desperation thudded. She crouched, ready to pull back into the shadows, taut limbs shaking, but forced herself to peer through the bars. No one was out there, trying to stop her escape, guarding, watching. But there was no one to help, either.

Something glinted in the grass. She squinted. A bolt-cut padlock. *He's cut off the lock the bat group had used, and put on his own?* Then she noticed tracks. She squinted. Yes, tyre tracks! Near the gate. She must have been brought here in a car. And perhaps if anyone was looking for her, they'd spot them.

Looking out across the heath, Nell spotted Furze Wood. So she was at the northern end of the tunnel, which curved around the west side of the heath.

If she could get to the southern end of the tunnel, maybe she could escape that way? She'd have further to run, to get to the car park. But she could do it.

But . . . what if he's cut that combination lock off, too? And replaced it with his own?

Still, it was the only thing she could try. And she might be running out of time. She didn't relish walking back through the tunnel on already tender feet. She inspected one, then the other. Mud and grit were ground into a hundred bloody cuts.

Dusting off the worst, Nell turned, took a deep breath and limped towards the other gate. She grimaced at more wicked bites of grit and glass, but tried to make her progress as rapid as possible.

The light dimmed with each step, until pitch blackness consumed her.

She hobbled on for what felt like an age. Her ragged breath and the blood rushing in her ears were so deafening that she feared she wouldn't hear her captor's return. She focused on the plips of water, still reassuringly loud. *How long do I have?*

Suddenly, she stumbled on something, her foot smashing into a mound of stones. She yelped, then realised something had pierced her foot deeply. Perching on one leg, leaning against the wet wall, she brushed her instep. Her fingertips found a syringe. Horror crushed her like an avalanche. Ripping the needle out, she speared it into the ground, right against the wall, out of the way. Panic pounded in her head. *Oh, God. Oh, God.*

Keep going. Especially if it's contaminated. Get out.

Nell staggered on, choking back scared sobs as she stumbled in darkness. She pulled mouldering air into sore lungs, trying to calm her racing heartbeat, trying to convince herself that her especially tender foot wasn't hot, swelling, infected.

She didn't dare believe the glimmer of light. It ignited hope, yet it was still so far away.

Gritting her teeth against the pain in her head, her neck, her feet, her wrists, Nell just kept going.

Finally, *finally*, she reached the gate, and the glare of sunlight blinded her. She grabbed the iron bars. Fresh air tasted delicious, even through her burning throat. She blinked bleached vision into colour. No one was outside.

She felt for the lock, passing the chain through her hands, desperate to *not* find a padlock.

Yes! A barrel! Relief surged through her, making her sag, panting. A flood of tears threatened to erupt, but she wasn't free yet.

She fumbled with the lock, turning the numbers to four-five-four-five.

But nothing happened. She yanked desperately at the chain, hoping that it was just stuck. But it didn't budge.

Nell tried to hold back the sobs. This had been her escape plan. Freedom was right in front of her. And yet out of reach. Pressing her forehead against the iron bars, she squeezed her sore eyes shut. When she opened them, she was staring right at the lock, in her hands. She frowned, shook her head, then turned the lock over. Realisation dawned! She'd been viewing the numbers upside down. So the code she'd put in was right but, with the lock upside down, she'd effectively entered it in reverse order.

She tried again, the right way up this time – four-five-four-five. The lock fell apart in her hands.

Sagging with relief, Nell heaved at the heavy gate, then closed and locked it behind her. There was still no one around. This end was further from the Furze Wood car park. But, if she could get there, if she was lucky, she might get away in the car. She didn't have the keys – but there was the back-up spare.

Nell glanced around again. No one – for miles. So she *ran* – full pelt, like a sprinter on their final stretch – towards the car.

After the shivering iciness of the tunnel, the heat of the heath *baked* her. The day had been scorching and, now, the early evening was sweltering.

She must have been in the tunnel for about an hour. Her captured snakes would be frenzied – and the snakes on the heath would be hunting. Underfoot, bracken, heather, thistles, spiky grasses all lacerated her already injured feet.

I'll have to risk a bite, it's fastest through the brush.

She flung herself across the tussocky, uneven ground like a zigzagging rabbit. Her feet, slapping sharp bracken and gritty earth, felt like they were on fire. Her pulse thundered, her sore eyes stung, her head hammered, each wheezing breath flamed. She forced cramping muscles onwards, feeling adrenaline kick in, swooping her through the pain.

The trees of Furze Wood loomed larger as she neared them. Then – the car park! A bobbing grey blur beside the gold-and-bronze heath. It was the best sight in the world.

Nell mustered a final burst of speed, fearing her hammering heart would explode through her chest.

She prayed that whoever had attacked her didn't know about the spare car key taped inside the petrol flap: a precaution that had been in place ever since Erin had dropped the key in Plunkett's Pond, during a survey, and lost it. Erin had been mortified, but now Nell pinned all her hope of survival on it being there. She'd never, ever, *ever* be annoyed with Erin again.

Her bare feet crunched gravel as sweat stung her eyes. Reaching the car, she skidded to the far side and yanked open the petrol flap. *Yes! The key!*

A wall of heat hit her as she fell into the driver's seat. Nell turned the ignition, the key slipping in her sweaty hands. Overcompensating, she gripped hard and the engine screeched but didn't start. *Oh, please, not now.* Nell nearly wept at the thunk of the engine turning, spluttering into life. She threw the car into reverse, spun the wheel.

The buckets in the boot slid sideways. The warm serpents churned inside them.

Nell's bloody feet slipped off the pedals. She ground the gear into first.

Then she jumped – *shrieked* – as someone body-slammed the passenger door.

It was him. It had to be.

Slick feet grappling, she floored the accelerator. But the passenger door flew open and the man tumbled in.

Nell yanked the wheel hard left, throwing him against the open door. He clung to the seat, hauled the door shut behind him.

He fumbled in his pocket, pulled something out and flicked her penknife at her. Nell's foot fell off the gas. The car shuddered, stalled, hurling them both against the dash.

Nell fumbled with her door. But he grabbed her, pulled her back, and she felt the sting of something cold and sharp against her neck.

She turned to look at him properly for the first time.

Drew pressed the knife to her throat. 'Take me to your mother.'

Chapter 24

James and his team raced to the tunnel entrance. He had to hold himself back while armed response formed up. An officer, wearing a bulky protective vest, bolt-cut the padlock and unthreaded the chain. His second officer pointed his bodycam down, scanning the ground.

As the lead officer gestured, the armed team jogged forward, guns at the ready.

Opening the gate, the team threaded inside. The torches on their guns painted bright stripes of light on the walls and into the tunnel's depths.

James had identified the other tunnel entrance, and he knew a second unit were making the same approach from the south.

Gripping his radio, James listened to the sounds of the team. But the crunches of footsteps and heavy breathing were all he could hear.

He approached the gate cautiously, looking for what the officer had noticed. His heart sank when he saw that the combination lock – the one whose code Nell knew – had been replaced, its padlock intact. Even if – by some miracle – she'd tried, Nell couldn't have got out.

Then James spotted the tyre tracks on a tiny patch of bare earth, disappearing into dense bracken – and he could picture all too vividly how Nell had been brought here. The attacker must have rendered her unconscious with her own chloroform. *But is this our serial killer? In that case, why take Nell hostage? Surely it's someone trying to stop Imelda and her bill, through Nell?*

His radio crackled. 'She's not here. And the gate at the other end was locked.'

James feared he'd throw up. Maybe these tyre tracks were her attacker taking her away again. Maybe this had only been the venue for the video. *So where the hell is she?*

Monday 18th July – 7 p.m.

Nell frowned at Drew, not expecting the request to drive to her mother's. *So this is about Mum's bill? Or is Drew the murderer? Or is this somehow . . . both?*

'Yeah, let's see how she negotiates with some real skin in the game.'

'What is it you want?' Nell's voice croaked.

'Well, we'll see what *you're* worth, for starters. With luck, she'll want *you* enough to give *me* what I want.'

'Which is?' She swallowed, trying to soothe the rawness of her throat.

'Right now, I want you to *drive*!' Drew roared. 'Stop playing for time and *move*!'

The blade stung as it pierced Nell's skin. A hot tear of blood trickled down her neck.

Desperation clamoured in Nell's chest like a rising mob of birds shrieking alarm calls. Her breathing became fast and shallow, and heightened her panic.

With effort, she steadied herself. She'd been trained to deal with this. But the scenarios hadn't evoked the same level of terror. She nodded. 'OK. I'll drive.'

Her hand shook as she put the car in neutral, started the engine – the actions as deliberate as those of a learner driver, as if she had to recite the steps.

Drew kept the knife at her throat, casting a wary eye around the car park.

Whip-fast, Nell slammed the car into reverse, floored the gas, shot back. A hard *thunk* jolted through them as the car smashed into a tree.

Nell had braced herself to avoid being flung towards Drew's blade. He crumpled against the dash, then pushed himself upright, facing Nell, his face flushed with fury.

'What the *hell* are you playing at?'

'Sorry. I slipped . . . My feet are a bit bloody. And it's a bit . . . nerve-wracking . . . having your knife there.' Nell tried an apologetic smile, but her dry lips pulled taut over her teeth. She had to maintain the driving position, and some control over where they'd go. 'It won't happen again. Promise.'

She didn't need to look over her shoulder to know. The faint sounds told her it had worked: her crash had dislodged the buckets' lids. And near-silent slithers of roiling bodies told her that her cargo had been disturbed into activity.

Nell took a deep breath. *Calm. If I can just keep calm, it will all be fine.*

Beside her, Drew jittered like a mouse. He stared in the wing mirror for signs of damage, as if worried that the car wouldn't be drivable, then at Nell, obviously unwilling to leave her and inspect it.

And Nell didn't want him to. 'The car's fine. She's a tank.' She put the car into first gear and eased away, her progress slow enough to buy the time she needed.

Drew's agitation subsided as Nell reached the road.

'We're heading south, keeping on country lanes, to Finchmere. We're not going through Pendlebury or past the police station. Got it?'

Nell nodded, turning left into the empty lane, driving as slowly as she dared. The bend curved around the woodland. Leaving the place that she'd signalled to Rav, and the place James would search, was frightening.

But she wasn't alone.

Humanise. Make conversation.

'Sure, Drew. You do know you can trust me, right? I'm not going to try anything. If I can help, you know I will. We've worked together, you know what I'm like. And you must have good reason to want whatever it is you're asking for. Maybe we could make a case?'

'Yeah, I know what you're like. A woman who wants everything her own way,' Drew sneered. 'Thinks too much of herself to make people a cup of coffee. And I already have a case. It's called your life. Your mother claims to put so much value on women's lives. So, let's see what she puts on yours.'

Nell attempted a conspiratorial glance. 'Don't think for one moment she'll go soft on my account. She's a ballbreaker.'

'Bloody mothers.' Drew's lip curled. He stared at Nell like he was looking through her, his body tremoring. The blade against her throat quivered.

'So, how do you think she can help?'

Drew snorted. 'Stop the bills she's pushing through parliament for a start. She's got no sodding idea.'

'About what?'

'About everything. No understanding about what it's like to have zero opportunities, that falling into crime might be your only option.'

'Mum's not talking about petty crime, though,' Nell said. 'She's talking about serious attacks. Murders. Like the ones here, on the heath.'

She watched Drew for his reaction.

His lip curled again. But he stayed silent.

What if I'm not just sitting next to a kidnapper . . . What if I'm sitting next to a serial killer?

Perhaps her plan had enough flexibility to deal with that.

Another hot trickle wormed down Nell's neck. She saw the neck of her T-shirt blossom with her blood.

'I've said enough.' Drew peered out of the window, checking around them as Nell drove. 'I just want to see your mother and strike a bargain. I'm a fair man. It's a straight swap.'

'You're swapping me for someone?' Nell asked. 'Someone you care about?'

'I'm not playing, Nell. So stop trying your tactics on me. I'm immune.'

'Look, Drew, I don't know what's driven you to this. But it must be something serious. If there's something I can do, all you have to do is trust me enough.'

Nell made her face as sympathetic as possible, feeling Drew's stare. She couldn't look at him or make eye contact while the blade still nicked her neck. But she kept her head high, tried to make her tone sound sincere.

'I'm going to swap you for my dad. Seems fair, doesn't it? A daughter for a father.'

Nell's mind whirled. 'OK. So, he's . . . in prison?'

Drew nodded.

'And you think he deserves to be released?'

Drew grunted.

'And Mum's reform bill might make it harder for him to meet parole?'

Drew nodded again.

'But not *impossible*,' Nell suggested.

'Well, we'll see, won't we?'

They drove on in silence until Nell reached a crossroads. She pulled up. 'Can you . . .' she pointed at the knife, 'so I can look, and then turn.'

The bite of metal eased.

As she turned, to wend her way slowly westwards towards Finchmere, she felt something glide against her arm.

An adder. She'd known this was coming. But it still sent a shiver down her spine.

She fought every molecule in her body, which urged to *shudder*, to stay rock-still. The adder slid up onto her shoulder and paused, its long forked tongue flickering against Nell's cheek.

Monday 18th July – 7.15 p.m.

Rav was staring at his phone and jumped when James's number flashed. He answered the call immediately.

'Rav? She's not in the tunnel. Her car wasn't at the car park. Any idea where she could have been moved to?'

Rav felt sick. He'd been imagining news of Nell's daring escape. He had no idea how she'd have managed it, but somehow, under the terror, he'd had some strange certainty she'd have done . . . something.

But now . . .

'Think, Rav, where could she be?'

'He'd have to get rid of her car. Anywhere near there he could have parked it?' He put the call on speakerphone and brought up a map. 'Maybe the Furze Wood car park? Maybe the hospital car park?'

'Righto. I have a team at the hospital. I can get them on it.'

'No . . . Wait. Furze Wood. That's the release site for the snakes. Her car might have been parked there, not the main car park. You could easily have missed it, if you just searched Furze Heath. The woods are to the north.'

Chapter 25

Monday 18th July – 7.30 p.m.

Arriving at Furze Wood car park, James leaped out of his car. It was totally empty. He scanned the bushes to see if she'd been dragged into the undergrowth. Nothing obvious. He'd leave a team here to search the woods and the heath properly.

But, if Nell *wasn't* here, and if this really *was* about Imelda, maybe Nell's kidnapper was taking her to Finchmere, taking the battle to the battlefield.

He radioed his team. 'Can we get Traffic to follow all routes from Furze Wood to Finchmere? I need checkpoints all along those routes, so no one travelling *from* Furze Wood can get to Finchmere.'

Or, if they wouldn't – or couldn't – stop, he'd at least know where Nell was.

But even James knew he was asking for the impossible: Pendlebury was the closest station to Finchmere, and Nell's attacker was already ahead of them.

So he checked on Ashley, who was with the hostage negotiation team. They should be at Finchmere, with Imelda and Conor, by now.

He could make out the activity in the house in the background. Imelda's clipped tones saying, 'Fine, what do you need me to do?'

'We're all set here, James,' Ashley said. 'Plenty of cooperation. Very little panic. Feels a bit like a test case rather than a real event. Maybe, if we prepare for the worst, we can hope for the best.'

Monday 18th July – 7.30 p.m.

As she crawled along in the car, Nell watched the adder on her shoulder out of the corner of her eye.

Its head lifted and the pinkish-grey forked tongue emerged fully, wavering up and down, as the viper – hot for hunting – sensed its surroundings.

'What the—?' Drew jerked back, the knife leaving Nell's neck.

The removal of one threat made her breathe a little easier. But the snakes around her were a very different danger. And she, unlike Drew, had to move to drive the car. If he wanted, he could sit completely still and not be affected by them at all.

But instead, he batted the serpent winding its way up his car seat. Its reaction was faster than his: with a threatening *hiss*, the snake shot forward like lightning, striking Drew's finger, then fell in a tangle on the centre console between Drew and Nell. Its scales rasped as coil looped on coil, then its head raised to fix narrow, orange eyes on Drew.

'What the *hell*?' Rubbing his red, swollen bite mark, Drew pressed himself against the door, staring at the snake. Then he jumped at the sight of another serpent gliding along the passenger windowsill towards him. Using the blade of his knife, he tried to flick the snake away, but it hissed, recoiled and then struck, sinking fangs into the veins cording his wrist. It hung on as Drew shrieked, then it released and withdrew, still hissing.

'Oh, my *God*! They're *biting* me!' he wailed. '*Do* something!'

'I can't right now.' Nell kept her voice low, calm.

Driving had already been tense – the knife at her throat had restricted how she could turn her head and look around; her blood-smeared feet were either slipping off or sticking to the pedals. The pressure needed to use the accelerator, brake and clutch gouged her wounds, grinding grit, dirt and glass deeper into the cuts.

The hot throb in her feet seemed to grow, but she tried not to think about her injuries being contaminated, going septic. She had to focus on keeping her movements gradual, or she'd risk making an adder feel defensive enough to attack.

Next to her, Drew wasn't helping. He was twitching and flinching and swatting snakes away – flinging most in her direction. It was impossible to ignore them, and even harder not to instinctively flinch. The effort not to react made her sweat, salty droplets rolling down her face, stinging her sore eyes, making her head prickle. Her whole body needed to *shudder*.

As Drew's eyes strayed to her, she glimpsed his jaw dropping. She couldn't help slicking with sweat again as an adder slid up her face, the reptile's muscles undulating against her cheek, a tidal rhythm through hard belly scales, propelling the snake upwards along her ear, over her temple.

It made Nell's flesh crawl. The idea of a snake slithering around her head and face was unbearable. She fought the desperation to knock it away, or move her head, knowing the snake's reactions would be so much faster. If she could just keep calm, keep still.

But Drew continued to make that a challenge. As another snake slithered over his headrest, he screamed and swatted at it. 'How bloody many *are* there?' The adder struck Drew's ear, before his whack sent the snake hurtling through the air and landing behind Nell's seat, hissing.

She drove slowly, about thirty-five miles per hour on the country road, in fourth gear. She couldn't risk moving her feet to use the pedals, without seeing if there was a snake in the way, or putting her hand on the gearstick without checking. She had to try to glide through any turns, across junctions, just praying anyone on the road would be forgiving.

But a car roared up behind her. With no opportunity on these winding roads to overtake her, he expressed his displeasure immediately – tailgating and flashing his lights, then blaring the horn.

Nell jumped at the sound, then froze. She glanced in the mirror to see the man make an indelicate gesture. Just what she needed.

Beside her, Drew was yelling again '*Holy* bloody . . . Bloody *hell . . .*' His voice was breathless now, the words thick through his swollen lips, and his shirt was soaked in sweat. The sharp odour in the enclosed, hot car rolled towards Nell, enveloping her, nearly making her gag.

He shrieked at the sight of a snake hissing in his lap, and clawed at the seat, as if futilely trying to push himself backwards, away. It just made the viper hiss again, then *strike*. Nell didn't like to guess where that bite landed, as it elicited such a *howl* from Drew.

As the car behind her flashed its lights again, Nell made herself ignore it. She couldn't pull over. There were no lay-bys or gateways. And, even if there were, she wouldn't stop. If she did, Drew would leap out.

He tried to trap me – now I've bloody well trapped him.

A viper tickled Nell's bare foot. She chewed her inside lip, fighting her reaction to flinch, battling to keep her foot steady on the pedal.

As another snake slid through the gap between Drew's seat and headrest, he jerked away, his arms twitching up in reflexive protection. The adder shot out and sank its fangs into his arm.

'*Argh!*' As Drew clapped a hand on his forearm, he jolted another viper sliding along his seatbelt and, quicker than Nell could register, it bit Drew's hand. He cried out again.

The snake curling across Nell's face tensed at the vibrations around it.

Just breathe, Nell told herself. Long, even breaths. She recollected the day she and Rav had been taught to handle these rare snakes – long before Amir's weird training day. Rav had helped her overcome her fear. She tried to hear his encouraging words: they're more scared of you than you are of them; just show calm respect, no fast movements.

Their herpetologist trainer had also reassured her. Adders might be venomous, but one bite was highly unlikely to kill, and anti-venom was readily available. But if you had an allergy to snake venom, or you were bitten multiple times, you'd need swift medical intervention.

Drew was only being bitten because his nervy movements and thrashing around made them feel threatened.

Feeling the viper's tongue flick her ankle again, Nell's foot froze at the angle needed to keep the accelerator pressed. Tension shot up her leg. Another serpent slid onto the top of her seat, while another coiled around the gearstick.

As the adder on Nell's face glided into her hair, parting it like a python through grassland, she glanced at Drew.

His face was red as a ripe cherry, sheened with sweat; his neck swelling, his breathing laboured. He yanked his shirt collar. 'Help me . . .'

Nell took the gamble to ask about the victims, wondering if Drew might give anything away. 'I wish someone had been able to help those women. On the heath.'

Drew gave a short, wheezing laugh. 'They . . . deserved . . . it.'

Her heart thudded. 'Why?'

'Selfish . . . negligent . . .' Drew's breath was ragged. 'Called themselves mothers . . . but neglected their kids . . .' he slurred. 'Destroying their . . . lives.'

Nell fought not to react to the personal tone of the accusation, keeping her focus on the murders. 'But the poor young woman who was left on the heath, Amy, wasn't—'

'Useless . . . druggie. Wanted a kid . . . but wasn't going to give up . . . her habits. Bloody . . . *selfish*.' Spittle frothed at the corner of his mouth and sprayed on his chin. His chest heaved.

The scene at the anniversary fair flashed into Nell's mind – when Tom's partner, Anna, had joked about having some wine while she wrangled their toddler. Drew's barely disguised revulsion had been staring her in the face.

There's only one way he can know all this, surely . . .

'What about the woman who was killed while her little child was playing? It must have been far worse for that poor child to lose his mother.'

'What, denying that boy his dad . . . his role model?' His words rattled.

What if the dad wasn't role model material? Nell wanted to ask – but she didn't dare disturb Drew's confessional.

'Kelly had family around her. Plenty of role models there?'

'Ugh. Knocking back . . . cocktails at all hours . . . Same as . . . Shirley.'

At the unexpected name – the one that *hadn't* been reported as being linked to these murders – Nell fought to keep her breathing calm.

Her suspicion was now a chilling certainty: *Drew is the killer.*

Dropping his knife in the footwell, he ripped at his collar. The top button flew off, firing past the snake coiled on the headrest. The adder flinched, then tagged onto Drew.

Unaware, Drew fluttered a hand. 'Please . . . Feel sick . . . I'm hot . . . too hot.'

The snake swayed, as it followed the movement's vibration, then struck with devastating accuracy, sinking fangs into the soft flesh of Drew's hand. The adder's body hung like a rope bridge between its clamped jaws and its tail, curled around the headrest's metal leg.

The car behind flashed, then honked again, and Nell struggled not to jump, to make herself relax.

Drew flicked his hand, trying in the worst way to dislodge the snake. The snake on his windowsill fixed its unwavering gaze on him.

His eyes rolled as his body slackened. His stomach gurgled. A foul, putrid stench of defecation filled the car.

Nell gagged, clamping down on the heaving waves in her stomach.

Diverting her attention from the biohazards in the car, she focused on the driver behind, keeping her company in the rear-view mirror with his excitable, expressive sign language.

Drew slumped against the door. The adder at the passenger windowsill struck, fangs curved, pink mouth exposed, as jaws latched onto Drew's throat. The serpent's body whipped around his neck, like a poisoned ligature.

There was no way Drew could move now. His only chance of recovery depended on her getting him immediate medical attention. With him incapacitated, Nell looked actively for places to pull over. She knew the manoeuvre would be a challenge, but it would be easier for her to sit still if she didn't have to drive.

A dip in the road coming up was just a passing place, and Nell wasn't sure she'd be able to use the gears and pedals as slowly as she'd need to, and still stop safely within the space.

She knew fields lay off the road ahead. She knew there was a gateway, often left open, with a long lay-by that the tractors used to ease their entry onto the road. She prepared herself to steer into it, knowing she wouldn't be able to indicate and warn her friend in the car behind.

With the viper still tickling her foot and the driver behind her still blasting his horn, Nell spotted the lay-by. She gradually tilted the wheel. The car behind gave another irate blast, before slowly swerving out. He sped past, giving Nell what she assumed was a parting wave.

Seeing that the gate to the field was open, Nell drove through it, meeting the uneven ground with jarring thumps. She held her breath.

The snakes around her hissed, but just hunkered down. In the field, with no obstacles around her, no cars to hit her, she could check the footwell to make sure she could slip the clutch, and prevent the car from stalling, without risking a snake bite.

Her foot on the clutch was the one that had been pierced by the needle. The pressure she needed to exert with her tender, swollen sole on the pedal made her whimper.

With great care, she moved her foot from the accelerator, beside the viper, to the brake pedal. The snake flinched, but didn't strike, as Nell moved away from it.

As the car came to a stop, Nell prayed that the snake around the gearstick would move so she could lift her injured foot from the clutch. But it didn't, so she had to keep that burning pressure on the pedal.

Carefully, she pulled on the handbrake, then put her hands in her lap, keeping herself contained, still.

Only then did she really look at Drew. Red, angry bite marks had puffed up on his finger, wrist, ear, arm, both hands and neck. His face was so swollen, his breathing so laboured, that he looked like he was on the edge of consciousness. He could barely speak.

But he was trying.

Wheezing, he pushed his phone towards her. 'Please . . .'

Chapter 26

Monday 18th July – 7.45 p.m.

From Furze Wood, James followed the obvious route to Finchmere that avoided passing Pendlebury Police Station and the main roads.

As side roads branched, there were multiple options, then multiple options of *those*, and James began to despair that he'd never find her as fast as he needed to.

He doubled back on a couple of routes to check other roads.

Nothing.

Finally, he *hared* along a winding road, one he could imagine Nell enjoying on any other day. Passing a gateway, he glimpsed a flash of something – *a car?* – in the field.

He stood on the brakes, hearing rubber screech on asphalt, then reversed hard to check. It was a clapped-out Volvo estate. Nell's site car.

He radioed in his location, and that he'd found Nell's car.

The warning to stay put until his team arrived was roundly ignored, as James crept over, towards the driver's door.

The engine was still running, and terror lumped in his throat. *Did that mean Nell . . . ?* He couldn't even bring himself to think it.

His brain registered the motionless bodies inside the car.

His heart lurched at the sight of Nell leaning back against her seat, eyes closed. *Is she unconscious?*

Then he clocked the man beside her. Drew. He definitely looked unconscious. His violently red face and neck were swollen up like balloons, and drool was dribbling from slack, puffy lips.

His phone was on the centre console. Beside . . . a . . . a *snake*?

Whoah! James jumped backwards, shuddering.

As he crept close again to examine things more closely, he spotted another serpent gliding along Nell's seat.

Panic surged. Nell would know that the best thing to do with snakes is keep calm and still. But surely she would have called if she was OK. She'd need help to get out of this. So if she *hadn't* . . .

With fumbling fingers, he called Ed, back at the station. 'I need an ambulance, and get DS Ezra's snake handler friend here, pronto. One possible fatality and Nell with God-knows-what injuries. Blue lights all the way.'

A pause, then, 'No, I'm not exaggerating. What we're dealing with here is a car full of venomous snakes. And I can't get help for Nell, or arrest that *monster*, until they're dealt with.'

Monday 18th July – 8.15 p.m.

The car door opened, and Nell looked at the unknown man without moving her head. She'd heard James making his assessments earlier, but she'd been unable to move. The cramp in her leg and the burning in her foot were an agony of fire. And she didn't know how much longer she could bear it.

'Nell? If you can hear me, keep still. We're going to move all the adders away, OK?'

Nell watched the unfamiliar man pluck up the adders around her with casual skill, as if he were choosing apples at the supermarket. He placed each one into a cloth bag, where they writhed, then settled.

'Are you OK? Have you been bitten?' James asked.

Nell whispered, instead of nodding. 'No. But I trod on a used needle with my left foot. In the tunnel.' After the man had leaned across her and unwound the snake from the gearstick, Nell carefully put the car in neutral, then let the clutch out with a groaning sigh of deep relief. 'And I have a few other injuries.' Her voice was still croaky.

'Has Drew been bitten?'

'Yes. Several times.' Nell heard the wail of a siren as the ambulance approached.

'Do you know how many snakes are in the car?' the handler asked.

'Twenty-four.' She added one for good measure. It would keep him looking for longer.

'I'm up to thirteen,' the man said. 'Can't see any more, I'll check the boot.'

Shooting a sidelong glance at Drew, Nell was pretty certain he was beyond help now. And the snake wrangler would probably find most of the snakes around the buckets in the car boot.

'Got all but one, now,' the helpful adder catcher said.

Nell ached to get out and into the ambulance. 'Did you find one in Drew's footwell?'

The catcher looked carefully. 'Nope.'

'If there's only one adder left, maybe we can get Nell into the first ambulance, and keep checking,' James suggested.

Before anyone could say no, Nell moved slowly, smoothly, reaching for James's hand.

But as she got out of her car seat, longing to shudder away the flesh-creeping prickles all over her body, desperate to check for herself that there was no lurking serpent in her hair, her legs buckled underneath her. Swaying, she collapsed into James's arms, nearly blacking out.

'*Medic!*'

James's yell swam through the fogginess. Nell felt herself being transferred to a stretcher and jolted over the field, then into the ambulance.

'I'm . . . OK,' she tried to convince them.

'No snake bites, but a used needle has penetrated her left foot,' James said.

The foot was gently inspected.

'Jeez.' The wince in James's voice was obvious, and as her other foot was checked, Nell heard him suck air through his teeth.

'I think chloroform has been used on her,' James said. 'And she's been choked or strangled twice now, over two consecutive evenings. Please also check her skull. She headbutted someone with the back of her head last night, and that's only two and a half months after she had a head injury.'

Nell felt the medic tracing her injuries, checking her, as James spoke. With a groan, Nell blinked her eyes open. 'I'll check on the other guy,' an unfamiliar voice said, and Nell heard the rustle of boiler-suited legs stride away.

'James?' Seeing him beside her, she said, 'He killed them. He told me. He knew about all the women. Even Shirley. I'll . . . make a statement.'

'OK. Thanks.' James's eyes filled with concern. 'Not right now, though, eh? Let's get you to hospital and on the mend first.'

'I'll need the defibrillator here,' the same voice called from the Volvo.

The medic helping Nell stopped, grabbed the kit and sprinted over. As Nell blinked and tried to sit up, she saw Drew lying on the grass, his shirt ripped open as the paramedics attached wires to his chest.

The snake catcher had shut the passenger door and was still searching from the driver's side. Nell wanted to admit to her lie.

'Clear.' The paramedic's shout was followed by a whine and a jolt.

'James, I added an adder,' Nell confessed. 'So, your catcher has caught them all. Ask him to release them in Furze Wood.'

'OK, I'll let him know.' Moments later, James was back. 'How the hell did you manage to keep your injured foot on the clutch all that time? That can*not* have been easy.'

'Had to. Couldn't risk the car stalling and jerking the snakes around.'

'How many times did Drew get bitten?'

'Clear!' Another whine, another jolt.

'I'm not sure how many exactly. Several. Something between five and ten times. I was trying to drive. With a knife at my throat, then surrounded by angry adders, then with an irate driver behind me.'

The paramedics lifted Drew onto a gurney and rushed him into the ambulance. 'We have to prioritise this patient,' one said as they pulled Nell's stretcher from the vehicle.

'*What?*' Nell spat disbelieving indignation. 'He's a *serial killer*. All my injuries –including God knows *what* in my foot – are down to him. And *he* gets priority treatment?' Sitting up, Nell fired an outraged glare at James. 'Seriously?'

The medics ignored her and tended to Drew.

'He has just put me through *hell* because he wanted to use me as collateral to spring his criminal father from jail. But if his dad's in prison and affected by Mum's proposal, he's not in there for nicking sweets from the corner shop, is he? He's in there because he's done something awful. Maybe as awful as his serial killer son. God knows how many people they've harmed between them. So, please!' She swept her hand through the air. 'Go *ahead*, look after *him*. Take care of *him* ahead of another of his victims.' She found herself making the gesture at the ambulance's dust, as it sped to the hospital with blue lights flashing.

'Look, they have to triage according to injury, Nell. Nothing else,' James said. 'Just keep calm. Help will be coming.' His brow creased. 'So you discovered his connection to Imelda is his incarcerated father? He was gunning for Imelda because her bills might make it harder for him to get parole?'

Nell nodded. 'And he was talking about the victims like he knew them well and hated them. Like he was doing the world a favour by killing them.' She folded her arms. 'Let's just hope the ambulance doesn't make it in time.'

James stared at her. Nell had the uncomfortable sense that he was re-evaluating her world view. *Let him.*

As he swallowed and looked away, Nell wondered if he was even more uneasy because he wasn't disagreeing . . .

Chapter 27

Having stood his various teams down, James now asked them to regroup with him in the incident room. They still had another murderer to find, one who'd known enough about this case to manage a copycat kill.

Just as he was wondering if Simon *had* had any connection to the case, Hesha raced in.

'I've finally got a reply from Simon Slaker, saying he would like to pick up his memory card, and is now convenient? He's outside. Didn't expect us to be closed.'

James nodded and walked with her to the reception, which was locked outside of standard working hours. Those limits didn't apply to his team.

Unbolting the doors, James opened them and came face to face with the moody-looking man.

But Simon did manage a smile. 'Oh, thanks, I thought I'd have to come back. I got a message saying you were finished with my memory card and that I could collect it.'

'Yeah, come with me.' James beckoned. As he steered Simon down the corridor, he asked, 'Can you tell me what you were doing yesterday night? About 9 p.m.?'

'Yeah, sure. I was helping a mate out. At his place. Over at Nye. He was in a mad panic. Imminent baby and hadn't finished all the things to, you know,' he flapped his hand, 'prepare. He had me painting walls, and building an IKEA cot and flat-pack furniture. And we only just got it all done in time, as it happens. His wife went into labour yesterday afternoon. I can't say the DIY was really playing to my strengths, but I owed him one.'

'Why was that?' James wondered if this was the same friend who had provided Simon with an alibi for the night Nell's house

223

had been broken into – and wondered just how much Simon owed him.

Simon's lips set in a thin line.

'OK, well, we can ask your friend when we speak to him. What was his name?'

Simon huffed. 'OK, look, he's let me borrow his camper van. He wanted something more reliable to take his family around in, and I'd been kicked out by my girlfriend and suddenly his old Caravelle didn't look so shabby. So we just swapped. Let's say the paperwork is still catching up. Needs must, and all that.' Simon showed James the contact details in his phone, and James noted name and number.

James tried to keep a neutral face as several pennies dropped. 'Well, let's hope that paperwork does catch up with you, before one of those surprisingly keen traffic officers pulls you over and needs to check your details.'

'Yeah, all right, point taken.' Simon rolled his eyes. 'Are you going to give me my memory card?'

'Yes, but I want to ask you something first.' James showed Simon into the interview room where the memory card was already inside a reader, attached to a computer. It had been prepped like this as soon as tech released it, ready in case anyone located the errant ornithologist.

'You certainly have an interesting range of subjects.' James clicked through the various shots of birds in bushes, variously framed, some images more blurred than others.

He stopped clicking at the picture of Amy, standing with her naked back to the camera. 'Care to explain this one?'

Simon squinted at it and tutted. 'Yeah, that was really sodding annoying. She got right in the way.'

James frowned and looked at the screen.

Simon wound his finger. 'Take it back a shot or two. See the little egret I was tracking as it flew across the lake?'

James looked at the set of blurred images that progressed across the lake, with barely a bird obvious in the frame – then the perfect, sharp shot of Amy – before more blurry snaps.

'It was an opportunist shot – I hoped to get a couple of photos. But it moved too quickly. It was only as I panned past Amy that the damn autofocus woke up and locked on her. Sodding annoying.'

'Yes, it looks very much like she was the focus.' James studied Simon carefully.

'Yeah, that's the problem with fast shutter speed and continuous autofocus. I'm taking several pictures every second but the autofocus snaps lightning-fast onto whatever it thinks is most significant within the frame. It's infuriating because, as you can see, it always favours people. It could really use a birder override.'

James peered at the screen again. He didn't buy it.

But Simon leaned in. 'Can you see those brilliant white feathers? As densely white as a snowstorm? Against jet-black legs and beak? So elegant. That's the little egret. They used to be rare here. They're becoming more common, but it still gives me a buzz to spot them. Such sharp monochrome. They always photograph dramatically.' He grunted. 'Unless some idiot spoils the shot.'

Monday 18th July – 9.30 p.m.

Rav had answered James's phone call, over an hour earlier, with shaking hands. Hearing Nell's voice had made him jerk forward in his seat, holding his breath.

She's OK!

He'd only had to wait this agonising hour for her to have a check-up at the hospital. He knew she'd had some pretty nasty wounds, and he was anxious that her head injury should be checked thoroughly.

But now, finally, she was in his arms, complete with tetanus booster and fast-tracked blood tests.

His family, who had arrived in the middle of the situation, and had stayed with him – tense and worried, taking it in turns to get tea, go for a walk, get some fresh air, all while he'd been glued to his phone – had absented themselves at Nell's arrival.

Rav was glad their reunion had been private. He couldn't hold back tears as he hugged her to him, checked her over and tried to grow calm after the awful tension.

But now, his parents and sister were hovering in the doorway, anxious to speak to Nell, to see for themselves how she was.

Aanya broke the ice. 'Nell? What happened? How did you get away? Tell me everything.'

As Nell finished recounting the events, Neeta squeezed her arm. 'I'm truly relieved you're OK. I can see how good you two are for each other.' She gestured at the door. 'Are your parents still here? I'd like to speak to them. I . . . I need to apologise for our behaviour at the hearing. This has not been an easy time. But—'

'Oh, Neeta, there's no need—'

'I think there is, *Beta*.' Neeta pulled Nell into a heartfelt hug. 'We haven't given your relationship the chance it deserves, have we? So let us make a fresh start.'

Monday 18th July – 9.30 p.m.

With nowhere else to look for leads, James had prepared his questions for Drew's wife, Nicky, and armed himself with the warrant that Val had secured to search the house and Drew's computer. He and Ashley were even escorting the SOCO team to the door.

As they walked up the sweeping drive, James took in the view: mock-Tudor detached house, a silver Lexus in front of the detached garage. It all oozed successful executive home.

Before he rang the doorbell, James glanced through the living room window. The woman, whom he presumed was Nicky, was sitting on the sofa, watching TV. As she moved forward to pick up a cup from the coffee table and drink, James gasped.

Her entire eye socket, and all the skin encircling it, was a dusky reddish purple, swollen like an overripe plum. Exactly as if she'd been headbutted the day before.

Beside him, Ashley exhaled. 'Good cop, bad cop?' she asked.

James nodded. He had a feeling Nicky would respond to Ashley's empathy. Especially if he put the pressure on and went straight to arrest.

An hour later, with SOCOs busy at her house, he faced Nicky across the table, interviewing her under caution. Her lawyer and James could both see that Nicky wanted to confess. She wasn't the hard-bitten type. It was festering inside her. And James knew Ashley would draw it out.

'We already know all about Drew's life,' Ashley was saying. 'And you must have seen a lot of it first-hand, growing up together.'

Nicky blew her nose on the soggy tissue. 'You wouldn't believe the things he had to endure. I don't know how he did, quite honestly. Those . . . *men*.' Her voice broke into a sob. 'He was always coming round to our place. My mum would always feed the waifs and strays, as she called them. So we got to know each other well. And I saw the difference a bit of kindness from my mum made. I thought he just needed someone to love him.'

As she sobbed, Ashley pushed the box of tissues across to her.

Nicky mopped her face. 'Everything teaches you that, doesn't it? From fairy stories upwards. Love can conquer all.' She sniffed. 'And these days, we're told to be kind. But the idea that you can love someone out of their torment . . . It just isn't aways true. And teaching people that, teaching *young girls* that, that's a crime in itself, in my book. It doesn't matter how much you want it to be true.'

She took the next tissue Ashley offered. 'Because what happens then is . . . is . . . if the *man* doesn't change, then it's the *girl*, isn't it? Who blames *herself*: "*I didn't love him enough. My love wasn't strong enough.*" When the truth is, there are some who just can't be changed.'

'When did you realise that Drew couldn't be changed?' Ashley rubbed her arm.

'I knew it whe-when . . .' Her face trembled so much that James feared they wouldn't catch the words, even if she said them. 'When I'd done what he'd done.'

James froze, waiting as Nicky took a long, shuddering, heartbroken breath. 'He was my world. I *believed* in the fairy tale, the happy ending, good over evil. I *believed* I could save him. I'd believed that, right in my soul, since I was seven. I thought he just needed more from me, more strength, more love. I thought it was *me* letting *him* down. So when he was here, under arrest, I had this . . . *idea*. To protect him, to show him I *wouldn't* let him down. By... doing something while he was in custody. When it couldn't have been him.'

She screwed the tissue into a ball. 'I'd seen a woman he worked with, who was his type. It didn't take much to work out where she'd be. I parked near the heath to see if she was there. Drew had said they were working at weekends, and I knew what the site car looked like. And she turned up! I'd been trying to psych myself up to do something, but then her colleagues joined her. I totally panicked. Crammed myself into these awful scratchy bushes to hide. And when I found that sleeping bag, in that sack, I knew it could help. I parked down the road, so I could watch them leave, and I followed her. She dropped off the girl she was with and drove off.'

Exhaling through puffed cheeks, Nicky winced and touched her eye. 'She went to this stately home place. I hung around, wondering what to do, and she came out again, and headed back to Pendlebury. To the Spinal Unit. I waited by her car. As it got dark, I was pleased. I thought it would make it easier.'

Nicky picked at the tissue, shredding it onto the table. 'I'd got myself all . . . ready to . . . to do it. And then I went for it. But she fought back. I was bloody terrified. She was like a wildcat. I . . . I had to get out of there, in case it attracted attention. I was angry at myself for failing, and at *her* for making it difficult. I had to find someone else. Town was too bright. Too busy. And if it was going to be difficult, I'd need to do it somewhere quieter. I found a country pub and waited in another dark car park.'

Her face contorted. 'It was . . . *awful*. So, so *awful*. That poor woman.' She rocked forward, keening. 'I'm so sorry. I'm so, *so* sorry.' Covering her face, she took several gasping breaths. 'I had to leave her somewhere she'd be found immediately. Drew had told me his team were doing surveys on the heath at night, so I didn't dare take the body there. So, I took it to that fancy house. I checked Google Maps, and saw that church and the nearby car park. I could, sort of, lay her to rest. And I knew she'd be found.

'I *hated* myself. And that's when I knew. I couldn't ever do anything like that again. But *he* didn't feel like that, did he? He didn't want to stop. There's not enough love in the world to change that. Yet, all I could think about was the poor little boy he *had* been. Who'd been treated so horrifically, been so twisted up by that chance encounter, beyond his control, that destroyed his whole life. And what a different life he could have had.'

Chapter 28

Tuesday 19th July – 7 p.m.

Nell woke abruptly and jerked up, grabbing her phone.

How is it already seven in the evening?

She kicked the covers back and dashed to the shower, desperate to see Rav, annoyed at herself for sleeping the day away.

Last night, Neeta's chat with Imelda had become an invitation to Finchmere for drinks and nibbles the following evening – *any minute now!* And Nell had invited Conor and Sylvia, along with James, wanting to know the details, hoping it was all over.

Before she'd left the hospital, Nell had stolen a few more hours alone with Rav. She'd curled up beside him, sharing a fierce yet restful stillness, glad to be close. It told Nell more than any words could. Rav was the only one who could have deciphered her code. He was the first person she'd wanted to see after the ordeal. She had no doubts now about their future, whatever it might hold. And judging from the strength of his grip around her, neither did he.

As she'd left, Rav's trainer had taken Nell to one side to warn her that Rav had been overdoing his PT. It seemed her kidnap – and the afternoon Rav had spent messaging and worrying – *had* at least been good for enforcing rest. But Rav needed to take a more moderate approach, or he'd do more harm than good. The solution was obvious. If Rav would agree . . .

She pulled on jeans and a jumper and ran downstairs, finding Rav in the hall.

'Oh, just in time for cocktails and company.' Rav grinned as he studied her face. 'You look better for some rest. How do you feel?'

'I'm fine. Have you been here all day?' Nell asked. 'I'm sorry I slept in.'

'You needed it. Besides, I've been essential as a canapé tester.'

She leaned in to kiss him, loving the sparkle that was back in his eyes, then walked beside him as he wheeled himself into the great room, through the ballroom and out onto the terrace. Her parents were chatting with Neeta and Rakesh, and both families were clearly enjoying sharing tales of errant offspring far too much for Nell's liking.

So, she was pleased – if apprehensive – to see James approach, with Ashley and Val. He delivered the news Nell had been anticipating, with no preamble. 'We've just heard from the hospital. Despite their best interventions, Drew died earlier today.'

Nell sank heavily into the seat at the end of the table, next to Rav. She took a few steadying breaths, swallowing hard, then looked up at him. 'Good.'

James winced, and Nell saw his personal opinion warring with his professional one. Eventually, he managed to say, 'It can't have been easy to hear that confession, under such stressful circumstances, after he'd attacked you and kidnapped you.'

'Quite. I'll save my sympathy for his victims and their families.' Nell crossed her arms.

'But his start in life was challenging,' James said. 'Not everyone has the privilege . . .'

Nell's cheeks flamed at what she thought was going to be a criticism of her myopic outlook, from her cosseted life, unable to put herself in someone else's shoes.

'. . . of having a family that loves them. Who can offer them a stable upbringing.'

Nell's discomfort deepened. She'd never had to contemplate her most basic needs as a privilege. She hadn't just had wealth, she'd had opportunities. And people who cared about her. She'd never really thought what alternative hand her accident of birth might have dealt.

'He killed his own mother, when he was just nine,' Ashley said, her voice low.

Nell gasped, looking from her to James, then Val, and wondered how the hell they managed to do it. To see the worst of human nature, yet still believe in the best of it.

'But he was in custody when you were attacked,' Ashley said. 'And when the other victim – Alex – was left here, by the church. So we knew we had a copycat killer, trying to prove Drew's innocence.'

'Who?' Nell asked.

'His wife,' Ashley said. 'They grew up together, so she knew about his awful start in life.'

Nicky? Nell remembered meeting her at the fair, trying to make her feel at ease.

'So if she tried to, what, kill Nell,' Imelda said, 'and then *really* managed to kill Alex, then she must have known Drew was a murderer? A serial killer?'

At James's nod, Rav gaped, then asked, 'Yet she *stayed* with him?'

'She hoped – *believed* – she could change him,' Ashley said.

'It's tragically common,' Imelda explained. 'Victims of domestic abuse often cling to the hope that their abuser is, deep down, a good person; that with enough love, they will change.'

'But *five murders*?' Rav looked aghast. 'How many would it *take*?'

Val gave a sympathetic shrug. 'She *has* confessed. And she gave us the boots she wore during the last murder, with your unique seed mix in the treads, Nell.'

'And we – *finally* – found the distinctive ligature he used,' James said. 'A drain snake, used by his dad, who was a plumber. Metal tightly coiled around a rubber core, which left a distinctive – but not easily recognisable – impression. Dr Saunders is swabbing it, just in case there are more victims. We don't think we'll find anything, but we have to be sure.'

'And we've seized his computer,' Ashley added. 'Tech have already found an account of saved posts he kept of all the murders. It's like a full confessional on there.'

'So, one way or another, the case is essentially closed,' James asserted. Looking at the table, spread with platters of canapés and sparkling wine in silver ice buckets, he raised hopeful eyebrows at Imelda and Hugo. 'Deserves a toast, surely?'

'Absolutely,' Imelda said, as Hugo opened a bottle of Finchmere sparkling wine.

As if summoned by a popping cork, Sylvia arrived, with Conor and a dazzling smile.

Nudging Nell, Conor pointed at his jet-black hair. 'It's a wonder I'm not white as snow, after yesterday. Can you imagine what it was like, getting those updates?'

'Try to imagine being in the car,' Nell sparred.

'Oh, darling, *don't*!' Sylvia shuddered, recovering enough to take a glass of fizzing wine. 'I can't believe what happened. Thank goodness you're all right. What were you doing on the heath in the first place?'

Nell frowned. 'It was your text, Sylvia. Asking me to do the translocation.'

Sylvia shook her head slowly. 'I didn't send a text . . .'

Leaning forward, Nell asked, 'Did Drew go into the office? Did he have a chance to use your phone?'

Sylvia's gasp was the answer. 'That . . . *swine*. He must have texted while I was talking to Elliot.' Her face darkened but she rallied as Nell reached for her hand and squeezed it.

Once everyone had a drink, Imelda raised her glass. 'I'd like to say thank you. To Conor and his team, and Ashley, all prepared to deal with the worst while being so kind.' Imelda's cheeks trembled as she turned to James. 'And James. For finding her.' As Imelda's arm slipped round Nell's shoulders and hugged her, she leaned into her mum's embrace.

Their emotions were drowned out by the toast. As it died down, James said, 'I can't take credit, Imelda. It was Rav who knew where to find Nell.'

Rav shook his head, downplaying his part. But Nell wouldn't let him. 'I knew he'd know,' she said firmly, holding his gaze and letting him know how invaluable he'd been. Despite being surrounded by company, the smile they shared was completely private.

Shaking his head, Rav explained. 'Nell made it easy. She gave me two clues on that recording, so I'd have no doubt where she was.'

Imelda stared at him. 'What? I've watched it a million times. What did you spot?'

Rav glanced at Nell. 'She twitched her thumb to give me the code of the combination lock of the tunnel she was trapped in.'

Imelda's mouth dropped open. 'What do you mean?'

As Rav imitated the movement, Imelda stared at him. 'You knew that was a *code*?'

Nodding, he added, 'And, when she tried to nudge her ear, I realised she was telling us there was a distinctive sound to catch. It was the nightjar. Which, around here at least, *only* nests on Furze Heath.'

'So we knew exactly where to start the search,' James said. 'Rav saved us hours. We wouldn't have been so close on Nell's trail without him.'

Conor tilted his glass at James and Rav. 'That's some solid teamwork. Trusting each other enough to make life-saving decisions on the basis of each other's deductions isn't something you find every day, you know.'

'And you believe Drew took Nell hostage,' Imelda clarified, 'to try to force me to release his *father* from prison?' When James nodded, she fumed. 'What a deluded fool!'

Val nodded. 'He hadn't really outgrown his hero worship of his father.'

'That might be down to the trauma he suffered as a small child,' Ashley suggested. 'A nine-year-old's logic could blame prison for keeping his father away.'

Val glanced at Imelda. 'What does this mean for the bills you were working on?'

'Pfff!' Hugo huffed. 'An end to it, I should hope.'

When Imelda just raised her eyebrows, Nell prodded her father. 'Dad! This is Mum's *career*!' She turned to her mother. 'If this is what you believe in, then you fight on!'

'But it's the *risk*, Nell,' Hugo stressed. 'Not just to your *mother*. To *you*, too.' He shook his head. 'It's too much. And you *must* agree, after what just happened.'

'That's exactly why I *disagree*,' Nell protested. 'The murderer *trapped* me. He'd got me *unconscious*. But he'd have killed me if I'd been anyone else *but* Mum's daughter. Her politics turned me from a victim to a hostage. So her work directly saved my life.'

'Oh, I give up.' Hugo threw up his hands.

'Fine. As long as Mum doesn't,' Nell said.

'Thanks for asking, Val.' Imelda ignored the outbursts. 'I'll give you my press soundbite, if you like?' She cleared her throat. 'This case has proved that change is needed more than ever. These bills aren't the *perfect* solution – we need cross-party, long-term systemic change for that, which I *do* hope to make progress on. But these bills *are* the line in the sand that must be drawn – a start. And I will continue to use my platform for this work.'

'Good.' Val grinned. 'I'm looking forward to working with you. This has been an ordeal for a lot of people. For the victims, and their families.' She turned to James and Ashley. 'This case has been opened *three* separate times now. But you were the ones who solved it – by upholding the *appropriate* rigour in our investigations.'

Nell wondered if she'd imagined the emphasis on the investigation being conducted *appropriately*. But Ashley must have caught it, too, because she asked, 'Oh? Is something happening with Trent?'

Val nodded. 'It'll be public knowledge by the end of the day. Trent is officially retiring. He's taking a month to hand over – and three weeks of that time will be holiday.'

'Who's he handing over to?' Ashley asked. 'Who'll be our new Chief Constable?'

Val couldn't hold back her smile. 'You're looking at her.'

As James and Ashley leaped to their feet, cheering, the others around the table clapped and raised their drinks. The excitement was infectious.

'Of course, my move will mean a reorg.' Val eyed Nell. 'Especially given the crime wave we seem to have round here. So I'm delighted to announce that, in no small part due to this case, I've secured the budget to open a new DI position.' She arched an eyebrow at Ashley. 'I'm just hoping the perfect candidate will walk through my door. After this case, in particular, I can see how valuable psychological insights and good teamwork are.'

Ashley's jaw dropped. Val smiled and sipped her drink.

'Well, if we're announcing news, then maybe I can share mine?' Sylvia asked. 'With Conor and I getting married, we've been thinking about our future. So when I found a perfect opportunity, I couldn't resist it.' She raised her glass at Imelda and Hugo. 'And I've been delighted to accept the position of Marketing Director for Finchmere.'

Nell gaped at her. 'That's amazing!' She'd been so distracted, she hadn't known Sylvia had applied – or, even, that they were *looking* for someone. 'But it won't be the same in the office without you.'

'Nell! Didn't we say nothing is forever? I'm surprised you're still there, given all you work on here, like your epic rewilding project. I'm *hugely* excited to be part of it.'

Absorbing the news, Nell beamed. 'Yes, it *is* exciting. I'm *so* glad, Sylvia!'

'I'll see the regeneration of Furze Heath through, first, of course. Oh! On that note, look.' Sylvia took her iPad from her bag, opened an email and clicked on a video. 'Simon and Erin cosied up together at her place yesterday to make this as a surprise.'

As Nell leaned in, James asked, 'Who's this Erin, that Simon was with yesterday?'

'Colleague,' Nell explained. 'Why?'

James looked like he could kick himself. 'Investigative black spot when we were trying to track him down. Never mind.'

Sylvia tapped the screen and the video faded in, showing Furze Heath from the air, back in the spring, pale buds hazing the birch trees. Nell gasped at the clip of her kneeling to examine a plant, then make a note, then a sped-up shot of her putting out the reptile traps.

'From Simon's wildlife cameras, darling,' Sylvia explained.

'I wish it was as easy as that makes it look!' Nell laughed.

A time-lapse sunset had the sun melting into a scarlet horizon over the dusky heath, then night-time shots of flitting bats and headtorch-wearing ecologists. A chorus of flurrying birds in an apricot dawn was followed by sped-up films of planting across the site, and Amir overseeing the reptile fence installation. Then the frame zoomed in on a still shot of him holding a smooth snake, and Sylvia nudged her. 'That's my photo. Rather pleased with that.'

'Yes, what happened to Amir?' Nell asked.

'Drug bust, apparently,' Sylvia whispered. 'According to my inside contacts.'

'Oh?' Nell wondered if Amir was supplying when he left his bag in the pub, but she was distracted by the powerful film of the tower block disappearing into a cloud of dust.

Another sped-up series showed trucks clearing the site, damping down the dust. Then an aerial shot overlaid the first image with the last. Littered, derelict tower blocks were replaced with a tidy construction footprint. The reptile fencing ringed the least valuable habitat for development, while around it, the sparse vegetation had been enhanced with planting which connected habitats across the wider landscape. And Collette's map over *that* showed the planned pond and bank, the playground and the new affordable housing.

'What a great way to show the progress and the plan!' Rav beamed.

'Brilliant, isn't it?' Sylvia said. 'It's going straight on the website. Rufus will love us.' She raised an eyebrow. 'And it seems like Erin and Simon are growing rather close.'

Nell poked her. 'Stop matchmaking. Tell me about your wedding! Who'll be there?'

'Your parents, of course, and mine. Do you know any of Conor's family?'

When Nell shook her head, Sylvia admitted, 'Me neither. But I'm looking forward to meeting them. I have to invite James, of course. And he's bringing his young lady.'

'Uh-huh.' Nell couldn't help her automatic reaction to the idea of Shannon being there. But, after seeing her at the gallery, Nell had to admit that Shannon was definitely mellowing. Maybe this time they'd enjoy a party?

After Sylvia rejoined Conor, the conversation flowed around them. Nell leaned into Rav, ignoring the sides of his wheelchair pressing into her.

He leaned his chin on her head and murmured, 'Fancy getting away from the crowd?'

Nell nodded and stood up as he winked at Imelda and picked up an ice bucket containing a full bottle, balancing it on his lap. He wheeled himself down a ramp that had been put over the terrace steps and headed over the lawn, towards the orchard.

'I've been thinking—' they said in unison, then stopped and laughed.

Rav looked up at Nell, waiting for her to finish.

'I think you need some TLC,' she said. 'I've been on your case, when really you need a bit of care and a gentler approach, rather than me pushing you to increase your training.'

'TLC, eh?' Rav smiled. 'Great minds.'

* * *

Rav enjoyed Nell's quizzical gaze as they continued to the orchard, right up until the lawn became rough wildflower grassland, and he puffed as he navigated the uneven terrain.

Nell seized the ice bucket that bounced on his lap – and then gasped.

She took in the lights threaded through the trees, making the orchard glow in the golden sunset and illuminating the wide rattan sofa spread with throws and cushions; the delight in her face made Rav's heart swell. Then she spotted the projector pointing at the whitewashed barn wall, and the chocolate ice cream in another ice bucket, beside a vast bowl of popcorn.

'I know it's only a tiny thing, after you've been so . . . unwavering. Over everything. But I wanted to do something. To say thank you. I know I've been a pillock. But I love you.'

'Oh, this is so romantic!' Nell set the wine on the flat arm of the sofa and snuggled under a cashmere throw. Rav parked, transferred himself to the sofa, and passed Nell the ice cream, arming her with a spoon.

When his free arm settled around her, strong and familiar, her long inhale drew in the fresh scent of grass, and she relaxed for what seemed like the first time in ages. Mellowing chirps echoed from the distant woodland as the birds' activity slowed.

As Nell excavated a chunk of chocolate and salted caramel from the tub of squidgy ice cream, Rav nodded at the downland valleys, gilded in the evening's glow. 'Film or view?'

'Oh, *view*, while it lasts. This is my favourite bit of the downs. Well, one of them.'

'Sure.' He poured them both some wine, shooting her a comedic grin. 'I wasn't sure if you'd like my film selection anyway. I mean, I downloaded all the classics for you to choose from. *Snakes on a Plane. Anaconda—*'

Nell thumped him playfully.

'Hey! Watch the wine!' Rav laughed and handed her a glass. 'I prefer the view. Quite something to think of all those acres being rewilded, all down to you. Sylvia's right, it's an epic project.'

'Yes.' She glanced up. 'I've been thinking about that. We'll be moving into the next phase soon. I'll need to recruit an ecologist.'

'Why don't you work here, then? Full time, like Sylvia said?'

'I mean that I'll need an ecologist, as well as me. Sylvia's right, I should take the reins here properly. So I need to build a team.'

Rav nodded. 'I can probably recommend a couple of—'

'Really?' Nell half turned, so she could meet his eyes.

'What?'

'*You*, you idiot. I want you.'

'Oh. Well . . . isn't that a bit unreal—'

'We'll get an off-road wheelchair. Or adapt a quad bike. Or horse and carriage. Whatever it takes. But there's no reason why you can't supervise, plan, ID, project manage . . . *if* you'd like to.'

'*Like* to? I'd *love* to!'

'Then I'll work my notice period and get Elliot to the end of survey season. And we can spend the week at Sylvia and Conor's wedding coming up with our business plan, and the detailed strategy for the next phase. I could really use your suggestions.'

'Oh, great!' His gaze turned away from her and settled on the view, a million ideas flashing through his brain. 'Yeah, I have a few thoughts. I can't wait to get started!'

'And . . .' She looked hesitant. 'Don't you want to move out of the Spinal Unit?'

Rav's smiled faltered. 'Yeah. But I'm not going to stay at my parents'. And I had to stop renting my flat. So . . .'

'Yes. *So*?' Nell stared at him, like he was failing to add something up. 'Are those really all your options?'

He frowned.

As she chewed her lip, a white flash soared silently past. Rav gasped. 'Did you see? That was one of our owls! From our nest box in the barn! The adult male!'

As they stared at the grey barn, where the owls had taken up residence in the box they'd installed, another ghostly white shape glided towards them, in silence. The flight was less certain, the tail and wings a little shorter. With a swoop, the bird landed on a fence post, ruffling his feathers like he'd surprised himself. The parent landed nearby, with a hissing call, and then they both took off, gliding low over the grassland.

'Fledgling,' Nell whispered. 'So they reared at least one! That's amazing, given their start, being ousted from their nest and breeding late. Having to start again, and adapt.'

'Uh-huh.' Rav leaned his cheek against her head. 'So if they can do it, I can do it. Is that what you're thinking?'

'No, it wasn't. But you make a good point!' Adjusting her grip on her glass, she moved her fingers: eight-two-eight-two.

Rav frowned. 'What's this? Greater horseshoe bats? Are they here?' He looked around.

He'd got the code, based on greater horseshoes echolocating at 82 kHz. But not the reason. 'No. But you might need it.'

'Why . . . ? Ah, you reset everything after the break-in. It's the code to your place?'

Nell shook her head. '*Our* place. If you'd like. Fancy moving in with me?'

He stared at her, half wary, half hopeful. 'Is it . . . practical?' But he didn't care if it was life on a pull-out bed, or a stairlift. Nell was right. They could adapt.

The fear that had constricted him from the inside, squeezing out all hope, for so, *so* long, suddenly released him. Without the wall of tension in his chest, his breathing became a deep, calm lungful. He'd forgotten what a deep breath felt like. His shoulders dropped. The knot in his gut melted away. He leaned in to kiss her, then drew back to gaze at her eyes, alive again with that sparkle.

'Yes, please, Nell. I'd love that.'

Acknowledgements

I still have to pinch myself at having the immense fortune to work with the most fabulous team at Embla books: Cara Chimirri, Anna Perkins, Emilie Marneur, Jane Snelgrove, Hannah Deuce, Katie Williams and Paris Ferguson – you put so much talent and care into evolving a manuscript and you make it a total joy!

On top of that, I get to work with the dazzlingly brilliant Katie Fulford, and wonderful Sarah McDonnell, at Bell Lomax Moreton. Your partnership, encouragement and advice means more than you know.

Part of the fun of writing a book is in the polish and working with the exceptional team of editors to get it just right. Emily Thomas – thank you for your brilliant insights and skilful attention – I always look forward to getting your edits back. Daniela Nava, thank you for your knack of smoothing out my manuscripts. And thank you for your eagle eyes, Jenny Page and Kay Coleman.

Lisa Horton, thank you for bringing such personality to the cover characters! You always strike it just right!

And I'm always delighted by how the audio team breathe life into the characters, with magical performances by Kristen Atherton. Seems like I'll never find an accent she can't do . . . ☺

Granny and Granddad definitely have a part to play in inspiring snake-related stories. Aside from knowing where you could find grass snakes and adders (including the unusual melanistic black adders) 'up the wood', at any given moment, Granny seemed to have misspent a lot of her youth snake hunting. Granddad's less predatory approach was immortalised when he vaulted a five-bar gate, clearing it better than any Olympic hurdler, at the fearsome sight of a lone grass snake, minding its own business, swimming in a river. And then there's the famous family story of the snake in my grandparents' bed[*] – *not* a euphemism, but my mum's idea of

---

[*] (No animals were hurt in the making of this family anecdote.)

revenge as a child, after being unfairly told off. There's no historic record of what Granddad vaulted on that occasion. But Mum didn't mind getting into trouble at all for something she *had* done.

Researching the prison system, rehabilitation and psychopathy has been fascinating, and I've had the chance to speak to some brilliant experts along the way. I'm truly grateful to Dr Sohom Das and Graham Bartlett for sharing their insights.

I'm also grateful to Dr Jo Martyr for expert advice on Rav's condition and recovery. And Rav's orthopaedic surgeon is named in honour of the real Mr Christopher Rennie, FRCS, a fabulous, caring doctor.

I'll be raising glasses on both sides of the pond to Jo and Rachel and Sabrina, Matt and Lauren and maybe *with* Mark and Esther (hurray!) as well as Nigel and Erin, Brenda, Julie, Alan, Bruce and Bob.

Mum and Dad – thanks again for all the reading, and for sharing the fun of writing these books! I couldn't ask for a better team to have in my corner. I love you, Mum. You're the best mum on the planet.* You're alright, Dad.**

My delicious husband, Ian, thank you for even more murderous fun over brunch (I think you need a new Murder Brunch loyalty card). For each book, we have to act something out so I can properly imagine it and write about it, and they usually tend to be the dangerous bits. This time, Cable-Tie Sunday will be hard to forget. I do love that you're game for anything!

And for those who have been kind enough to read this book, or to have shared Nell's adventures this far – thank you. I hope this book has been as much fun to read as it has been to write.

---

* (Please don't put a snake in my bed.)
** (Zero risk.)

The Nature of Crime

Like Nell, the job I enjoyed least as an ecologist was translocating reptiles.

So, it may be reassuring to know that I have taken a little artistic licence with the episode in the car: adder bites in the UK are rarely deadly and are very treatable; multiple bites and/or anaphylactic shock would be necessary to cause a serious reaction but, even then, death would be unusual. And adders, the UK's only poisonous species, prefer to hide than attack.

And spare a thought for the snake's point of view: translocation is not fun for the species being collected and moved. As much as it can be a very pragmatic mitigation method for a population on a site being developed, moving reptiles to a new habitat can cause stress, which reduces their capacity to reproduce. So minimising that stress is essential for species which are protected already due to their rarity.

If you ever see thigh-high black plastic fencing snaking across fields, it's one of the first signs of a development happening. That fencing, described in this book, separates areas where reptiles are from the rest of the site, so the species can be translocated out of harm's way.

Reptile surveys are always labour-intensive, especially laying out the refugia. One memorable survey used thick, industrial conveyor belt rubber (instead of the lighter tins, or squares of roofing felt) as the heavier material was deemed safer near the motorway. With limited parking spots, I had to lug these for miles to set them out in the right habitat, mapping them as I went. Only being able to carry two at a time made it essentially impossible to get all the refugia out in the days available, necessitating 5 a.m. starts. On the third morning, aching and sore from two days of lugging, I really went for it, despite the fog, and set out nearly a hundred traps . . . only for the mist to clear and show me I'd put them all out in the wrong field.

The upside of that project was that some of the site skirted a police dog training ground, which was fun to watch as I surveyed. I didn't know then that it was providing inspiration for a certain Hercules.

Budding herpetologists will find refuge in their county's local Amphibian and Reptile Group (ARG), often delighted to have volunteers to survey sites to help grow the population records for our six reptile species.

Grass snakes, adders, common lizards and slow-worms are our more ubiquitous species, sometimes popping up in gardens. Like the examples at Nature Fest in the book, there are always opportunities to share your garden with wildlife. Ponds are ideal as they can support so many species, and any rough edges that are seldom disturbed are likely to be colonised by something hopefully cute but at least interesting. And it's the best excuse for any garden untidiness! And even compost heaps welcome wildlife – a female grass snake may lay her eggs there to incubate them.

I think of grass snakes as quite a gentle species; they don't have fangs but instead have very small teeth, and they've rarely been known to bite a person (if ever). They prefer to play dead (thanatosis) than confront, and will even emit a foul odour to deter predators and add realism to the playing-dead act. Talk about commitment to a role.

The sand lizard and smooth snake are our rarest species, usually found on heathland. Both are quick and rarely seen – so treasure that moment if you ever have it!

And the other rare heathland species in this book is the cryptic nightjar, who gave the crucial clue to Rav. Like the team in the book, I've been lucky enough to go heath-hiking at dusk with a skilled ornithologist to catch a glimpse of a nesting female – not an easy task, with that incredibly camouflaged plumage – and to hear first-hand the nightjar's very strange and distinctive call.

Outside of ecology, and resurrecting my other biological disciplines, research into the MAOA gene and the causes of psychopathy has been fascinating. While I'm sure our understanding and knowledge will continue to evolve, the current insight into psychopathy being triggered by extreme abuse (and potentially preventable), is utterly heart-breaking. And the accompanying evidence shows that psychopathy can only be triggered when there is a specific type of brain damage combined with specific genetics.

Which is just one more example of how outcomes depend not only on the nature we have, but how we nurture it.

About the Author

After spending sixteen years as an ecologist, crawling through undergrowth and studying the nocturnal habits of animals (and people), Dr Sarah Yarwood-Lovett naturally turned her mind to murder. She may have swapped badgers for bears when she emigrated from a quaint village in the South Downs to the wild mountains of the Pacific Northwest, but her books remain firmly rooted in the rolling downland she grew up in.

Forensically studying clues for animal activity has seen Sarah surveying sites all over the UK and around the world. She's rediscovered a British species thought to be extinct during her PhD, with her record held in London's Natural History Museum; debated that important question – do bats wee on their faces? – at school workshops; survived a hurricane on a coral atoll while scuba-diving to conduct marine surveys; and given evidence as an expert witness.

Along the way, she's discovered a noose in an abandoned warehouse and had a survey derailed by the bomb squad. Her unusual career has provided the perfect inspiration for a series of murder mysteries with an ecological twist – so, these days, Sarah's research includes consulting detectives, lawyers, judges and attending murder trials.